The Hungry

Love will keep us together, hunger will tear us apart

Book 1

Of the Ravening Trilogy

Author

Shalynn Cavanagh

Copyright
© 2015 Shalynn Cavanagh
All rights reserved
ISBN - 13: 978-1517383718
ISBN - 10: 1517383714

PRINTED IN THE UNITED STATES OF AMERICA

Dearest Donna & Chris,

Thank you for always sharing your crazy stories + enspiring me to write my own!

All my love,
Shalynn

Acknowledgements

To my Nan and Pop who cultivated a love of reading and writing within me surpassed only by the love I have for them, and their love for each other.

I always promised you would see the book, Pop. This one, and every one that may come after, is for you.

Secondly, to Courtney and Alyson.
I couldn't have done it without you, not any of it.
You were there from the very beginning.

Lastly, to the people around me who continuously prove that the absence of fear is less powerful than the abundance of bravery.
You have shown me who the true heroes are.

Thank You.

4

Sandra

All my life, I have wanted to travel: free to do as I liked; go where I wanted and take what I desired. To have the ability to just pack up and leave without a second's thought, without a moment's regret. But I have now come to realize that being a traveler wasn't so far off from what I was.

Just a scared girl with no home and my bag packed and ready to go.

6

Chapter One

October

"Dad?" My voice echoed in the front room of our house as I called for my father. I didn't expect an answer, normally I had to go searching for him.

He surprised me today, popping out of the kitchen, "Hey, Sandy baby, what's up? How was school?"

He was cheerful, and it left me dumbstruck. My father hadn't called me 'Sandy baby' in over a year.

"Um... it was good. I was wondering if my friends could come over tonight?" I asked. I was almost afraid to voice the question now, seeing how happy my father was. Perhaps I should just stay at home and hang out with him. I rarely got to see him anymore, not like this.

He still didn't meet my eyes, but it was something I had gotten used to in the past few months. His blue eyes, so different from my own, were always focused just a bit above my head.

"Who's coming? I'll make pizza!"

I grinned at his excitement. It had been so very long since he had been animated about anything. "Just the usual crowd; you know, Rhea, Jason, Eva, Gabby, and Andrew."

"Not Anne?" He laughed, "She doesn't go anywhere without Andrew!"

"Apparently she's busy," I replied, "it's a family dinner, or something."

"Well, it's okay with me. When are your friends going to be here?"

"Probably within the hour." I told him, heading down the stairs to my room in the basement.

I threw myself on the bed and stared at the ceiling, hearing my father bustling around. It was the oddest thing, hearing him moving around with purpose. I half expected him to start humming, the way he used to do.

The shower beckoned me, and I headed to the bathroom, clicking on the radio before I stepped into the water. I sang along to some mindless tunes, scrubbing my hair. I had been thinking about cutting my hair again, but it had taken so long to grow out; maybe once spring came I would consider it.

An announcement started, interrupting the song I had been enjoying. I stuck my head under the jet, successfully blocking off the talking. I despised talk shows; I was all about the music. It was one of the traits I shared with my father. There wasn't much else we had in common, other than music. My mother had been the one I had been closer with; both in our stubborn personalities and looks.

She, however, had been a wild child; the type of girl that could never really be tamed. Went and married my father on a whim, when he had proposed after a week of dating. That had been her style, though I couldn't even imagine my father doing something so reckless. He was the rock of the family, the cautious one; my mom hadn't been afraid of anything.

The water went cold on me, a shock to my previously daydreaming system. I leapt out, wrapping a towel around my chilled skin. The radio announcer was still going on about some freak car accident. I tossed on my favourite jeans and t-shirt, turned off the radio, and waltzed to my room.

"Sandy!"

I shrieked, whirling around to face Gabrielle, one of my best friends. I could have murdered her for sneaking up on me.

"You scared me! What if I had been naked?!" I scolded.

She shrugged, "We've been friends since we were kids, I'm pretty sure I've seen all of you."

I didn't have an argument, and even if I had there wasn't really a point. Gabby was right, I had known her since we were children, and I knew by now that she was impossible to argue with. Even if you were right, you always somehow ended up looking bad.

"Whatever."

She jumped on my bed, gathering a pillow to her chest, "So, who's coming tonight?"

"Pretty much the whole group, minus Anne."

"She busy?" Gabby asked, her forehead wrinkling in confusion.

I laughed, "Yeah, she's got a family dinner. I think Andrew will head over there afterwards."

"Probably, he never seems to leave her side." Gabby narrowed dark, accusatory eyes on me, "Does that bother you?"

I rolled my eyes, "Are you joking? Gabby, seriously, why would that bother me?"

"Cause you loved him first." She responded easily, baring my deepest secret with a casual shrug. I scowled at her.

"Gabrielle," I hissed, "seriously?!"

She grinned prettily, "What? It's true, and you know it!"

"I did love him. A long time ago. We dated. We broke up and he's with Anne now. I love Anne, I'm happy for him." It was the truth, and no matter how many times I told Gabby that she never let it go. It was Gabby's nature to be jealous though, and she didn't really understand how I could watch Andrew be so happy with Anne and not hate every minute of it.

"Doesn't it *bother* you? Seriously, it would drive me nuts."

I laughed. "I know it would drive you nuts. I'm okay, honestly."

Most of the time. I didn't love Andrew anymore, not in *that* way, but it did bother me sometimes how much happier he was with Anne. I would never admit it, of course.

"Well, if you're over it, I would like to hook you up with Zack." Gabby announced dramatically.

I rolled my eyes, "Gabby, please, drop it. You know I'm not interested!"

She smirked, "I thought you were over Andrew though?"

I scowled, "I am, that doesn't mean I'll date anything that can walk upright!"

"He likes you though! You should have invited him tonight!" Gabby whined, slamming me with her best puppy dog eyes.

"He was invited," I told her triumphantly, "I invited him when I invited Jason. He said he was busy."

Gabby rolled her eyes, "You invited Jason? He doesn't even talk!"

"For your information I like Jason! He's very nice. Plus, Eva's friends with him."

Gabrielle flopped backwards, laying down in my unmade bed. She was put off with me, I could tell. The good thing about Gabby was how quickly she got over things like this, though, and within seconds she bounced back.

"Hey ladies!" Rhea came bounding into my room, not bothering to knock. I supposed none of my friends bothered knocking anymore because my father had stopped answering, and I always told them to just come inside.

"Hey, Rhea." I smiled; Rhea grinned back and dropped beside Gabby on the bed with a bounce.

"Sandra, your dad is... umm, cheery?" She informed me cautiously.

"I know, right?" I murmured, "It's bizarre. I don't know why he's suddenly being normal again."

"Well, it has been almost a year." Gabby sat up, frowning at me.

I sighed, "Still not enough time. He's not over it. He never will be."

"A year is a lot of time!" Gabby protested.

I shook my head slowly, "Not for him. No amount of time would be enough for him. There's no one else on earth that could ever compare to mom for him. He's biased. He knows it, too. She was the one for him."

Rhea's smile was sad, "I wish I could have met your mom. It sounds like he really loved her."

I couldn't help the rueful smile that took over my face, "He definitely did."

"Eva texted me, she's with Jason. They're on their way." Gabby informed me.

"Awesome, and Andrew told me he would be a bit late. Dad said he would make pizza."

Rhea clapped her hands together in excitement, "What are we going to do tonight?"

"Probably watch a movie and do what we do every Friday." I scowled, "We really need a hobby."

"Do you think she likes him?" Gabby asked abruptly, ignoring my words.

I was lost. "Who?"

"Eva? Do you think she likes Jason?"

Rhea laughed, "No way, Gabby. She thinks he's fun, they're friends."

The thought of Eva liking Jason was almost comical, although I didn't say anything. Jason was too quiet for her; it already drove Eva crazy. Jason took his time to think through his words, which was nice, especially since his brother Zack said anything that popped into his head at any given time.

"Come on, let's go to the living room." I said, distracting my friends from their conversation. I headed out to the room my dad had made for me before my mom had died,

Rhea and Gabby in tow. It had a couple of couches, tons of bookshelves, and a big TV with an even bigger DVD collection. I spent most of my life hidden down here with a blanket these days.

Eva came racing down the steps, Jason walking behind her. She was carrying a huge bag of treats, and her energy showed just how many she had already eaten.

"Hey all!" She flopped onto the other couch, "How are you guys?"

Her treat bag started making its rounds, Jason settled himself onto the arm of my couch, looming over me. Jason dwarfed me in height and breadth, something which could be a little intimidating.

"We're good," I answered, "Zack's not coming?"

Jason shook his head, "Busy."

I nodded, pleased. Zack was an okay guy, but I didn't want to spend all evening listening to him talk about his bike training for his upcoming race.

"Did you hear about that weird accident?" Eva asked suddenly, "It was bizarre; some guy jumped out of his car at an intersection and got into another car and mauled the driver. Like an animal, seriously! He didn't even know the guy he attacked. They're calling it a mental case."

I realized this was probably the radio announcement, "Weird, did the guy live? The one who was attacked?"

"Yeah, but he was in critical condition last I heard."

"Sandy?" My dad's voice surprised me. He hadn't been in my basement in months, and even now he stood at the top of the stairs.

I got up and climbed the stairs to stand in front of him, "Yeah, Dad?"

He had a jacket on and his tool belt, "I'm just going to go fix the shed door you've been complaining about. The pizzas are in the oven, they'll be ready in half an hour."

"Thank you." I said. I hadn't complained about the shed door in a year, mostly because I wouldn't trouble my unstable father with something so trivial, but I wasn't about to end this new streak of cheerfulness by telling him that. "We'll save you some pizza."

I heard the front door open, and my dad turned around. "Hey, Andrew. I think the whole gang is here now."

Andrew smiled at my father, probably just as surprised as I had been that he was up and about. "Hey, Mr. Carter. Doing some handy work?"

My father nodded, "Yes, I was going to reinforce a step."

I bit my tongue so I didn't correct him. If the only slip-up my father made tonight was confusion as to what he was fixing it was a good night.

"Wow, good job." Andrew told him.

Dad nodded aimlessly, "Thanks. Alright, Sandy, don't forget the pizza."

"I won't, dad."

He smiled, the first one in forever, "Love you, Sandy baby."

I choked up, I couldn't help it. "I love you too, dad."

He started humming and headed out the front door. I heard the door close before I sunk down onto the top step, forcing back tears.

Andrew whispered, "You okay?"

"Barely." I muttered, "He's humming again. He's humming, Andrew."

"This is good, you know that, right?"

I smiled, "I know. It's just weird."

He reached over and squeezed my hand, "Everything's going to be okay now."

I smiled at him, thankful for everything he had done for me. He had always been there for me, especially when my mom had died.

"I know."

Chapter Two

"This show is so unbelievably predictable. He's obviously going to survive, and they're going to live happily-ever-after. I hate happy endings." Andrew was sprawled out on a couch, his lanky body taking up too much space. His hair flopped into his eyes, and I wanted to remind him for the millionth time this week to get a much-needed haircut.

"Shut up, Andrew. I love a good happy ending." Gabrielle laughed at Andrew's gagging face. He threw a pillow in retaliation, and Gabby rolled her eyes.

This Friday was turning out to be pretty average, despite my father's strange behaviour. The pizza was laying half-devoured on my coffee table, and I couldn't imagine eating another bite I was so full.

Gabrielle, Andrew, Rhea and I were sitting on a couch watching a movie that Rhea had picked — which only guaranteed it would be boring; Jason was playing a card game with Eva, her good-natured teasing only emphasizing his silence.

"You seriously have no taste. Love stories are overrated," Andrew turned back to Gabby to restart their argument, "action is where it's at." I couldn't help but agree with him, however, I was smart enough to keep my mouth shut and stay out of their debate.

Rhea sighed dreamily, "I think love stories are beautiful!"

Andrew rolled his eyes, "Of course you do, Rhea."

Rhea laughed at his words, knowing just as well as we all did that she was a complete sap when it came to animals or kids or love. Despite our teasing, I envied the way she made everyone comfortable just with her presence. She had been there for me when my mom had died, more so than anyone else, though we hadn't known each other that well at the time. I couldn't count the times I had phoned her crying, and how often she had driven over in the middle of the night just to talk to me.

My mother's death had brought us together in a lot of ways; she was one of the only people I could talk to. She understood it, since her sister had died only a few years before.

We were drifting again, though, I could feel it. Although we were still friends, it was the type of friendship that grew stronger with adversity, not the opposite.

A crash was heard upstairs, and I figured my father had caused it, since he was the only other person in my house. Terror gripped me for an instant as I recalled the time I had raced to my father after hearing a shattering noise, only to see my dad's furious and forlorn face staring into a broken mirror, blood dripping from his sliced fist.

The mirror mom had gotten for her birthday.

"What the hell was that, Sandra?" Andrew asked, movie forgotten. Andrew and I were always a little jumpy, and the foreign noise in my otherwise familiar house had set my nerves on edge.

"My dad?" I replied.

Andrew shook his head, "He's outside."

I flew to my feet, panic gripping me. I was about to race upstairs to see what had caused the crash, but then my neighbour walked down the stairs. He had blood down his coat, and on his hands and neck.

It was probably the most surreal moment of my life to see the neighbour I rarely talked to heading towards me like we were friends. I wondered if he was injured, there was so much blood all over him.

"Luke?" I greeted him cautiously, back-pedaling a little at his appearance.

He surged towards me at his name, blue eyes filled with malice. His body jerked, like he was unwilling to go any further. His teeth were bared in this weird animalistic grin, somewhere between pain and fury. And hunger; there was so much hunger in his gaze, I shuddered.

I jumped backwards again, away from him; I was so startled by his appearance, and the way his eyes cruelly roamed my figure. There was no lust in his gaze. It didn't make sense, I knew that, but he looked at me as if assessing the nourishment he might gain from it. From my flesh. From me.

"You have to run!" he choked out. "I'm going to hurt you; I'm going to kill you!"

This was all the encouragement I needed; I was so spooked by the blood and his appearance I grabbed the antique sword that hung beside me on the wall, in honour of my grandfather who had fought in WWII. It was heavier than expected, and I wondered why I had never thought to even lift the stupid heirloom before this moment.

"Go away!" It was *supposed* to come out strong; it was supposed to be demanding! Instead it was just a whine, slow to rise from the recesses of my throat.

Finally, the image of pain faded from his eyes; the restraint on his figure disappeared. Whatever had possessed Luke had gained full control. He grinned maliciously at me, like he knew everything about me, knew what I was thinking.

"I'm going to eat you," he promised, "like I ate your father."

The words incited something in me, something that had always lain dormant. A deep-seated need to protect, and rage-- rage against the world for taking away my mother, and rage against this monster for threatening my father.

I snarled, as if whatever beast was holding my neighbour captive in his body had jumped into me. "I'll *kill* you if you touch us."

I heard the movie end in the background, a cheerful tune to accompany the credits. It was out of place. The world was still going on around me, while I stood still because everything I had ever known was wrong now. Everything had changed.

I didn't actually plan to kill him, I just wanted him to be so afraid of me he left my house and never came back; but he lunged at Gabrielle, looking like he wanted to hurt her!

I would like to think that if it had been any other of my friends in the room, I wouldn't have reacted as I did. I couldn't help it though — Gabby was my best friend, and had been for longer than I could remember, I could remember her standing up to bullies in the first grade for me, and holding her when she had cried after her first breakup. I was protective of her; and why wouldn't I be? She was a part of my family, now that my blood family was nearly decimated— and before I could try to hold back, I was throwing every bit of my strength into swinging the sword in my hands.

I knew that this *thing* —whatever it was— could not be my neighbour: whatever he had been before was now gone. I also knew that no matter what or who he was, no matter how strong or how evil or how powerful he was, he, just like anybody else, wouldn't live if I cut off his head.

If I didn't kill him, Gabrielle would die. It was this knowledge, this one thought that solidified my resolve. My arms suddenly felt like they were being ripped from their sockets. The sword fell from my grip, and I was staring into the dead eyes of Luke's head.

It was at an odd angle, not completely severed from the neck. There was blood everywhere, and I managed to only stare at the gore around me, as I felt tingles race up and down my arm muscles.

I should throw up; it felt *natural* to throw up. I didn't vomit. I met the horrified expressions on my friends' faces, seeing the screams that I had tuned out dying on their lips. I searched out Andrew's eyes. It was instinctive for me, the type of reflex I couldn't control; something leftover from when I had been with him, depended on him fully. He would know what to do. He probably had the same instinct I did.

His green eyes were ruthless, there was no fear or shock, just a sense of relief and a desperation I knew could be seen in my own face.

His voice was soft and gentle, the only thing that could have possibly broken through to me in that moment, "We need to figure this out. We need to know what's happening. That was *not* normal, Sandy."

Calm descended into my veins, some type of adrenaline survival instinct, and I knew that I had to harness it, use the clarity of this moment to survive the turmoil of the next. I schooled my face into the closest thing to a neutral expression I had, and kept myself steady. This was the only way to handle it. The appearance of my neighbour had so rocked the reality we lived in, and my friends were only just realizing it, as was I.

I had read so many horror books, and seen so many monster movies, the ideas all blurred into one. I had never seen gore like this in real life. I had seen death, more than my fair share of it, but it had always been at a hospital, slow, a withering of life more than a sudden end.

However, it didn't matter what Luke was, or what had happened. It didn't matter if he had gone crazy, or gotten sick, or whatever else. The only thing that mattered is that he had been hungry for my flesh, and he had been able to think. I knew it, because before I had killed whatever Luke had become, he had known exactly what he was doing. He had told me his intent even before he had carried it out.

"Of course it wasn't *normal*," I hissed, trying to keep my volume low. I could hear someone crying behind me.

"It was like a zombie." Andrew said softly, horror etched into his expression. I wasn't entirely sure I believed in zombies, and I didn't really want to believe in it. Anytime the idea of a zombie apocalypse came about it pretty much meant the end of the world.

I nodded, trying to keep the calm that Andrew had tried to inspire, "He could think, Andrew... that isn't exactly a 'zombie' thing. He could speak too, and he was telling us to run. He was telling us how hungry he was." My voice cracked at the end, and I knew the thin facade of control we were trying to put over the others' was fading.

"Zombies!?" Rhea let out a laugh, borderline hysterical. "Those aren't real. They aren't possible." She dropped to her knees, her face sinking into her hands. I was amazed she didn't start screaming, but her silence was almost worse.

Eva nodded desperately, "Yeah, they're... horror stories! This guy just... lost it."

Jason was white as a sheet of paper, and the only words that left his mouth were: "We killed him. Oh my god."

"We need to phone the police!" Eva said, snatching her cell. Before anyone could stop her, she had 911 dialed.

Her cell fell from her hand as her jaw slackened, "It's... It's busy?" The sentence came out as a question and I felt just as dazed as she looked.

The possibility that this was an isolated incident from whatever cause, whether it be that my neighbour had gone insane, taken too many drugs, or been infected, had just gone from slim to none.

"What do we do?!" Rhea's voice was almost a breathy shriek.

"We stay calm." Jason snapped; his hands were shaking.

I nodded blankly, "Yes, I mean, it could just be that he was deranged?"

I didn't believe my own words and the others could tell. I knew he couldn't be mad, I had talked to him only a week ago and he had been a kind man. He had a great sense of humour, I remembered that now.

I wish I would have taken the time to know him because now he was gone; now I would never get the opportunity. I had killed him! I was a murderer.

Andrew took the sword gently from my hand and touched the blade, "This is fairly sharp. Did you recently sharpen this, Sandra?" My brain scrambled to comprehend what was happening, still caught up in guilt and pain.

Andrew knew something, or at least had a theory. He wasn't willing to share, and the memory his aimless question had evoked left me with no desire to share either. My dad had sharpened the blade not too long after mom died. I'm not sure if it was to kill himself, or just to remember the man who had fathered the love of his life.

"My dad!" I cried, "My dad! He was outside. The blood, the blood on his coat. He said he ate my dad!" I whirled to sprint outside to find him, my poor father who could barely keep track of time, let alone withstand an attack.

Jason grabbed my arm and pulled me back, almost bruising me. "Sandra, no. You can't go out yet. What if... what if there's more?"

"But my dad?" I whispered, "I have to help him."

"You can't. Not yet." Andrew told me.

I choked, "He won't fight back. He'll let them hurt him."

"Sandy, calm, please." Andrew commanded, "We will go for him as soon as we figure this out. What do you think happened here?"

"I don't know, Andrew. He was normal only a week ago. His name was Luke, he lived across the road. He was nice!" My voice was rising slightly, and I gestured to the nearly decapitated body on my floor. I was near hysterics, and it took every bit of strength I had to swallow it all down.

"I want to cut it open." He said softly. "Cut him open."

I gaped at him, absolutely horrified, "You... you what!?" Andrew was the least sadistic person I had ever known, and the thought that he would so defile a body disgusted me.

Andrew frowned, "To see what's inside. If whatever he became affected him internally, or if he's the same. It could narrow down whatever this thing is."

"You aren't a goddamn doctor, Andrew!" I smacked him on his arm, as hard as I could. The slap resounded in the basement quiet, and I thought of the sound his head had made when I swung the sword. My stomach rolled.

"Oh, shit. Oh god, I killed him." I dropped to a crouch, forgetting entirely about Andrew's idiotic autopsy plan.

Andrew took the silence of the others for acceptance, although that was a far cry off what I had been thinking.

He used the sword to slice a long cut in the corpse's abdomen. I lifted my eyes to watch, despite the fact that I knew it would disgust me. For a moment, I believed I would throw up, reflexively. I held myself back, watching in horror at the sight unfolding in front of my eyes.

I heard the thud of a body behind me, and I suspected that Rhea had fainted. It wasn't Rhea though; it was Gabby. Jason rushed to her side, rousing her from what must have been a nice reprieve from this reality.

Every organ was practically decimated. It looked as though they had all slowly collapsed over time, disgusting and almost eaten away. The fact that I knew which organ was which reminded me of bio class, and the nausea rose again at how much my life had changed in so little time. I had never thought dissections would actually become commonplace.

"What in the hell could cause that?" Jason asked incredulously.

Rhea was gaping at the sight, "Intense starvation?"

"He doesn't look starved to me. Thin, yes, but no ribs or anything," I said numbly. It was true, my neighbour was fit but still had meat on his bones, and the starvation theory seemed wrong.

Andrew took the sword to the stomach, the only part of the body that seemed intact. Nestled inside lay chunks of what looked to be meat, and not the kind that I had eaten last night off my barbecue.

I fell on my butt, graceless and wounded in the face of what I was seeing.

"What if that's my... dad. My dad!" I turned to the wall and threw up violently, my body shaking with sobs and stress.

"My god," Rhea murmured, "His body literally started devouring itself from the inside."

Eva was shaking so hard I thought she would fall as well, but when she spoke, her voice was still dead steady, "This isn't zombies. They don't even exist, and even if they did, none of this really fits with the myths. It has to be some sort of virus, like a biological weapon. Maybe it's an act of warfare."

As unappealing as the thought of zombies were, I knew that the virus idea was much, much worse. Because there was no defense to a sickness, a sickness which could be airborne.

Zombies at least could be destroyed.

"No. It can't be. We've have had no signs of military aggression towards us, Canada is rarely a country of war. And besides, if it were a virus why would the first place it showed up be Edson? We're barely on the map. But even if it is a virus, it can't be airborne!" I said emphatically, wiping my mouth on my sleeve.

"Why can't it be airborne?" Jason questioned.

Andrew sighed, "Because then we don't have a hope in hell. We're all dead, already."

Gabby started to cry, "But... but..." She didn't even finish her though, she just collapsed into sobs.

"We assume it's not airborne because we don't have a choice. Until proven otherwise we're all safe as long as we do not allow any direct contact with these infected people."

My friends dissolved into whispers, and I knew fear ran rampant in them. However, it was true, there was absolutely nothing we could do if this virus was airborne except wear masks and stick together. It was a far better idea to believe the virus was transferred some other way; that way we could believe that none of us were infected, and we could just stay together until there was a cure. If there was a cure.

One glance at Andrew told me he was thinking the same thing. Virus or no virus, it was now a 'kill or be killed' world, and he was planning on living. I snatched the other antique sword from the wall and touched the blade. This one was blunt, not sharpened like the other one; but with enough strength behind it, it could work.

"Guys, we need to get out of here and to a safe place. We could lock up in the house, but these *infected*," I hissed, "can think, and therefore get into the house. And they know we're here. We need to get all the weapons, survival items and valuables we can, get in the car and get out of here."

Gabrielle nodded to me from her spot on the ground. She was paler than usual, and shaking like a leaf, but I was heartened by her show of agreement. Jason helped her to her feet.

"We need everything we can get. Food, camping gear, winter coats and boots." Andrew said, pointing around my basement to where he knew things were stored.

Eva stared at him, "Winter coats? Andrew, it's barely October."

"We don't know how long we'll be gone." He told her, the sentence brutal in it's simplicity. Everyone went silent at his words.

From the basement we quickly gathered a suitcase full of matches, flashlights, coats, blankets and a first aid kit. It was a rather good start to safety, but everything else we needed, including weapons were upstairs.

With my dad. I hoped, at least. I hoped my dad was up there, completely fine and wondering why we were screaming. It didn't seem likely though. My father could be dead. He could be worse; he could be one of those creatures too.

I didn't think he was alive anymore. Not since Luke had said he had eaten him. Not since he had blood coating his hands. Not since I had seen his insides. I didn't think my father was alive.

After all, why would he fight for his life as I had fought for mine when he no longer cared whether he lived or died?

I prayed he was safe, because if he came at us, hungry for death and murder, I would have to kill him to save my friends and myself. I would have to kill my dad.

I didn't know if I could do that, even if it meant my own life. He was too fragile, and I couldn't dare disrupt the barely living existence he had finally carved out for himself. Especially since he had seemed so much better tonight.

Especially since he had told me he loved me.

As I went up the stairs, Jason set a hand on my shoulder reassuringly. I realized that he meant to comfort me, and to tell me that he would take care of my father should it come to that.

Perhaps Andrew and I weren't the only ones ready to survive whatever this was, to give ourselves over to the killer's instinct that had once been an integral part of humans. I nodded weakly and opened the door, thankful I had left the hallway light on. It didn't lessen the chance of discovery or death, but it made it seem less imminent.

Like rats we scurried to the kitchen, and my ears strained to pick up the slightest noise from my dad, or anyone else. We encountered nothing, and I quickly gathered every knife I had including all the kitchen knives and a few hunting ones, and all my extra batteries. Everything that wasn't perishable I took, every soup can I owned, and the metal can opener and all the water bottles.

Gabrielle gasped and I looked to her quickly. She was staring out the kitchen window, her already pale complexion so white it glowed, and I feared for her life for a second. It looked as though her heart was about to give out.

"They're coming. Sandra, look, there are dozens of them."

Eva choked out a whisper, "They look hungry."

I didn't bother to look, immediately Andrew and I were ordering our friends about.

"Check every room, take a knife, kill anything and everyone that comes towards you and threatens you. Get sweaters, get extra clothes! Take anything else useful, and meet in the garage in five minutes. Go. Go!" The last word was nearly a yell on my tongue, and before I finished saying it, every last one of my friends was dispersed through my house. I ran to the front door and locked it. I raced to the back door, planning to do the same.

The screen was hanging in the frame, but I tugged the glass door shut and locked it anyway. At my feet I found my father's tool belt, and my heart sunk. All I wanted to do was to just sit down and die. Curl up on the couch where I had spent hours with my family, safe and warm and loved.

"Sandra!" Andrew's voice shocked me back into reality, and I sprinted back to the kitchen. I scooped up my cat, Dara, wondering whether I should leave her or take her.

Leaving her was logical.

Leaving her was cruel, and condemned her to death.

I didn't have the heart to just leave her here, so I grabbed the small bag of cat food and headed to the garage.

They were all there, panting and holding bags and armfuls of supplies. I could hear my front door rattling in its frame, and I knew it was a matter of moments before those things were inside.

"We have to go." I murmured. Solemn faces met mine, and I heard a final, echoing crack from upstairs. I yanked the door to my garage open and headed for my van, thanking my dad fervently for a moment when I realized he had locked the garage, but left my van open. He had saved us.

We would survive today, but I wasn't sure about tomorrow.

Andrew was already packing everything in the trunk, "Everyone get in. Grab those Gerry cans; we need all the gas we can get. That air pump too! Yeah, and the jumper cables."

A chill went up my spine, I heard movement behind my father's SUV, and I froze. Everyone froze, and we all pivoted to see what was happening.

My father was standing there, staring at me, death in his eyes. I fell against the van, scrambling for my knife. I couldn't do it, I knew I wouldn't be able to hurt him, even though he barely resembled the man that had showered me in kisses and hugs as a child. He was thin, and covered in blood, and a sickening wound made up of teeth marks marred his neck. He should be dead, or at least incapacitated. He shouldn't be stalking towards me like a lethal animal, ready to rip out my throat.

Andrew stepped forward, and he didn't hesitate the way I had. The sword, the blunt antique I had given him in the basement, was swung against the back of my father's knees as he lunged at me, and he went down with a thud, legs torn up. Andrew was panting, watching my father as he started to claw towards me, and I couldn't move from where I had sunk to the ground in front of him.

Jason snatched the toolbox from my father's workbench, stepping in front of where I had fallen to my knees. He dropped it down on my father's temple, spraying blood around us. The toolbox caught him in the temple, again and again, and I just watched in horror; frozen in the sickening nightmare that was a reality.

He stopped, finally, and everything was silent as we all stared at the destruction on my garage floor.

"Sandra?" Jason whispered. The toolbox had slipped from his hands, lying bloody and half open on the floor. Andrew had picked the sword up once more, and he looked hardened and cold in a way I had never witnessed before.

"Dad?" I murmured, my fingers reaching out to settle on my father's hair. It was coated in blood, and I felt so horrified, brutalized, a million other emotions. My father was dead. Not just absent, or suicidal, or sad, or lonely, or any of the other things I had gotten used to in the last year; he was gone.

A slam against the door made me jump and I stared up at the white door that was the entrance to my house. They were in my house. Those things, those horrifying creatures that had torn out my father's throat.

"Sandra!" Andrew was yelling at me. "Sandra, move! Come on, we gotta go!"

Gabrielle was screaming, "She lost her dad, shut up, shut up!"

Jason's hand encircled my bicep and he tugged me to my feet, leaving bruises I was sure would haunt me. He practically threw me towards the driver's side of the car.

"Get in and drive!" he snarled, rushing to the other side of the car.

I stared at the handle and opened it, slowly. I felt like I was in shock, although I wasn't sure since I had never been in shock before. But I was... relieved. Horrified, distraught, sad; of course I was feeling all those things too, but I was also relieved. Because my dad was gone, and my mom was gone, and I had my cat, and everyone else I loved inside the van.

It was this moment, more than any other, that I swore to protect my friends. Swore that I would spend the rest of my life —which probably wouldn't be very long— protecting the contents of the van.

I launched myself into the driver's seat, turning the car on. I was breathing too heavily to be normal, but what else could be expected in this moment? I locked the doors and turned to face my friends. They were all staring at me, as if waiting for me to decide something, or breakdown again, or cry. They didn't know what to do. I had to take charge, I had to do everything in my power to get us out of this alive.

I would protect my friends.

"Phone everyone you know and love, make sure they're themselves. Tell them to get out of this town, secure themselves until we can find a safe place and help them escape there." My voice was shaky, but no one questioned it.

They had already started; I could practically hear the thoughts and prayers circulating in their heads. Jason, who sat in the passenger seat, snatched up his phone and placed it to his ear.

"Hey, Zack?" His voice was nervous as he waited for a response to confirm his brother's normality.

"Yeah, it's on the radio? Well you need to get out of town. We can pick you up from somewhere safer." Jason responded to a question.

"No, you idiot, don't come here!" Jason snapped. His expression grew angrier at whatever Zack said. His eyes slid to me for a second.

"We're all safe, and we'll meet you somewhere. Find mom and dad if you can and take them with you. Be careful."

He hung up and stared at me, "Parents were at the mall. Zack can't get a hold of them. He's going to call us when he's out of town."

I nodded, "Good, we'll pick him up. This van is going to be cramped. Anybody else have news?"

"Anne's fine." Andrew responded to my question, "She locked herself in the basement because her brother started annoying her by telling her he was going to eat her. Then she realized it was real. She needs us to come get her; she has no weapons down there. Not that she would use them if she had them."

Andrew's face was fixed in a frown, and it was an unusual sight. He was usually the light-hearted one, the joker. However, he adored Anne, and we both knew she was not the 'survival' type. Gentle to the core of her soul, she wouldn't touch a weapon, even if it was life or death; she just didn't have it in her.

No one else told me anything, and I stared back at them to see only faces filled with grief and despair. The expression of Eva's countenance however, stole my breath.

Anger and desolation more extreme than I had ever witnessed devastated her usually smiling face.

"What happened?" I asked. I knew I would not like what I heard.

Eva sighed, "My mother is gone. My sister told me so. She said she had eaten her. Then she told me I was next."

"I'm sorry," I breathed.

Eva laughed bitterly, "It's not your fault. It's no one's fault. I've lost my mother. I have a sister out there, but she is as good as a monster. I have no one."

Then she seemed to realize who she was talking to: *me*, the girl whose mother had slowly suffered for months only to die on her birthday, and whose father had now been brutally slaughtered on the floor of her garage. I was the epitome of 'nothing left'.

That didn't take away her right to grieve. I hated when people did that, when they seemed to believe that because I was hurting, they weren't allowed. As if I would think their pain wasn't good enough. Every pain was good enough; there were no expectations or standards of hurting.

"You have us." Gabrielle promised. Eva nodded sadly and gripped her hand, tears tracking from her dark eyes.

"What about your parents?" Eva asked.

Gabrielle frowned, "They didn't answer, but they were in Phoenix. Maybe things are safer in the States?"

Eva nodded encouragingly, "Maybe. So we just have to go in and get Anne, and then it looks as though we will be safe to leave."

"Sandra, you okay?" Rhea asked softly. "Your dad-"

I started the van. "He's gone." My voice was brutal as I interrupted her, and I locked the doors in preparation to open the garage door before anyone could say a single word. I was proud, extraordinarily proud, of myself in this moment. I had done it, I had gotten us organized and out of the house. It was something my mother would have done.

"Get ready," I told them, and pressed the button. The garage door opened infinitely slowly, and people --infected people-- came swarming inside like bees drawn to honey. They smashed into the sides of the van, yanking on the handles and hitting the windows with their fists. I could hear Gabrielle crying, and Rhea's face was white in my mirror.

I threw the vehicle into drive and floored the gas. I hit people going out, and the thuds they made against my van will never escape my memory.

The sight of the open garage door as I drove away haunted me; all I had was a memory of evil being enclosed in the place I once called home.

Nowhere was safe anymore.

Going into town was strange, there were still cars and trucks, and most people looked as if they didn't even know what was going on. Then abruptly, some cars would swerve, and the drivers would leap out of the vehicles to dive at other people's cars. I could see what the bizarre accident the radio had mentioned earlier had been about.

It was obvious the news of whatever this attack was hadn't spread to everyone, and I turned on my radio to find out exactly what was publicly known.

"There is some chaos on the streets of Edson today with a new outbreak of insanity. Edmonton and Calgary are both having the same things happening, and we are receiving word that other areas in the province are the same. The Premier has been contacted but has yet to comment on the strange antics of some of the citizens, but with the build-up of an –and I hate to say the word- *infection*, it is advised that people lock themselves in their houses and wait until this insanity calms down. There is no need to worry. I repeat, there is no need to worry."

The radio announcer nearly made my temper explode, and I knew that the others in my van felt the same way.

"Stay in your houses!?" Gabrielle gaped, "That's just begging for death! You saw the way those... *things* swarmed Sandra's house! There were tons of them, and she lives far enough out of town that there shouldn't have even been that many."

I switched radio stations, to a much less popular one, but one I had always preferred. With good reason, as the advice the newsman was giving out was much better.

"We are unsure as to what is causing the anarchy in our streets today, however, it is suggested that you find a highly defensible area, and prepare to defend it and stay there, or get out of town until things quiet down. If you are leaving town, head for a less populated area. Do not, under any circumstances, come into contact with the infected people. We will be broadcasting this and any changes to the situation for as long as possible."

I looked grimly at Andrew and he shook his head sadly, "Well, at least it's better advice. And we now know that the radio stations think it's bad. If they aren't sure how long they are going to be broadcasting, they probably think the province is going to hell. I wonder if it's like this anywhere else in the world."

I pulled up to Anne's house, and glanced around my cramped van. Andrew was watching me from behind the passenger seat with an empty seat beside him, hopefully where Anne would sit if this rescue went well. Gabrielle was in the far back with Eva and Rhea beside her, all three of them looking pale, and trying so hard to be brave.

Jason was in the front with me; I handed the keys to him. We had enough room for now, luckily, but the Gerry cans, food and clothes we had brought were taking up key space.

"Andrew and I are going in. If we aren't out in ten minutes, and anything comes out that isn't us, leave. Protect the others. If we aren't out, but no one else is coming out of the house, send Eva to do a quick scan. Do *not* let her come in to help."

Gabrielle didn't like this plan, I knew it by the way she was glaring at me. I smiled at them all, and I deemed that one smile the best bit of acting of my entire life. It lit up my face with confidence and love.

"We *will* be back in ten minutes."

Andrew grabbed the sharpened sword and I pulled the two largest butcher knives from the knife block we had taken from my kitchen. Jason moved to the driver's seat and kept the car idling for a quick getaway. Andrew and I stalked up to the front door, and I reached for the handle. He stopped me, fingers laying briefly on my arm where Jason had pulled me so roughly.

"You okay?" He murmured.

I glared at him, "Peachy. Stop asking, I'm fine. We have to do this and get out."

His green eyes saw too much when he looked at me, but I kept my scowl focused until he finally looked away.

Together, we opened it as quietly as possible. Immediately we could hear yelling, but no one was near us.

"They're by the basement door, off to the left. Sounds like two of them." Andrew whispered, focused completely on the task at hand. I could hear it now, the shouts that came from Anne's family. Unless we could head them off, we would have to kill them. That was the last thing I wanted to do, I adored Anne's parents, they were lovely, and her mom had been especially supportive when my mother had died.

I smiled grimly at my best friend, "Charge?"

He snickered, "I'll run through the house, yelling, and go out the backdoor and loop round to the car. You get Anne and get out."

I didn't like it, he risked too much, but it was also the best plan we had. I knew he would do anything if it meant Anne would get out safely. "Stall, we're going to need time. Go." I murmured.

He immediately took off, yelling like a madman. Gratitude filled me that his long legs could move quickly. I could hear Anne's parents scramble after him, and as soon as they were out of eyesight, I ran to the basement door.

"Anne!?" I called as softly as possible.

"Sandra? Was that Andrew?" She asked as she emerged from the basement. She was lugging a duffel bag, and I was glad that her tall, willowy frame was stronger than it appeared.

"Yes, he's distracting your family. Come on, we have to get out of here. I hope you grabbed as many supplies as you could."

"I did. But there's no food down here. It's in the pantry behind you." She opened the door, lugging a big black bag. I whirled around and opened the pantry door. Every soup can on the shelves was thrown into the garbage bag I grabbed.

Anne's soft gasp alerted me to danger, but it was almost too late. Anne's mother was advancing on her, but if I hadn't known Anne's mother as well as I did, I never would have recognized her. Her normally conservative auburn hair was wild about her face, and the way she bared her teeth gave me chills.

I knew she was the enemy, just as I had known it with my neighbour; but Anne hated violence, and I knew she would never defend herself against her own mother.

This was wrong: mothers were supposed to protect and love their children, not eat them! I rushed Mrs. Hines, a woman who had made me dinner in the past and comforted me when I had cried, and pulled my knife from my belt.

I knew Anne was trying to stop me, but she wasn't fast enough.

The sight of the knife I had once used to chop vegetables entering a human's skin was surreal; Mrs. Hines dropped to the floor, the knife still embedded in her usually blue eye. The blood pooling beneath her was scarlet on the ivory floor, and I felt as though I had somehow defiled a beautiful thing.

I turned and grabbed the bag of food, and Anne, whose face was blank and broken. Tears were coursing down her cheeks, and I knew that I had shattered something deep inside her when I had murdered her mother. Yet, she didn't resist my powerful pull towards the door; Anne never was a fighter. She would rather die than hurt anyone else.

As swiftly as possible, I raced to the car, Anne being half dragged behind me. Gabrielle looked like she was having a heart attack, Jason was as calm as always. He opened the trunk, and we shoved everything into the already half-full space. I had never seen my van so full, not even on the spontaneous road trips my mother had once made my family go on.

I jumped into the passenger seat, and Anne sat on the empty two seater where Andrew would have to sit as well.

I looked at Jason, who dwarfed my height in the drivers seat, "Thanks."

His steely grey eyes met mine, but he didn't say a word, and I didn't really expect him too. Sometimes I could swear I knew what he was thinking or trying to tell me. He may have been Eva's best friend, but he was my rock. He never really changed, and I just counted on him for support.

I needed support so much now; I had killed two people I had known in one day. How could I murder the people I knew? I had loved Mrs. Hines like another mother. What would have happened if Anne had been the one trying to hurt me? Or Gabrielle? Or Eva? Would I have stabbed my kitchen knife into Gabrielle's eyes as easily as I had Mrs. Hines?

I didn't want to know the answer to my question, and I vowed that it would never be necessary to find out. I would devote everything I had to protecting my friends. From now on, that would be my purpose. I would forget everything; I would be whatever they needed me to be to save them.

Andrew came sprinting around the corner, Anne's brother and father fast on his heels. Eva threw open the back door, and he leaped in, practically crushing Anne in his rush. Rhea slammed the door behind him, I locked them, and Jason sped away from the curb.

As we drove away from her house, my heart pounded from adrenaline and pain. I was a murderer, and only Anne and myself knew it. Somehow I had to break this stressful silence, and share the weight on my shoulders. I had to make everyone understand I wasn't a monster.

I wasn't a monster, was I?

"I'm sorry." My voice sounded too large in the crowded vehicle, the music was barely background noise at this point.

Anne's blue eyes, the exact same eyes as her mother's, landed on me, "You should have let me die."

That got everyone's attention.

"Nobody is going to die while I'm around." I whispered, "I'm sorry. I know how you feel."

Her face twisted angrily, and it was the first time I had ever seen her express rage, "I want to say that you will never know how I feel, but I can't. Because you *do*. That's the only reason I don't hate you. You knew exactly what you were doing, and exactly how I would feel and you still did it. Even if it meant I hated you."

I nodded sadly and repeated, "I'm sorry."

I started to cry. I cried like a child who had broken its favourite toy, and Anne cried with me. Everyone watched, part of this mourning, and yet not, because they still did not know what I had done.

It was time to tell them what they were travelling with. They had watched me kill my neighbour, but I didn't think it had set in yet. I didn't know him, I had never hugged him, or laughed with him or cried with him. I had killed Mrs. Hines though, a mother we all knew.

Murderer.

I swallowed and stemmed my tears, "I killed her mom. I killed Mrs. Hines."

Jason didn't flinch, just closed his eyes for a long moment. Andrew's face twisted and he clasped Anne's still crying form even tighter. The other girls started to cry, even Eva, who was usually too collected to take to grief. She hadn't even reacted this way when she had found out about her mother, but I had to leave it to her to care so much for others. She was sorrier for Anne's loss, and perhaps for my actions, than she had been about her own devastation.

My voice was small, and tearful, "I'm sorry."

It felt stupid to keep saying it, but there was nothing left for me to say. I turned back toward the road, staring straight into the setting sun. My eyes had dried, and I wished I had taken more time to cry, a longer time to mourn, not only for Anne's mother, but for mine, and my father, and my house, and my whole life.

My eyes found Jason's form, which was sitting stiffly in the driver's seat. He glanced at me, and gave me a smile that was pure support. I felt that maybe I had grieved in his special way. No tears, or sadness, or anger, just silence.

There was magic in silence sometimes, and I noticed that with every passing minute, the sorrow seemed to lessen. Or maybe it just got easier to bear. Anne had cried herself out, and was now asleep on Andrew's shoulder. Rhea was sleeping as well, with Gabrielle stroking her blonde hair comfortingly.

I wanted to be held and comforted. I wanted to be selfish, because I was the one who had killed those people. Anne's grief was stronger, because it was her mother who had died, but in a way, my loss was greater because I was never going to be innocent or a child again.

I would always look at people and see my neighbour's head on my carpet, his body fallen and broken, or maybe Mrs. Hines blood pooling beneath her corpse.

Jason's soft murmur chased my morbid thoughts away, "Where are we headed now, Sandra?"

"Out of town. Follow Highway 16 until you hit the 32 on the left. It's less busy. We need Zack to call us, but until then we'll go north until we feel safe, then we'll find somewhere to sleep and continue on tomorrow." I replied, my voice still sounded weak. "Wake me when it's my turn to drive.

Chapter Three

Dara was crying, soft kitten whines, and I knew it was because she hadn't gone to the bathroom in hours. She was the only one voicing the complaint, but we were all in the same situation. I was driving now, and there were some cars on the road. They were obviously running like us, people crammed into the inside. I wondered if they had thought to bring extra gas, or food.

The worry extended to us as well; there was no way for us to get food when we finally ran out. If we had guns, we could maybe shoot down an animal. I knew Andrew was a good shot; he'd been to the shooting range before with his dad. I should have thought to bring my fishing rod, because trout was better than nothing.

However, we had enough food to last us a while, which was probably more than any other car of survivors on this highway could say.

"We need guns." I said, my voice barely a mutter. Everyone was awake, which surprised me. Jason nodded from beside me. He was holding his cell phone, and I knew he was willing it to ring. Zack still hadn't called, and we had been driving for almost six hours now, taking highways as long as they were fairly empty. The gas tank was low, but I was grateful that at least the van was good on gas.

We had just entered Saskatchewan, outside of a small town called Pierceland; we were now the furthest East I had ever been.

I had a feeling Zack wasn't going to call, although I would never voice that opinion. Jason wasn't stupid anyway.

Jason sighed, looking away from his phone. "Zack would have had one. If he had grabbed it. My parents always had a handgun."

"He's going to call." Eva reassured.

Jason didn't answer, and I didn't expect him to. I could hear everyone shifting restlessly in the back, and I knew they were facing the same problem as my cat. She hadn't stopped meowing yet.

"Bathroom break?" I questioned. My voice was weary, and my eyes were starting to blur.

Jason nodded, "We should stop at a station. It's not the safest, but we could get gas. It's better than using one of our Gerry cans so early."

"Yeah, and I could use the walk." Andrew chipped in from the back.

Almost twenty minutes later I was pulling into a gas station. It looked old, and I was hoping that would mean it was deserted. I grabbed another knife, regretting for a moment that I had left my last one in Mrs. Hines' eye.

I shook my head to rid myself of the callous thought. I had always believed that humans were essentially still animals, but I had figured it would take longer than a day to revert me to that bestial stage.

I had always been a survivor though.

"Boys, don't use the bathroom, just go outside. Stay close though, and grab a knife." I had two huge butcher knives for myself, both tucked into the belt of my jeans.

Andrew nodded, "We'll gas up while you go."

"Thanks. We're going to try to find an actual bathroom, but if not, we'll go around back."

Gabrielle's face was disgusted, and I marveled that she seemed to react better to an apocalyptic situation than peeing outside. Trivial worries, but maybe that was all that was keeping her together. Worry about the things that had always been constant.

I grabbed Dara, stroking her soft fur, and got out of the car that had become a sanctuary. Rhea, Anne, and Gabrielle followed and Eva hung back with her knife out. I approved of her caution, and was grateful that at least two of us knew the basics of how to defend ourselves.

The bathroom was a slum, but it was better than nothing. I let Rhea, Eva and Anne go in first while Gabby and I waited outside. I set Dara on the ground and prayed that she would not stray far. I didn't have the time to find a lost cat, but I didn't have the heart not to search for her if she did wander off.

It was Dara however, that saved my life. I heard her hiss and watched as all her fur stood on end, and my knife was out instantly.

"Dara, what is it?" I soothed, my eyes straining in the half light. I wished we would have held off until daylight, but our gas never would have lasted that long.

I wanted to yell for Jason or Andrew, but I knew they wouldn't make it in time. Also, any yelling from me would draw more of the hungry things, and it would make Rhea and Eva come out of the washroom.

Even if whatever was coming at us killed us, it would never think to look in the bathroom. I hoped.

My cat was still hissing, and Gabrielle was holding her knife determinedly but unsteadily. I vowed to protect her with my life.

Dara launched herself in the air and I finally saw my assailants. There were two huge men, the type of guys that I would have avoided walking past on a sidewalk. They looked greasy and tough, and their harsh eyes shone with hunger.

It was the hunger that scared me the most.

My cat was going feral on the biggest one, her claws ripping into the skin of his face. I didn't hesitate to use the advantage she had given me, and I leapt at the other man.

He grabbed me and pulled me closer, teeth going straight for my throat. I struggled with him, taking all the bruises in exchange for no bites. In every zombie story I had read, biting or exchanging fluids would change me into one of them. I would rather die, and I was starting to get pretty good at not dying.

His meaty hand finally let go of my arm he had been restraining to pull my head harshly to the side, exposing my fragile neck. I twisted my body wildly, determined to escape his hold. My hand was finally freed and I managed to swing my knife upright, ready to stab in every direction until the man dropped me.

My knife entered his temple, and I pulled it out viciously and stabbed it again and again until my feet finally touched the ground. His body started to crumple against me, and I struggled to stay upright. The weight of him was double my own, and I fell hard on the gravel, pain ricocheting up my arms. The other man with the shredded face lunged towards me, and I wriggled underneath his partner's body, desperate to get free. His hands grabbed at me, and I thought that I was probably about to die.

A rock hit him in the temple, knocking him just slightly off balance in his crouch. I leapt to my feet, adrenaline keeping me steady. I went after the stumbling man, my bloody knife already going after more death. I felt insane, and a quick scan around the area showed Gabrielle's pale face and the bathroom door opening. My cat was mewling pitifully on the pavement, and I knew she was dying. I locked my gaze on the evil creature, blind and stumbling in front of me; I tightened my grip on my knife as he recovered his balance. He was already searching for me, and I knew that this man had killed her.

He had killed Dara, my mother's precious kitten.

I felt my lips turn into a snarl, and I wasn't sure in that moment who was hungrier for blood, the monster or me.

In fact, I wasn't even sure which one of us was the monster anymore.

I was on him in an instant, and he fell to the ground, his already unsteady form easy to knock over. He was face down and defenseless, and I raised my knife in the air and brought it down to chop at his neck.

Eventually, someone pulled me off of him and I collapsed in the dirt. I saw that it was Jason who had come close enough to me to do so; everyone else was pressed against the wall in fear.

I looked back to the body I had mutilated; his neck had been torn up until it was held on by little more than a few ligaments. There was a gun on his belt and I grabbed it. The other man had one too, and I pulled at it until it came free. I stood on my shaky legs, adrenaline and fear and anger flowing through me. I kicked the man I had killed as hard as I could in the ribs, satisfied when his body jerked. It hurt my foot, but I didn't regret it.

A soft, sad noise brought me out of my stupor. Dara was wheezing on the ground, her kitten-soft fur matted with blood. I knelt beside her and picked her up gently, careful to keep her mouth away from my skin.

I was unsure if she could get infected, and I probably shouldn't be holding her as though she was a sick child, but no one stopped me, and there was no way I would just leave her there to suffer.

"Oh Dara, baby, what have you done?" I cried. She hissed at me, and I felt her broken little ribs sticking out from her skin. I deserved to be hissed at.

"Oh Dara, darling Dara." My words were incoherent, and all I could picture was my beautiful mother coming home with a gentle little kitten. All I could see was her snuggling with me on my favourite reading chair, or licking the food from my fingers when I let her. I could see her throwing herself at that *creature* to save my life.

Her hiss died out, and I knew that my hands that had been tightening like a vice on her neck had finally stolen her life. The life that had been sacrificed to save me.

My face turned up to see my friends staring at me in horror and fear. I felt like maybe they didn't know who I was, this blood-stained, violent girl who had managed to kill two men twice her size, and the cat that she had loved. I felt like maybe I didn't even know myself.

I made no excuses, "She might have been infected. I would rather kill her than have her be a monster. I expect any of you to do the same if it had been me."

"But-" it was Gabrielle's voice, aghast at what I had just implied. She would never kill me, not even if I came at her hungry for her flesh.

I stared her down, "I would rather die than be one of them."

I stood and glanced down at my torn shirt. There was blood all over me, and I was thankful that none of it was my own. I could not get infected.

"I have to use the washroom." I said to no one in particular and walked into the bathroom.

I shut the door behind me, sinking to the floor where dirt and mud caked the tile. My breath was shaky, and I could feel the sickening burning feeling in the back of my throat that meant I was about to cry. I stood and washed my face, and my hands, scrubbing away at them. The blood wouldn't come off, even though I scrubbed until my hands felt so dry they would crack.

I faced myself in the mirror, staring into my own golden eyes. I looked the same; a little bit sadder, a little dirtier, but the same.

"I am a killer." I whispered, watching the mirror form my words with my mouth; familiar features on an unknown girl. "I'm a murderer."

I sucked in air wildly, trying to control my emotions. In this type of world, I couldn't have emotions, not out in the open, not if I was going to live.

I swallowed all my pain, and all my tears, glaring at my image. "I will protect my friends. Doesn't matter who I am. What I become."

I nodded decisively, the mirror echoing my resolve. It was all that was keeping me going.

I opened the door, completely in control again. Everything was back to as normal as it could get outside the bathroom. Gabrielle and Jason were waiting for me, Dara's little body was covered with a rag of some sort, and I had washed most of the blood off my face and hair.

Gabrielle went to the bathroom and I waited with Jason for her to come back out.

"Was I wrong?" I asked. He was the only person I would ever ask, because he would never tell anyone else I had ever questioned my actions. He would also tell me the truth.

"No, Sandra." He replied, "I don't think so. You had to kill the men. They would have killed you. And I don't know about Dara, but if I was infected, I would rather have you kill me. I don't want to lose control and hurt anyone I love."

It was probably the most he'd ever said to me about feelings and emotions. Probably the most personal thing he had ever said to anyone. I would do him the same honour he would have done to me and take it to my grave.

"Thank you, Jason." I picked up the rag-covered bundle, and when Gabby came out of the washroom, we all walked to the car.

The others stood in front of an indent in the ground, and I saw that they were holding the cat food and some rocks. Rhea was holding a flower, it was only a dandelion weed, but it was a flower. I could have hugged her for her kindness.

That's how Rhea was though, the kindest of our group, and probably the least likely to survive, perhaps other than Anne. I had the sudden urge to protect her with my life, the way I always vowed to do with Gabby. I could understand why I felt that way though: Rhea was the type of person that made you want to look after her. She was the epitome of kindness and fragility: a flower never destined to grow in this world.

"I dug a hole. Over there," Andrew said gently. We all walked in a sad procession to the small hole dug beside the gas station. I laid Dara sweetly in it, and Rhea set her flower on top. I grabbed the cat food and opened it. Dry food mixed with dirt as I poured them on top of my cat, and I wished that I had more than just that to leave with her. I wish I didn't have to bury her beside some run-down gas station.

"Dara was a good cat," I declared, "she saved my life. And she loved my mother. They are together now. And maybe my dad is with them. I hope so anyway."

My speech was pathetic really, considering I had once wanted to be an English major. But really, what else was there to say?

We walked back to the car, and Andrew drove. I let Anne have the front, not wanting to sit beside her, left to study the similarities of her face: her copper hair and penetrating blue eyes, features she had shared with her mother.

Eva and Rhea took the two-seater, their heads bent together, black and blonde hair mixing as they whispered, and perhaps even mourned together. I sat in the middle of the far backseat and Gabby laid her head on my shoulder and fell asleep. I pretended that it was just another road trip where we were too tired to stay up, and snuggled together in the backseat.

I didn't want to curl around her the way I used to; I didn't want to touch her with all the blood staining my hands. I had changed my clothes, but I could see still flecks of it under my nails, even though I had scrubbed away until my skin was raw.

Instead, I turned my head away, towards Jason, and cried. I had promised myself I wouldn't cry anymore in the bathroom, but there was no holding it back now that I wasn't in danger again. I had never cried this much in my life, not even when my mother was killed, but I decided it was allowed. Just today.

Tomorrow I would have to be strong.

Chapter Four

    I was woken up by the type of sounds I expected to hear in a rainforest, not a van full of frightened people. For the first time since I had beheaded my neighbour I woke up and I wasn't frightened. Surely, if the rainforest was around me, nothing was about to jump out and eat me.

    "Zack!" Jason's voice ended my surreal moment, and I shot up from where I had fallen asleep on his shoulder. Jason had answered his cell, and I remembered then that he had a rainforest sound ringtone. Guilt flooded me for a moment, because I hadn't thought of Zack once since Dara had died.

    "Where are you?" Jason's voice was a mix of worry and happiness, and I couldn't help but smiling for him. Zack was alive!

    "Okay, we're surprisingly near. How are you travelling?"

    I wanted to beg Jason for answers, but he had a warning finger held up to the rest of us. Everyone in the van was wide awake and staring incredulously. We had obviously all believed Zack to be dead. Zack wasn't exactly the most intelligent guy around, but he was as bulky as Jason, and he knew how to use his muscle; it made sense that he had survived, he was a fighter.

I couldn't count the number of times class had been interrupted because Zack had gotten in a fistfight in the hallway. He was hot tempered and violent, and that was why I had never liked him. He was a nice enough guy, but with a temper and a jealous streak, and I had never been interested in him the way he was in me.

"You're what?!" Jason eyes widened, "A bike? Are you insane?"

I couldn't help the laughter that emerged, and it felt so good to laugh that I could barely contain myself.

"Yes, I know you needed to train, but you couldn't have taken the car instead of the bike? You're ridiculous." Jason paused, listening to Zack's reply, "Just keep going, we're past Pierceland. Yeah, head East on 55. It's an hour driving I think."

"Where is he?" I asked quietly.

"Near Cold Lake." Jason murmured.

Gabby snickered from beside me, "He's biking?"

"Has he run into any of those creatures?" Rhea asked.

Jason held up his hand, ignoring their questions. "Batteries dying Zack. Call someone else's phone if you need help. We'll wait on the road for you. We're in a silver van. Be careful."

The beep was audible, and Jason lowered his phone and stared at it. His phone was the first to go, and almost without thought I pulled mine out to check it. I had two bars, but how long would they last?

"I'm going to try my parents." Gabby whispered, "The lines have been down for so long, but if Jason got through, maybe I can too."

She pulled out her phone and started dialing.

"That's what Zack said." Jason muttered, "He couldn't reach us."

I smiled at him, "But now he's on his way. We're all going to be safe, and have to squish."

Jason frowned, "He's going to kill us when we tell him he has to leave his bike."

Andrew scowled. "He doesn't want to lose a bike? Anne lost her mom, Sandra lost her dad. We've all lost people. And he's worried about a bike?!"

Jason muttered, "Zack doesn't see things the way normal people do. He's an idiot."

"Damn right." Andrew growled.

Gabby's voice was panicked, interrupting Andrew's annoyance with Zack. "Mom? Dad? What's happening, are you safe?!"

The crackling on the line was obvious, although words were coming through in pieces. Gabby's eyes filled with tears.

"I can't hear you," she cried, "I can't hear you!"

I grabbed her arm, "Tell them you're safe! Maybe they can hear you! Tell them what you want them to know."

Gabby gulped in air, nodding at my words. "I'm safe, Mom, I'm safe. I'm with Sandy. We're all safe. I hope you are too. Love you. I love you so much. I'll find you!"

She hung up, unwillingly, letting her finger linger over the disconnect button.

I hugged her, as best as I could sitting down. "They're probably okay, Gabby. They're smart."

"I couldn't hear them. They were there, I recognized their voices. But I couldn't hear them! What if they needed my help?" She started to cry again, great heaving sobs that shook her athletic frame.

"Gabby. You couldn't have helped them even if they needed it. They're in the States, we're in Canada. We're too far away. If they were safe enough to answer a phone, they're as safe as we are."

Gabby nodded into her hands. "Okay."

"Alright, find a spot to pull over." I called to the front. After about five minutes Andrew pulled over, locking every door and turning off the engine. We sat in silence for a few minutes, watching every side of the van closely for movement. We didn't want to get ambushed and blocked in.

"Are we just going to sit here and wait?" Rhea asked.

Jason nodded, "Yes. We have to wait for Zack, and now would be a good time to make sure all your cells are nearby. He'll probably call either Eva or Sandra, he knows them best."

I grimaced at that. I knew nothing about Zack, we'd only ever spoken a few times at school. It made sense that he knew Eva, because Jason and Eva hung out all the time. I didn't relish the thought that he would probably call me and I would have to answer the phone.

We settled into the van more comfortably after a while with no movement outside. The longer the van sat with the engine off, the more unlikely it was for any hungry creatures to come get us. Quiet conversations were being held in the van, and Anne had climbed into the driver's seat to cuddle with Andrew.

Gabby was staring dolefully at her cell phone, "It's dying. They won't be able to call me back."

"Text them?" I asked, "Tell them to text you if they need anything. Or leave a voicemail. I doubt you'll be able to hear them. I'm surprised the lines are back up actually."

Gabby scowled, "Probably because enough people died."

No one argued, it was probably true.

"We need food." Andrew said, Anne curled in his lap.

I scowled, "We brought lots, we have some. If we're hungry there's granola bars."

Andrew shook his head, "No, Sandy, not right this second, but we need to learn how to find food outside. Hunt and stuff. I'm a good shot, but I've never been hunting, only to the shooting range. I don't know how to clean anything I bring down."

"Well, we're halfway there if you can shoot it." Eva said softly, "That's impressive on its own. We can figure the rest out."

"I don't want to wing it. Not when it's this important." Andrew murmured.

"Zack's a good shot. I don't know if he could clean a deer, but he knows how to hunt." Jason informed us.

Gabby was silent, still staring at her phone. I could tell she would be melancholy for a while, especially now that she had heard her parents' voices. It was almost worse, knowing they were alive, having something else to worry about.

I was almost thankful, in that moment, that everyone I cared about was in the van with me. I could look out for my group without anything else in my mind. It was probably the reason I seemed to be appointed leader.

"Are you excited Zack's safe?" I muttered to Jason.

He shrugged, "Yeah."

"He's a hazard." Andrew commented to us, "I'm not trying to be cruel, but we all know it. He's hot tempered and stupid."

"That's my brother. Watch your mouth." Jason's words were even, but I was surprised he had even spoken out.

Andrew shrugged, "Jason, I'm sorry, I respect you, but-"

"Then respect him." Jason snapped.

"Calm down." I interrupted. "Andrew, he's a good fighter, and he's stayed alive on his own. Keep your opinions about his personality to yourself. I know he's hard to handle, but in this world you don't need to be nice to get by."

Andrew closed his mouth and nodded. "You deal with him then."

I scowled, "I will, thank you."

Jason turned his head to the window, shutting his eyes in what I knew was fake sleep. I didn't bother him though, I was already angry enough that within a matter of days we had all started to fight.

Our wait was silent, and awkward. Despite Eva and Rhea's attempts to talk, the oppressive anger surrounding the rest of us cut any conversation short.

"Damn!" Andrew's curse made me jump. He started the van, and I scanned outside.

A man was staring at the van, grinning. I didn't recognize him, and I snatched my knife and crawled over the seats, crouching by the side door.

"Hungry?" I asked softly.

Andrew shrugged, "I don't know, but either we move, or we kill it."

I opened the door, "So we kill it."

I stepped out, facing the man in the ditch. I heard scrambling behind me, hoping the others were trying to get weapons to back me up.

"I see you," he called, stepping towards me.

I brought my knife up, attempting to look menacing. I wasn't exactly frightening, seeing as I was just over five feet. He would underestimate me, and that would kill him.

"Are you hungry?" I asked.

His smile was malicious, "Starving." He burst into a sprint, moving towards me at a shocking speed.

He was only feet away from me when I was shoved to the ground. Jason dove out of the van with the old sword from the backseat. It went through the man easily, pinning him to the earth. Jason was panting above the sword, watching the man grab for him from the ground.

I jumped to my feet, absolutely furious that Jason would shove me out of the way. I had been ready for him, ready to kill him.

As it was, the man just lay on the dirt, hands clawing at us. Every move he made jerked the sword around, destroying his insides.

"He should be dead. Normally, a person would die from that type of wound." Eva's voice was quiet behind me.

I plunged my knife through his temple, stopping all movements. "He wasn't normal. He was Hungry."

Jason pulled the sword out from his stomach, disgust written all over his face. "So they aren't human anymore? Is that what you're saying? We just kill them whenever, with no care to who they might have once been."

I glared, "Yes. We just kill them. Otherwise, we die. You can't think about who this man was; whether he had a wife, or kids, or parents. You shred their brain, and you walk away and forget about it."

Jason's steel eyes were full of judgement. "How could you just forget that? That you killed someone? You killed Mrs. Hines! You can just forget that?"

"Yes." My voice was icy. "I forget that, because if I don't, I get weak. And then I die. If I hadn't killed her, she would have killed Anne and I!"

"Who are you?" Jason asked; his voice was scared, as if for the first time he wasn't completely sure of me. It hurt, more than a little, but I steeled myself and stared him straight in the eye, knowing every single one of my friends was watching me.

"I'm a survivor. We're all survivors now, and if you aren't prepared to put your life above these creatures, you aren't going to be one for long."

I bent down and pulled my knife out of the man's skull, brushing past Jason and heading for the van's back. We needed water and granola bars, and I needed a moment for myself.

I wiped my knife on the grass beside the van, holding back the nausea that was threatening to empty the contents of my stomach. I wasn't sure if I was nauseous because I had killed the man, or because everyone seemed to think I was a monster.

The sooner Zack arrived, the better. Then we could keep moving, keep safe. Also, the one good thing about Zack was his inability to be serious; he would break this awkwardness that had settled about my group with ease.

It was Eva that came to talk to me, and I should have known that she would never fear me. We were so alike, and she probably knew how alienated and brutal I felt right now; still, I would make no apologies. I was saving their lives.

"Sandy, what if there's a cure? What if all these Hungry go back to normal in a few days?" her voice was frightened, as if this was the possibility that scared her the most. The possibility that I had killed people I loved, and I could have just waited and they'd be alright.

I shrugged. "I'm going to grieve either way. But not killing them will get all of us killed a lot faster."

Eva sighed, "I trust you, Sandy. Always have, always will."

I smiled at her, the first smile in a long while. "Thanks Eva."

"Jason trusts you too, you know? He didn't mean to question, he's just scared."

I nodded at her, handing her a granola bar and a water bottle. "Share the water bottle for now."

Eva thanked me, and although her eyes were still worried she got back into the van and left me to my guilt.

Chapter Five

Zack took longer to arrive than anyone felt comfortable with. While there had been no more attacks, the van's atmosphere was uncomfortable and cramped. Silence had reigned for hours, except for the small chatter between Anne and Andrew, who seemed to be the only people still getting along.

Hell, it had been less than a week and we were already being torn apart by our differences. The end of the world was obviously not about to bring us closer.

I supposed there were only two ways a small group could go when running and fighting for their lives though; either they came together -unbreakable, one armada of soldiers that could take on anything- or they fell apart: fighting each other, dying alone.

I did not want to die, whether it was alone or with those I loved.

Still, we had made it farther than most probably had, we were all still alive and about to gain another member. It pained me to think of all the people who had most definitely lost their lives in the last seventy two hours. It also pained me to think that those people would not be dead in their graves but out roaming the land looking for flesh.

"Sandra." The voice came at me, slow and reassuring, once more bringing me from sleep peacefully. Considering I had dreamt of blood and death I was getting good at waking up gently. Jason was watching me, and I wiped at my face, suddenly self-conscious I had been drooling.

"You have blood on your cheek." His words were blunt, a knife to my gut. I stared at my hands, seeing the stain that had transferred to my face. Quickly I snatched a sweater from the ground, wiping my cheek once again. How could I have been worried about saliva when I had blood on my face? The world had changed so drastically.

The blood left a dark maroon stain on the sleeve of the sweater. I threw it back to the ground, willing myself to forget that I had ever tainted it.

"What do you want, Jason?" I asked, my irritation from being awoken from my nap showing in my tone. He sighed, whether because he was annoyed with my own behavior, or because he didn't know how to answer my question, I would never know.

His dark eyes met mine, and whatever silent communication he wanted to have with me failed. I lived on words, actions, and Jason was only staring.

"What?" I snapped.

"I'll listen," he muttered, "from now on. I'll listen to you."

My heart sunk as my temper crackled, "I don't want you to listen, Jason. I want you to think for yourself, argue with me, tell me what you want, live your own life!"

Jason eyes widened, and I thought perhaps I had overwhelmed him with my words, as sometimes happened to him. He wasn't meant for words, just actions, emotions.

"I'm sorry. I just want you to continue what you're doing. I don't want you to like killing them, I want you to hate every second of it. But I also want you to love every second of living enough to keep doing it. Does that make sense?"

Jason's mouth tilted in a funny sort of smile; crooked and sad, but understanding. "I know what you mean."

I turned my attention on the others in the van, of which most were sleeping, trying to catch their rest when they could. Gabby was braiding Eva's hair, which seemed silly to me, but it was a nice way to pass their time, and at least it was breaking some of the silence up. Jason was sitting beside me still, looking stern, although at least he didn't seem angry or unsure about me any longer.

"Are you driving once Zack gets here?"

He nodded.

Gabby swiveled to look at me, flashing a smile. "We need a destination, Sandy. Can't just keep driving aimlessly."

I shrugged, "I don't know Saskatchewan that well, Gabby. We'll stop as soon as it's safe. The last thing we need is to run out of gas or blow a tire. This van is... safe."

Safe, such a foolish word to describe what the van meant to us now. It worked, of course, since it was a synonym of what I truly meant. Safe could also mean home, or a type of heaven, or devoid of danger.

The van had become our safety net -like children, hiding under their duvets- nothing could possible harm us inside these metal walls.

It wasn't true, of course, but the thought was comforting, and that was all that really mattered.

"Zack's coming down the road." Andrew's voice surprised me out of my thoughts, and I scrambled out of the van with my friends. Jason was surprisingly slow to get out, almost seeming weighed down by worries. Zack came skidding up to us, breathing hard. He was banged up pretty badly, and it looked like he needed stitches in a gash above his eyes which was bleeding profusely.

He ditched his bike, catching Jason in a hug that seemed to surprise the older brother, although it was returned. Jason finally let out a rare grin, and I knew that the only time that smile was present was with Zack around. So despite being a pain in the ass, he was worth something to us. To Jason.

"We gotta move." Zack's voice was cheery, but also filled with the type of fear I had never expected to hear from him. He ran his fingers through his thick hair, his cut still bleeding into his eye.

Andrew scoffed, "What the hell happened to you, man. You look awful."

"Took a fall on my bike trying to get away from some of those freaks," Zack's voice was rueful, "but you know I look good, Andrew."

I laughed, I couldn't help it. Zack just looked so ridiculous, his hand still in his blood soaked hair, telling Andrew how good he looked while trying to escape Hungry monsters. It was exactly the type of comment I had wanted, something to wipe the slate clean, bring out the best in myself.

Zack ingratiated himself to me in that moment, and I knew his wry comments would probably never fail to make me happy.

"Let's move then." Jason ended the moment, glaring at me for laughing. I wondered if he was trying to stop me from encouraging Zack to be so careless; if anything, I thought we needed some outlet of humour here.

Zack snatched his bike, and turned to the van looking ready for anything. He looked deadly, unlike the rest of us who just looked like wayward, lost children. Covered in scrapes and cuts, the raw muscle he had earned from an athletic life was a testament to how tough he was.

How was that fair?! I was the one who had done most of the murdering in the last few days, and I still looked like a wide eyed, scrawny kid. Still, I had always looked young, and perhaps that would work in my favour in this new hell.

"Can't take the bike." Andrew declared to Zack, his eyes flashing victoriously. I had never seen him look so wicked, Andrew was nothing if not calm and friendly.

Zack did not end up throwing the fit that was expected of him, instead he just rolled the bike to the ditch and turned back to the group, his expression beyond eager.

Jason stared blankly, "Zack, you told me once you loved that bike more than you loved me. I didn't think you'd just leave it."

Zack shrugged, "Man, there are like twelve freaky zombie things not that far behind me and I don't really care about a hunk of metal at this point."

I swung towards the direction Zack had come from, panic making me ready for battle. There were no Hungry in sight, but that didn't mean they weren't coming. We raced to the van, fitting everyone in once more; it was cramped and awful, but it was a haven, it was life.

Jason started the van and took off down the road at a breakneck speed. I could almost hear Eva's thoughts of car sickness invade her brain, and even though she didn't voice a complaint I pitied her.

"Ladies, check out my guns." Zack's voice was smooth and flirtatious, and I rolled my eyes at him. My mocking soon turned to a gasp of surprise though when I found Zack brandishing one handgun and a rifle for our inspection. Pleasure surged through me at the rifle, Jason's words assuring us that Zack could probably take down game to feed us ringing in my ears.

Jason nodded, "Told you he'd get our parent's handgun. Whose rifle?"

"Our neighbour. She was dead, so I figured I needed it more." Zack's response was clinical, despite the fact that it made me uncomfortable.

Andrew's green eyes were ruthless as he stared at Zack. "How did she die, exactly, Zack?"

Zack's infamous temper raged in his eyes, his ears turning a brilliant shade of scarlet. "Oh, I don't know Andrew, maybe it was the bloody flesh eating *monsters* out there?!"

"Calm, Zack." Eva's voice was soothing, but I thought she might have wanted us to all shut up because it was only worsening her nausea.

"You want me to be calm!? He accused me of killing our neighbour!" Zack's voice was rising, along with the burgundy flush of his face.

I flinched, "So what? It's a reasonable assumption."

Zack whirled on me, but something in my face stopped him from yelling at me. "Why is that reasonable, Sandy? When is murder *reasonable*?"

I looked away, out the tinted glass that hid me from the world. "It's reasonable when there is no other choice. Like when I killed my neighbour."

The van went quiet. Zack had been bicycling off on his own this whole time, what could he possibly know about the danger and pain we had gone through? It had only been days since I had last talked to him, but suddenly we were so very different; the hot tempered violent boy I had known was suddenly so much more naive and kind than I seemed to be.

"I'm sorry."

I shrugged. "Me too."

And wasn't that the goddamn understatement of the year.

Chapter Six

It was starting to blur into one long hellish nightmare as we drove East, which was why I was so glad when we finally ended up in the middle of absolutely nowhere. I wasn't even sure which province we were in anymore, probably the Northwest Territories, or maybe even Manitoba. All I knew is that we had followed highways through prairies for hours, North, and East; sometimes we backtracked West. There were less and less encounters with the Hungry.

We had been driving for days, almost a week, and Jason had gotten very good at siphoning gas. We'd gone through a Gerry can, but had gotten a refill at a deserted car. Soon we would need to stop for another fill up, and my body was screaming at me to find somewhere to sleep.

The car atmosphere was pleasant, and it surprised me that everyone had been content to forget the disasters that had happened. Anne didn't bring up her mother again; in fact, she barely showed any resentment towards me. No one brought up

Dara. I felt like I was living in this fragile bubble of ignorance.

We had tried using our cell phones many times, but the lines were all down. We assumed it was because of the overload the servers would have had as soon as everyone realized what was happening. Eventually, every one of our phones had died, our charging cords back home; little bits of hope extinguished with just a quiet beep.

It seemed like fate when I spotted a potential safe house to sleep in just as night had taken over the day. It was a skeleton in the dark, and the menacing shape of it frightened me. I knew it was probably the best bet for safety though, because it looked as though no one had been inside of it for years. It was just outside of a provincial park, and the road we were on didn't seem as though it was going anywhere special. We needed somewhere to regroup.

The girls had been napping when I saw it; Eva, Gabby and Rhea curled together in the back, and Andrew holding Anne's sleeping form in the two seater, with Zack on the ground on some blankets and clothes. None of them wore their seat belts, and the thought of berating them for the unsafe practice almost made me laugh. To die in a car accident after all we had been through seemed like a mercy.

I had turned off my music, which was unusual for me; I liked to have some background noise. I was jumpy, and the small house looming on the side of the road startled me enough to make me step on the brake, flight-or-fight breaking in on the small serenity I had found while driving on the deserted road.

Gabrielle scrambled to sit up, her head whipping from side to side as she assessed the situation. The sight of a tiny house seemed to please her, because her face, so drawn with stress immediately started to glow. She reminded me so much in that moment of the girl I had known only a week or so ago. Unbelievably beautiful, and able to handle anything life threw at her.

"You're sure it's safe?"

Jason glanced at me out of the corner of his eyes; we were probably both having the same thought: nowhere was safe anymore, but neither of us was willing to voice that aloud. Plus, driving any longer was probably more dangerous than taking a chance on this house.

"I'm exhausted," I murmured. I didn't want to make Jason drive again, and I had no will to keep going. I just wanted to lie down and stop thinking--reliving the people I had killed... Dara's funeral.

Jason dark eyes showed his smile and he nodded, "Yeah, I know. Hopefully it's safe, and we can get some sleep."

I nodded in agreement, but we both knew we would never truly sleep again.

"We'll go in, scan the whole place and make sure it's really safe. Take no chances. Kill everything that moves," Gabby declared. I nearly beamed in pride; the girl could be innocent and naïve but deep down she had a core of steel. If I could be half as strong as her I would be doing great.

"Do you think anything would have followed us here?" Rhea wondered, "Will we finally get to sleep and then get ambushed? I don't know if I want to stop."

Zack sat up from the floor and grinned, "Don't worry, if they haven't already flocked to the house, there probably isn't a lot in the area. In most legends anything that is

Zombie-like can't hear very well, or so it's said. Usually they go by scent."

I smirked as the others gaped at Zack's words, "How do you know this crap?" Eva wondered.

Zack shrugged and gave me a devil-may-care smile, "I like to be prepared."

I rolled my eyes, and enjoyed the weak laughter from my friends. We were so tired and tense, and I knew we needed a break. We needed to try this dilapidated house; it was the only shot we had at keeping our sanity. It looked abandoned and old-- the gas station had looked similar and look how that had turned out. The thought soured my stomach, but I ignored it. We needed to sleep.

I pulled up the drive and made sure the car was ready for a quick getaway. Neither Rhea nor Anne could stand violence, and I knew they would be useless if we had to kill anything, so I left them in the running car. I took the sword and a gun, and handed out knives to the rest of the group. Zack had his handgun, Jason had the rifle on his back, Andrew got the other gun. I trusted that Zack and Andrew could hit their targets, it was only Jason I feared for with the large rifle; he had never held a weapon in his life, but I supposed if the target was close enough he couldn't miss.

I drilled them, "If anything so much as moves, kill it. Go for the brain, we know that a sword through the stomach didn't work-- but no mythological thing can live without its head."

Eva shuddered, "Sometimes snakes can live for days without their heads."

She was terrified of snakes and the reminder of such a strange fear when there was flesh-eating-hungry things on the loose made me wistful. "I'm pretty sure you're thinking of cockroaches or earthworms. Snakes need their heads."

Eva frowned, as if she didn't really trust my words about snakes, but I knew she trusted me on these hungry things. Her knives were gripped so tight in her hands, her knuckles were ivory.

"Follow me," I murmured and took the lead. Jason was right behind me, his presence a shadow in my peripheral vision; Eva and Gabrielle were in the centre, and Andrew was taking up the rear with Zack. The door wasn't locked. The entrance was pitch black, and I snatched the flashlight in my pocket. The beam scoured the area, and all I saw was ragged old couches and a scratched up table. There were no sounds.

"Knives out," I whispered, my own hand curled around the handle of a wicked butcher knife. Then I shouted, loud and quick. Anything that was inside the house would come running.

Nothing did; and for that I was eternally grateful.

Eva's nails were digging into the flesh on my arm, "What the hell was that, Sandra?"

Zack tried to pry her off, "Easiest way to find out if there's anything in the house. There isn't, if you didn't notice. Stop it, you're hurting her."

Eva let go. She had been hurting me, but I would never say anything. If she wanted to scratch my arm to ribbons I would let her, we all needed some sort of release, and the stress of survival was killing us, ironically enough.

It had only been a week. How were we going to survive any longer?

"Sorry," Eva said softly. I caught her hand and squeezed it.

"No problem. Eva, why don't you and Jason scan the house and lock it down just in case? We'll go get the girls. We all need a good night's sleep."

Jason had his knife out, and with a nod to Eva, they headed farther into the house. The image they made stung my heart a little bit, two teenagers who should have been worried about the rest of their lives, instead worried about creatures that wanted to eat them.

I turned to go back to the car, Andrew, Zack, and Gabby behind me. The car was off, which angered me a little. The only thing we wanted them to do was keep the car running.

After that thought came the fear, because the girls weren't stupid, they just didn't know how to fight. They would *never* have turned off the car.

Andrew started running, his long legs eating up the distance to where Anne was. I was hot on his heels, knife in hand. My heart pounded, and I had never been so grateful that Andrew and Zack both had guns. The thin beam of my flashlight seemed measly against the night sky.

The sight in front of the car made my blood run cold. A man was holding Anne by her auburn hair, a long, wickedly curved knife at her throat. He was huge, bigger in both height and width than Zack was, and his military brush cut only emphasized his obvious strengths. Immediately, I was frightened: this man was dangerous.

Rhea was behind him, but I knew she would never make a move to save Anne. It wasn't because she didn't want to save her, I knew Rhea would rather die than watch anyone else get hurt, but she didn't know *how.*

I should have stayed with them! I should have made Jason, or Andrew, or even Zack stay with them! I knew my regrets were nothing compared to Andrew's; he was the one standing idly by while the girl he loved had a knife to her throat.

I had promised nothing would happen to anyone while I was alive! Out of everyone, Anne didn't deserve this; she had already watched me slaughter her mother-- she shouldn't have to die.

"Let her go." My voice was deadly. I was rather impressed with myself.

He snarled, "Why?"

I stared straight into his eyes, so full of death. "None of us here are Hungry. We're trying to live. We wanted to stay in the house for a while, because it seemed safe. Do not hurt her. You will regret it."

He smirked, and I knew that he was the wrong person to threaten. He was ice cold to the bone, whether because life had made him cruel, or because this infection spreading across the globe had created a monster. It didn't matter.

He threw Anne towards us as a distraction and Andrew dropped his gun to grab her. Zack's safety clicked off the same instant I lunged forward, knife out, trying to get the upper hand.

Rhea threw herself in the middle of us.

"Stop!"

I stopped dead, shock penetrating my system. Rhea, the peacekeeper, the one who was *terrified* of violence, had just thrown herself in front of my knife, and Zack's gun.

For a man who had held her friend hostage.

He looked stunned too, and pity surged into my heart. He had probably never had anyone stand up for him before this moment, and Rhea doing it now had thrown him off guard.

She had just managed what I had been trying to do. He was off his game. He didn't know what to expect.

"Rhea. Move. Why are you defending him?"

Rhea stared incredulously at me, as if I was the one who had hurt her friend, "Because this is obviously *his* safe house. He was making sure we weren't crazy, and he didn't hurt anyone. Wouldn't you have done the same to a big group of people if you were alone in a scary house?"

My rage and shock turned to embarrassment at what I had done. Really, the strange man had done the one thing that wouldn't get him killed. Had he tried to talk to me in the house, I would have killed him on sight.

I inclined my head slightly, "I'm sorry. I didn't think. My name is Sandra Carter."

He stepped forward but left my outstretched hand untouched, "John Reid. How many in your group?"

I frowned. "Eight."

"How many did you start out with?" he asked.

My eyes narrowed. "Eight."

I got the distinct impression I had just gained some of his respect.

"Your group?"

I glanced around. "I guess so."

There was a long beat of silence, then finally, "Do any of you know first aid? Or how to sew?"

"Why? Are you hurt?"

He raised an eyebrow, as if the thought of him getting hurt was ridiculous. It infuriated me.

"No, but someone's hurt in the house. Cut on her leg."

I smiled. This was the first sign of humanity he had shown. "Yeah, We have some solutions for infections, and Eva Redson-- she's inside-- is good with a needle and thread."

"I'm not bad either," Rhea added, smiling cautiously.

He gestured that she should go ahead, and I followed Rhea, not willing to let John anywhere near her. Andrew and Zack went after me, and John followed at the end, as if he feared anyone at his back.

I knew that John holding a knife to Anne's throat destroyed any chance of a friendship between him and Andrew. The safety was off on Andrew's gun, he was completely ready to use it if he thought John needed to be put down.

Then again, I doubted the gun would ever be not at the ready again.

Upon reaching the door of the so-called safe house we found Jason and Eva panting at the door. "We have to go, there's somebody living-" Eva was cut off by Jason's dry laugh.

"Looks like they already found him." Despite the chuckle coming from him, Jason's eyes were taking in every inch of John.

I sighed, "Yes, this is John. John, this is Jason, and here is Eva."

John nodded, ignoring every hand that extended in invitation towards him.

He was a man of very few words. We would probably have to drag any information we wanted out of him painfully and slowly. I didn't care enough to try. I had enough on my plate trying to keep the eight people I had started with alive. I didn't have time to make friends.

However, I doubted my lack of interest would have offendèd John. He didn't care about us, and I noticed that when one of us came to close to touching him he glared and moved away. He didn't like company, and didn't want it either. He'd let us stay tonight to fix up whomever he had hidden, but I doubted it would go farther than that.

John seemed like a very dangerous man.

"Follow." He didn't ask, just brushed past Eva and expected her to follow. Andrew, Anne and Rhea followed John and Eva, leaving Jason, Zack, and I alone.

Zack was furious, although he had kept his silence and his cool for longer than I ever would have expected him to. Still, his hands were clenched around his gun, and I wouldn't be surprised if he decided an impromptu fight was in order tonight.

"He's not some high and mighty lord, Sandra." Zack's hiss caught me off guard, "You don't have to listen to him. He's got to be close to our age."

I stared at him, "I'm not listening to him, but we are imposing. And don't go after him Zack, he's obviously capable of handling himself."

That didn't help, and Zack threw me a withering glare, "We're nearly the same size, I'm not worried."

I hadn't realized the difference between Zack and John wasn't very much, they were both huge, broad men. Still,

Zack still seemed like an overgrown teenager to me, while John seemed like someone who could had taken lives.

More like me.

I supposed appearances really were deceiving, then. I glared at Zack, "Just leave him alone!"

Zack's fury was something to be reckoned with, but for now he retreated away from Jason and I. My temples were pounding, and I tried to calm my racing pulse. Jason waited in silence, letting me collect myself.

"Where's Gabby?" I asked quietly, finally noticing her absence.

Jason nodded at the group that had left, "We found a woman in the basement. She was delirious and injured. The basement is obviously being used as a hideout, and we left Gabby down with the wounded girl."

"Okay." I was still staring after the group, thinking on John, and how Rhea had so easily thrown herself in front of my knife.

Would she die so easily for anyone?

The woman had absolutely no survival instincts, and she was going to be the one to get killed.

"He's interesting, isn't he?" Jason's voice was cool, and measured. I shook myself out of my thoughts and concentrated on his words, staring up at him. He had always been much larger than me, but after meeting John I didn't think of Jason as some sort of giant anymore.

"Who? Zack?" I was baffled. Jason never initiated conversation; hence why I felt so comfortable around him. I never had to speak if I didn't want to.

"No, John." Jason was eyeing me curiously. I didn't know what to think. What did he even mean by interesting? I had met John three seconds before Jason had.

"Uh, yeah, I guess so. He's obviously tough to survive this long, and he's got the whole attitude down, he's very..."

"Evil."

I cocked my head at the word, mostly because I wasn't sure if that was how I would classify John. He wasn't talkative, and he was definitely cold. I wouldn't call him evil; he had saved a woman's life, and he hadn't hurt Anne when he could have.

Yet I had killed an innocent kitten.

No, John was not the evil one here.

"Not evil." I corrected, "Just dangerous."

Jason was still watching me with his dark eyes, and I felt blood rush to my face. I rarely blushed, and I couldn't figure out why I would now of all times, but still my cheeks heated.

"Why are you blushing?" he asked suspiciously.

"Because you're staring at me and asking me about John! What the hell, Jason?"

He flushed too, as if he had just realized what he had been doing.

"Sorry."

"Whatever." I snapped, finally following everyone down to the basement. I regretted my final snap at Jason within seconds, but my pride wouldn't allow me to apologize. I had gone through too much today to care about hurting his feelings.

The basement was lit up, but the windows had been all boarded up to prevent light escaping. Two makeshift beds were on the floor, one empty and immaculately made, and one containing the body of a woman.

She was pretty, and that was the first thing that flashed through my mind: she had long brown hair, and ivory skin. She was older than I was, definitely. Maybe in her early thirties, although it was hard to tell. The hand that escaped the blanket was thin and graceful, and even the ring circling her fourth finger was delicate.

The second thought I had was that she was probably going to die.

Blood was seeping out of her leg, the bandages already soaked through. Her skin was clammy, and the luxurious hair that I envied was stuck to her forehead.

I gagged, "Oh god, I need to leave." I spun and walked to the opposite end of the basement. I crouched down and hung my head between my knees.

I heard Eva and Rhea taking charge, Andrew was holding the woman down and Anne was handing the right supplies to Eva at the right moment. Rhea was commanding Zack to heat water, and he rushed away on her request.

"What's her name?" Rhea asked John.

"Sophie."

Jason left me to help hold her down and I held my pose to combat nausea. Gabrielle eventually came and sat beside me, watching me with both caution and amusement. Her dark hair was lank and matted, and I couldn't help but think how different it was, now that trivial things like hair and makeup weren't worth our time.

"Are you afraid of blood?" She asked.

I groaned, "It makes me nauseous sometimes." I recalled that moment in the gas station bathroom, scrubbing my fingers viciously to rid myself of it. I hated blood.

She was kind enough not to point out that it was still all over me, and that I had so easily slaughtered three people this past week, and a cat. She did laugh nervously, and it was at that moment that I realized I scared her. Gabrielle was afraid of me.

I looked up, "Are you frightened of me now?"

Gabby had the grace not to lie, "Yes. But I love you, and I trust you. I know you had to do it. But can I ask you a question?"

I nodded, sick to my stomach with blood, murder and fear.

She barely whispered, "Are you frightened of yourself?"

I stared at where she had been sitting long after she left, my nausea at the injured girl's —Sophie's— blood gone in the wake of her question. I knew the answer of course: yes. I was terrified of myself, and my new talent for violence. I was scared one day I might lose who I was, just lose myself, and all I had left would be my talent for killing. But I was also scared of what would happen if I chose to be like Rhea, or Anne. Sure, we would always be calm, and humane and beautiful, but we would die.

I knew this as surely as I knew that the muffled screams coming from the other side of the room were a good thing. Sophie was being fixed.

When finally, they went silent, I moved to where she was. Black string, the kind I would have used to sew a button on was being used to hold together her leg. Everything stank of vodka, the only cleaning solution we had. I couldn't imagine having it poured on a gaping wound. I think I would have cried and screamed too.

She had screamed but there was no trace of tears on her cheeks. She was dirty except for her sanitized leg, and her eyes were frosty blue and totally lucid. They glanced briefly at Zack, who had returned with boiling water. All the bloody clothes were in it, and I remembered Andrew saying the Hungry could smell. I didn't know if he was right or wrong about that, but it wasn't worth the risk.

Thank goodness someone was thinking.

Her eyes passed over Zack, finding John quickly. He watched her without emotion; he was a total blank slate.

"You should have let me die."

John nodded, "I know."

She lay back down and finally, finally started to cry.

My heart had turned to ice, because the words she had just spoken to John were the exact same Anne had said to me. I had killed Anne's mother to make her say that to me, so what had John done!?

Everyone returned slowly to the basement, gathering around the cot Sophie cried on. She sobbed without shame, and I noticed that even crying made her pretty. When I cried, I looked like a puffed up baby. The jealousy I felt in that moment shamed me.

Sophie's sobs slowly died off, and she finally whispered, "I let him die. My... my... Alex. My husband. He died to save me. And now that he's gone, I don't want to be saved." Here she stared once more at John, who stared back unflinchingly.

This woman was broken, and no amount of stitching or healing could fix her. I didn't know what to do. I wanted to apologize; I wanted to help-- but all I could do was stand there and stare, the same thing I had done when my mother had died. I couldn't even speak, or cry.

Rhea, though, she always knew what to do. She got down on the ground and scooped up Sophie and held her. She was careful of her leg, and with every bit of strength she had, Rhea held on. Sophie looked shocked at first, as if she didn't know what to do with this strange woman hanging off of her.

After her initial shock, she burst into renewed sobs and grabbed Rhea as if her life depended on it. I had never seen anything like it. Instantly, these two women who had nothing in common just bonded. Rhea held her, and Sophie poured out everything she had.

I must have watched for an hour or so, shocked and bone tired. The others stood around me, and I realized that once more we were all mourning with this girl we had just met over someone we didn't even know.

We had to mourn, because no one else would. Because we had to hope that one day when we were dead, someone would do the same.

Chapter Seven

November

John never asked us to leave, and I think that's why we stayed for so long. The house was one of a kind, the only bit of civilization left on a dead end road. I realized we were safer in that house than ever before, mostly because I had never seen anyone more deadly than John.

I had watched him closely the first day, after we had mourned with Sophie. She had finally fallen asleep, and Rhea promised to stay with her in case she needed anything. Anne and Andrew disappeared into a bedroom to take the time we had to sleep and recuperate. I made sure they nailed boards up on the windows before going in, just to block any light from escaping. We didn't want to draw any Hungry to us.

Eva sat with Gabrielle a lot, and I think perhaps they were comforting each other in their own way. Our old lives flashed before my eyes, where we were inseparable: one person in three bodies. We were different now, on the outside and on the inside, but we were also still the same. We had been best friends, the three of us, but now that I had become someone I didn't even recognize, they were growing closer without me.

I resented it, in a lot of ways, but I didn't blame them. I wouldn't want to be my own friend these days, yet Jason and I seemed to be getting closer. I couldn't really tell, since we never spoke. We went everywhere together though, and it was nice to sit in mutual silence with someone who held some of your secrets.

Zack sometimes came with us, filling our silences with quips and jokes that would make me smile. He was endearing when he wanted to be, but often he would disappear for days from our company, and I wondered if he was training. Zack had always been dedicated to a goal to the point of obsession, and I feared that his new goal was to be as strong as John.

We watched John a lot. He was deadly. Rest and relaxation were not something he was familiar with; he took every second of spare time to practice fighting and surviving. On the second day there I realized he could kill with a knife at twenty yards. I could barely throw a baseball that far.

He could shoot a bow, and I watched him bring down a small deer in the woods outside the rickety house. I wondered briefly where he had learned to hunt with a bow, but I never gathered the courage to ask.

John still frightened me with how silent he was, how deadly he could be, but it was the way he had reacted to Zack only a few days after meeting him that lingered in my mind. Zack —after getting over his initial dislike— had been amazed at John's abilities, and at the first chance he got he had praised him and clapped a hand on his back.

I had never seen anyone move that fast, John had him pinned on the ground within seconds, a knife we didn't know he had on him pressed into Zack's neck. It was probably the only time I had seen John become undone; he had been panting, fury leaking out of every pore. I thought Zack was as good as dead.

Instead, John had hissed out, "Don't touch me." Pulled himself up and disappeared into the woods for an entire day.

Zack had been shaken, he wasn't a small guy and he knew how to fight, and John had him by the throat within seconds. I knew there was no love lost between them now, hence why Zack was pushing himself to be better, although I had high hopes that Zack would get over it and go back to being his cheery self.

John hadn't spoken since that incident. He was terrifying, and it didn't help that I knew he was the best fighter we had ever seen.

I wanted him on my team for his skill, but I never wanted to see him again because in truth, he terrified me.

Yet he never told us to leave.

So two weeks later, we were all still at the safe house with him. We were eating fresh meat from John's kills, and saving every soup can we had for when surviving became a matter of hoarding food. Sophie was up and walking again, slowly. We had been feeding her more meat and vegetables than we could really afford to, but with the blood she had lost she needed iron. Rhea was considering taking the stitches out in another week, although she wasn't sure. She wasn't a doctor, she had only ever hemmed curtains, sewn buttons. I had no real opinion on the matter; I still got nauseous just looking at them.

It was the afternoon of the seventeenth day when everyone seemed to gather in the kitchen. We had had these meetings almost every day, so it wasn't unexpected, but even John had come to this one. I knew it had to be important to draw John away from his knife throwing, so I sat up and paid strict attention.

Sophie was wearing hiking boots and a backpack. A hunting knife was slid into her belt, and I noticed she had cut off at least eight inches of her hair. It was jagged and brushed her shoulders, and her eyes had grown lifeless.

I knew that she wanted to die, and I understood why. Since her first mention of Alex it had become obvious that she had loved him more than anything else in her life. Losing him was killing her. Despite healing her injury, we hadn't saved her. She was unstable, and I couldn't trust her. A woman with a death wish was a liability.

My father mirrored Sophie in every way. He had become a shadow of the man he'd been when my mother was alive. They had loved each other with every fibre of their beings, and when my mom had died, my father was left as only half of a person. I used to envy that type of love; now I couldn't imagine having that type of weakness. It was terrifying, to think that a single person had the power to destroy you without ever raising a weapon to you.

Sophie never told us how Alex had died, only saying he had sacrificed himself so she could escape. I could almost imagine it, watching the Hungry take down her husband as she ran for her life, only realizing she would have rather died with him after she was safe.

"I'm leaving." Sophie stated, "I need you to take my stitches out."

I expected Rhea to agree and go along with her demand, even though I thought it was too soon to do it, mostly because Rhea was a pushover. Eva wouldn't remove them but Rhea would if Sophie ordered her to. I was proven wrong however, when instead, Rhea rose from the table, fury all over her face.

"Those stitches aren't ready to be taken out, and therefore you will not be leaving!" Rhea shouted, "We did not work to save you, only to have you die!"

Eva nodded forcefully, but I knew Anne's shocked expression mirrored my own; usually Rhea was placid and as easy to manipulate as a docile puppy.

Sophie was stunning in her rage, "You can't control me, and I never asked you to save me! I didn't even want to live! So either you take these stupid things out, or I rip them out myself!"

Rhea composed herself, but her voice was cold, her eyes merciless, "Then rip them out, because I won't be responsible for your stupidity and death."

Then she whirled away and stormed to the basement, leaving all of us to gape at her exit.

Sophie emitted a frustrated shriek and slumped to the table, backpack squishing into her. "Is she always this stubborn!?"

Zack laughed at Sophie's question, digging his knife into the already destroyed table.

"No," he said, "usually you wouldn't have to ask twice, but apparently she feels strongly about this."

Sophie sighed, "Just my luck. I guess I'm stuck with you for a while."

I didn't like the way she referred to us, as if we were a clan of lepers, so I snapped at her, "I'm so sorry you have to deal with the people who saved your life. You could always go ahead and rip out your stitches."

Sophie laughed, "See, I expected that type of reaction from you."

I had no response, and the thought that she had expected my anger threw me. Once upon a time I had been a fairly calm and level headed person. I hated her. I hated her so much the feeling burned inside.

So instead of yelling, I stood and walked away, but my exit had nowhere near the impact of Rhea's, because apparently it was becoming common knowledge that I had a wickedly quick temper.

Chapter Eight

Three days later John spoke again. They were the first words I had heard since the Zack incident.

We were gathered in the kitchen once more, and John appeared, looking as deadly as ever, sporting knives and a raptor gaze. This only happened when something important was going on, so I managed to drag Sophie from her sulking in the basement back upstairs.

"There is a town about two hours from here, near Black Point, and it should be empty of people now. The radio signal has been dead for days, so obviously the world has gone to hell. We should do a raid and get more food, gas and weapons. First aid, too."

For a moment I waited for him to elaborate, to give us the plan, but nothing else came from him. John wasn't a leader; he was a fighter.

Planning was up to me.

I nodded. "That actually sounds good. We have a good food source here," I looked to John to give him credit for his hunting, "but when we leave we will want gas, and there aren't enough weapons to go around right now. Also, if we have any more accidents, we'll need bandages and antibiotics. Penicillin will literally be a life-saver later."

When we first had escaped my house I hadn't even thought about infection or sickness. Truth be told, if Sophie's leg *had* gotten infected, she would have died. So we needed to get our hands on some penicillin, and painkillers.

"Alright, let's get going!" Sophie demanded. She wasn't one to sit around planning; she was always in action.

"No!" I knew if Sophie came she would probably die. "Jason, Sophie, Zack, Anne, and Gabby: you stay here. We don't need everyone, and what good would it do us to have a van crammed full of people when we need to fill it with supplies? Also, we need to keep the house on lockdown. No Hungry get in, we stay safe."

I could tell almost all of them hated this plan. Jason and Zack both liked to be close to protect everyone, and Sophie really just wanted to pick a fight. I was in charge though, and Jason knew that with John on our side, we would be safe. Zack would just have to get over it.

"You need more fighters!" Zack's voice was immediate, and even though Jason stayed silent, I knew he agreed with his hot headed brother.

"We have fighters; what we need is a cautious group who will come back alive." I told him bluntly.

"Not that I don't love Rhea, but why are we bringing her? She can't fight." Andrew's reasoning was sound, but I actually had already thought about it.

"Because she's calm in most situations, and if anyone gets hurt we need her. I can't stomach injuries, obviously." I glared at Sophie for a second, ashamed of my weakness, "And I doubt anyone else would know what to do, either. Well, except for Eva with her stitching, but we need her to be a fighter."

Rhea nodded, "I don't like to fight, but I will help anyway I know how."

"Also," Eva added, "the only thing I can do is stitch, and to be honest, it grosses me out."

I laughed harshly for what felt like the first time in forever, surprised at her words.

My rag-tag group eyed me strangely after my laughter, probably amazed I still could laugh. I sobered and stared at them proudly. They were so much stronger than anyone could have ever predicted.

I prayed we wouldn't run into any trouble, but entering a town that at one time was full of people pretty much just guaranteed the Hungry.

"Let's go. Gather weapons and a first aid kit for Rhea and go. We should use the daylight we have." John's words were curt, and as soon as he got the agreement he was looking for he left for weapons.

Exactly fifteen minutes later, John, Andrew, Eva, Rhea and I were ready to go. The van had been almost completely unloaded in the hopes we would return with it full of everything we needed.

John, Andrew and I carried the only guns we had, because we were the best shot. John and Andrew were an almost flawless shot, and I could probably hit something if I needed to. I was nowhere near as exact as them, but I didn't have to be precise, I just had to survive.

I let Andrew drive, and exchanged my plan of action with John. He was a good strategist, even if he didn't like leading.

"So we're entering the town on the west side, closest to the pharmacy. That's good, because we need to storm it and grab anything that we might need: painkillers, bandages, cold and flu medicine and *anything* behind the counter. Even if we don't know what it is, we better find out. If there is a book containing medical information, grab it. We don't want to hurt people trying to help them."

"In and out in five minutes. Rhea, go with Eva and get the behind the counter medicines. I'll go for the cold and flu stuff, painkillers, whatever. Sandra: bandages and soap, shampoo. We need stuff to live on." Andrew was always thoughtful, shampoo and the like hadn't even occurred to me.

"I'll watch the doors." John added.

"What if... what if they're waiting for us?" Rhea asked.

I frowned. "Why would they be waiting?"

Rhea hands twisted nervously in her lap. "They can think, can't they? What if they can plan?"

"I think their hunger would block out any rational thought." John's voice was authoritative, and Rhea's hands stopped twining. I wasn't exactly reassured, Rhea's question had raised some of my own worries; however, we didn't have a lot of options anymore, we had to continue with the raid.

We didn't speak for the rest of the trip, and luckily didn't see any Hungry. I had expected to see some, so I hoped that maybe they could starve, and had done so in this town. I doubted it.

The pharmacy came into view and we parked at the back entrance emergency doors. Windows were shattered around the place, and I realized that other people had looted before us. I wondered if other survivors were in the area, or if I was just seeing remnants of the past.

We exited the van silently, and I thanked my father briefly for buying me the automatic starter last winter, because I was going to leave the van running, but locked. I could only do that because my keys didn't have to be in the ignition.

The doors weren't locked, and one of the windows had been cracked. Rhea was the only one not holding a weapon. She was carrying a large duffel bag, ready to pack it with anything she could find. The rest of us only had plastic bags.

John opened the door and scanned the inside for a second, he entered with all of us tight behind him. The pharmacy appeared empty, but looks could be deceiving. I didn't even want to try my yelling-then-waiting idea again, this place was too large.

"Go, weapons out, kill anything that moves." John ordered in a harsh whisper, shooing us down the aisles.

Eva and Rhea moved quickly, hopping over the counter and dropping all the leftover prescriptions into their duffel bag. I opened my grocery bag and started snatching soaps and shampoos, razors and conditioner. Half of the shelves were on the ground, and I knew that some of what we needed wouldn't be here any longer.

My bag quickly filled, and I used the second one to get anything the girls would need. I was out of bags, and I scanned behind the counter to see how the other girls were doing. They were already gone, so I took off back down the aisle, heading for John and escape.

The shot was horrendous in the silence, and as soon as I heard it I knew we were in serious trouble. The gun that had gone off somewhere in the pharmacy was so loud that anything in the store would come running.

I found John, Rhea and Eva waiting, but Andrew was nowhere in sight. I shoved my bags at Rhea and gripped my gun tight.

"Get out of here. I *have* to save him." My whisper was vicious, and they didn't even question the order. John watched me silently, questioning me with his gaze. I knew he would go with Rhea and Eva, otherwise they would have no protection. At least two good fighters were stuck together in the shop.

I raced away, scanning aisles just looking for Andrew. I saw a few shadows on the other side, or even just standing and staring at me. I didn't even pause to consider them; I just kept going.

All I could see in my mind was Anne's desolate face if I came home without Andrew.

I had killed her mother, and there was no way in hell I would let the only thing she had left disappear. I knew what it felt like to be the girl who had nothing left, and I never wanted Anne to feel that.

She needed Andrew, and I would give him to her.

I found him in a grocery aisle, something I hadn't even considered. He had five bags stuffed full of cans and treats, and I realized that the bags were making it hard for him to hold his gun. Three people surrounded him, two women and a man.

One of the women was barely fifteen years old; it seemed much, much younger than me, even if it was only a few years.

I knew the gun would only draw more of them, so I pulled my knife in my other hand, and dove at them. The man went down instantly, his throat torn apart.

Andrew swung a bag around and made contact with the youngest one's head. She hit the ground, but I knew she wouldn't stay there long. I threw my knife, something John had grudgingly been showing me how to do, and was rewarded with a sound that meant the knife had hit home in the girl's brain. I didn't have time to retrieve my knife before the teenager was on me, so I just started smacking her with the butt of my gun. It wasn't doing much, just giving her bruises and making her angry, but it was keeping her teeth away from me.

Then abruptly she was slumped over on me, blood pouring onto my chest. Andrew was standing over me, one bag left on the ground for his knife.

He had killed her.

My heart was so heavy as I threw the girl off of me and grabbed the bag. I didn't realize that I wanted more than my friends to just survive, I wanted them to never understand murder.

I was supposed to be the killer.

Not Andrew. He was too good, too kind to be a murderer.

I didn't have time to think on that any longer, because then we were running. I had never been very fast, only muscular. Andrew was a sprinter, and I couldn't feel my legs by the time we reached the door. We had knocked a few

Hungry away from us, and one of the bags had split open and cans spilled out. Andrew didn't even pause; he just kept going with whatever he had left.

We burst out of the emergency door, and straight into the waiting doors of the van. We slammed them shut and John pulled away. I gave myself one minute to catch my breath, and silence reigned for that time.

"Well, we knew we would run into trouble," I said, a hysterical laugh trying to escape my throat.

Andrew frowned, sweat beading on his pale skin, "Yes. But you know you weren't supposed to come back for me."

I looked away. "I know. But I did. Get over it."

He laughed, still breathing heavily, "I'm not saying I'm not grateful, or I don't know why you did it. I'm just saying that you shouldn't take chances like that."

I shrugged, letting the subject drop.

"There's a small food store up here, which might be a bit safer than a big one. There's a liquor store beside it, and we should grab some."

At this, Eva burst into laughter, "Planning on becoming a drunk, John?"

He didn't laugh. "I was thinking more along the lines of explosives. But a drink does sound good about now."

John was brilliant: completely insane, but brilliant. Molotov cocktails, why didn't I think of that? The easiest and most effective weapon on earth: alcohol and fire.

We reached the food store and parked in the front. I didn't like the open area of the parking lot, but there wasn't a rear entrance so we didn't have a lot of options. John was going to the liquor store alone, and while I didn't like that plan, I wasn't going to argue. He was the best fighter, and if I had to lose anyone on this trip, I'd rather it be him.

He left us with the car running, and the rest of us entered the grocery store. There were six aisles; the sixth one contained pet food and books. We didn't need those, I doubted I would have the time to sit and read ever again.

"Andrew, take aisles four and five, you're the fastest. Take anything that won't rot. Rhea, take three, and Eva, two. I'll take the first one and watch the entrance at the same time." I barely breathed the orders, afraid that anything in the building might hear me.

Andrew took off without another word, his gun out, and another empty bag in his other hand. Rhea looked uncertain, and I handed her my gun. I was better with my knife anyway.

"Rhea, your aisle shouldn't have much in it. Do a quick scan and go to Eva. Take the gun, and pull the trigger on whatever moves. I've already taken the safety off."

She held the gun gingerly, and I thought that perhaps she was more afraid of it than of being eaten.

Eva urged her to go to the aisle, and then started down her own. I had taken the row with packaged candy and such, and I took as much of it as I could fit, along with every beef jerky packet I could see. We needed the protein, and jerky lasted longer than fresh meats.

I was nearly at the end of the aisle when I saw the tiny figure cowering underneath the frozen section at the back. I hadn't bothered assigning the back, because we wouldn't be able to keep anything perishable.

The shadow was petite and instantly recognizable, mostly because the figure behind it was completely in the light, and at least three times the size.

There was a child underneath the shelf, and there was a man standing over her, bulky and definitely Hungry.

I didn't even think twice, I just took off, sprinting towards the figure. I heard Eva's cry in the midst of my running, and my head told me that I should protect her, not try and save some child I didn't even know, but my heart wouldn't let me turn around.

I loved kids. It was probably the only thing that could have made me forget my best friend.

The man didn't stand a chance; I launched myself over the shelf and drove my knife into his shoulder. I had been aiming at the head, but he had dodged. It didn't phase me. I just pulled it out and drove it into his eye.

His blood pooled beneath him, and for a moment I thought of Mrs. Hines who had died the same way: my knife in her eye. After a second I whirled back around to see a dirty, thin little girl.

I held my knife up, and she shrank back, terror springing into her bright green eyes.

"Are you Hungry?" I demanded, my knife still ready to go into her face. She didn't hold any of the traits of the other Hungry I had seen; her mouth wasn't bleeding, and her eyes were frightened, not crazed. She didn't make fear leap into my heart, just the absurd need to protect her.

She shook her head fiercely, fright still controlling her actions. I knew that she wasn't infected, and I had to save her.

"Good," I said, then grabbed my bags in one hand and pulled her out of her crouch and over my shoulder with the other. It still held my bloody knife.

I stood, the only thought I had was of saving Eva, who I knew had been hurt somehow. Her scream had been one of pain, and I prayed that she hadn't been bitten. I would have to kill her if that happened. I couldn't take any chances.

What I saw, though, froze my blood.

Rhea was standing over Eva protectively, who had a vicious looking cut down her stomach. I doubted she was conscious. Rhea was holding the gun in her hands, and pointing it at another man holding a knife. Blood sprayed out of his mouth with every breath, and starvation I recognized instantly danced in his eyes.

He was Hungry, and he had a weapon. They could think, and they knew what they were going to do before they did it, then perhaps they could also retain information on how to use weapons.

I wanted to scream at her to shoot him, but I also didn't want to draw anything else. My heart was pounding, and I knew the instant the man stepped forward that Rhea couldn't do it.

She was afraid of the gun.

I was going to watch both Rhea and Eva die, because a stupid fool was afraid of a weapon that could save her.

My shriek was cut off in my throat as the man lunged at them. I saw Rhea crouch defensively, and I knew she would sacrifice herself so that I could try and get there in time. She wasn't afraid so much as weak; she just couldn't fight. She could die, selflessly, but she couldn't save with violence.

Tears burned my eyes, and I started around the shelves, attempting to reach my friends in time to save them. I wasn't going to succeed, I knew, but I had to try.

The man didn't get there. His hands had been grabbing Rhea's sweater, and then suddenly he was on the ground, dead.

For a bizarre moment I thought that Rhea had shot him, but I saw the gun I had given her on the ground where she had dropped it.

Then I saw John, and every single time I'd seen him practice throwing knives flashed through my head. He had saved Eva and Rhea both, and only because he could throw a knife faster than most people could pull a gun. He was completely still, as if he was taking a second to take in all the destruction he could create with a single knife toss. His eyes were rapt on the body of the fallen Hungry, another knife spinning in his fingers. He was ready if it even so much as twitched.

He was standing by the frozen section too, but on the opposite end. I wondered how he had gotten there, but I didn't have time to think about it. I was rushing at Rhea, ready to hug her, scream at her, or perhaps just beat her until she learned some survival instincts.

I didn't get there, though, Andrew came out of nowhere and started herding us back towards the van. He had more bags than me, although I was carrying a child as well as food. Three bags were around Eva, but she wasn't moving anymore and I hoped she wasn't dead. Rhea grabbed the bags, and, to my shock, the gun. John grabbed the knife he had thrown into the Hungry man's head, and picked up Eva, holding her carefully for a man who despised weakness or kindness. We hurried to the exit as fast as we could, considering our load.

We reached the van and tossed the bags in. John lay Eva gently down on the backseat, and I let Rhea crawl in with her first aid kit next. Andrew got in the drivers seat, and John and I managed to cram ourselves into the front. The little girl was on my lap, and clinging to me so hard I thought my spine might snap.

We drove out of the parking lot, and were about to head left toward the pharmacy, and the safe house when John stopped Andrew.

"No, we have to take a different route home. We don't want them to follow us."

The thought made my blood run cold. I knew they were capable of thought, and if they found our house, they could easily sneak up on us.

Andrew turned right and sped through the town, still heading west.

John eyed the child but didn't say anything, and Andrew sent her an exhausted smile.

"You're a pretty little thing, aren't you?"

The little girl stared at him and hugged me tighter, refusing to answer. I wondered how often she had been scared or hurt to be afraid of Andrew.

No one else spoke.

Chapter Nine

Not even an hour later we had taken so many ridiculous turns that I felt lost, but John knew exactly where we were. We had finally started back on our way home, and I hoped our precautions didn't cost Eva her life.

Andrew was speeding, going faster in the van than ever before. The fear of speeding tickets was long over, and I figured the worst case situation in the car was a car accident.

I almost wished that would happen, because then at least I would die in a way other people expected. A way that didn't leave me filled with horror.

We reached the safe house just as night started to fall. Jason was on the porch and pacing, I felt terrible for worrying him.

Abruptly it occurred to me that I had no idea how it was that John managed to save Eva and Rhea, even as fast as he is, when he wasn't even supposed to be in the food store.

"John, how did you get into the grocery store, when there was no rear entrance?"

"There was a hallway in the back that connected the liquor store to it."

Silently I thanked whoever had designed that hallway.

I was still furious with Rhea, because she was such a liability. At least Sophie would have shot the man, because she would never let someone else die when she could save them. She just would have gotten herself killed alone.

Rhea had put Eva in danger, and she could have gotten both herself and her friend killed or infected if John hadn't arrived there in time.

I got out of the van, the little girl in my arms. I grabbed as many bags as I could carry and brushed past Jason and into the kitchen. I wanted to talk to him, but with Eva injured badly we didn't have enough time.

I tried to put the girl down in the kitchen, but she was holding on like superglue. I eventually stopped holding her back, and let her just hang off of me like a monkey. I made two more trips to the van for bags, and saw that John and Rhea were bringing Eva in. Andrew locked the van and finally, finally we were all safe inside our house.

I had never been more thankful in my life.

I turned around to face Jason, and to unleash my wrath on Rhea at the same time.

He was furious; I knew it as soon as I looked him in the eye. For the first time I could see exactly how similar Jason and Zack were, because both the brothers had identical thunderous expressions. I had seen it before on Zack, but it was a new thing for Jason, and considerably scarier because of it.

Gabby, Anne and Sophie were all staring at me like I had grown an extra head, but it was the rage on Jason's face that concerned me. He had never looked this angry at me before.

However, the small form in my arms, squeezing my neck so tightly I feared she would break it, was worth all of this. I didn't even know her name, but her dirty face was sweet, and the large brown eyes that stared out at me melted my heart.

"What's your name, sweetheart?" I murmured. I knew she was terrified, and I wondered how long she had been running and hiding in the gutter to survive.

"Dana." She answered. I felt tears pool in my eyes; her name was so close to Dara's that sadness almost swamped me. I had failed to protect my kitten, but I would not fail to do the same with this child.

Jason stepped towards me, "Sandra, could I talk to you for a moment?"

Dana stared at him for a moment, stark terror plain on her face at Jason's obvious anger. I almost wanted to berate him for scaring her, but I knew that I deserved all the trouble I was about to get. He must have heard what happened, and how I had abandoned Eva to grab a kid. I turned to Gabby.

"Dana, this is Gabby. She's going to introduce you to everyone, make you some soup and clean you up a bit. Sound good?" Dana's hands were twined in my clothes, and I knew that she didn't want to let go of me, I was the probably the only one who hadn't been trying to eat her in weeks.

Eventually she let herself be settled into Gabrielle's arms, and the arms immediately enclosed her in a hug; the best part about Gabby: she loved kids, and they loved her.

Jason half dragged me into another room, Zack attempted to follow, but Jason slammed the door in his face. I almost laughed, wishing I could have seen the affronted expression Zack would no doubt be wearing. Jason whirled on me as soon as we were alone, and for the first time, I saw the debilitating fear behind his anger. He was terrified.

"Do you know what Andrew just told me? That you dropped everything you were doing, while in a dangerous area, to rush out and fight a Hungry because you thought -*you weren't even sure*- that an uninfected kid was there!? Is that true?"

I swallowed, he was angrier than I thought, and my actions sounded worse when he said them out loud, "Pretty much."

He snarled, "And while you were off being stupid, you left me here to watch a stupid run down house that no Hungry have gone near for weeks?!"

"I needed you to control Sophie and protect-"

"*Shut up!*" Jason said furiously, "Don't you ever, *ever*, do that again, Sandra. I didn't learn to fight and kill with this group only to have you die on me. How dare you throw away everything you have worked for and rush out to save a child we have *never even met*! Are you insane?!"

It stung, the way he said these things to me, but I thought perhaps that behind his fury was fear. Fear that his friend would die, fear that they would be left leaderless, and fear that he wouldn't be there to protect me. I couldn't exactly blame him, I would be just as frightened and angry in his place.

"Jason," I whispered, "I'm fine. I know it was stupid, I do. It went against everything I've tried to do, and it went against all my rules; I know! But she is barely more than a baby, she is what? Five at most! How could I let a child die? Especially when I could save her. I'm sorry I scared you, but isn't she worth it? Did you see the way she clung to me, like she knew that if we hadn't come along, she was dead? We *had* to save her."

Suddenly Jason was holding me, his arms tightening around me to a point where my ribs ached. I didn't complain, I had never felt so safe or so comforted in my whole life as I did then; his hand rubbed circles in my shoulder blades, and I could hear his heart thudding against my ears.

He was shaking though, and I felt so guilty for making him worry about me. I didn't really need to be worried about anymore, considering I was the most accomplished killer of the group. It still felt nice to be held though, and I knew Jason was probably the only one left who wasn't afraid of me these days, other than maybe John, who wasn't afraid of anything.

I held him as tightly as he was holding me for a moment, and then pulled back so he could see the honesty in my eyes. A blush clouded my cheeks, mostly because I knew my dark hair was matted from sweat, and dirt caked my skin.

"I'm sorry I scared you. I'll try not to do it again." I promised.

He held my close for another second, and then let me go. Jason cleared his throat gruffly and stared at me with hard but once more smiling eyes.

"You better not."

It was in the way he knew when to stop showing how much he cared that I realized how much I needed him. I had never been very good at expressing emotions, especially since my mother had died.

Jason never pushed, and he knew exactly when enough was enough. I supposed I had known it before, but it became so crystal clear in that one perfect moment that he was my best friend. He was my rock, the one person who wasn't afraid of me, and who still believed I was the same girl I had been before all of this killing.

He was part of my family.

Jason smiled, one of the first true ones I had seen in a long time, "Sometimes I think I'm going to have a heart attack every day. You sure keep me on my toes."

I laughed, "It was worth it this time. We saved a little girl!"

He stared straight into my eyes, "No, Sandra, *you* saved her."

I felt the tears I had been holding back fall down my cheeks, and I was surprised to understand they were tears of happiness, something that hadn't happened since the world had gone to hell.

Jason's smile turned rueful, "Awe, I'm sorry. Don't cry, please."

"Sorry!" I frowned, wiping away my tears. I felt stupid for being so emotional, but I supposed I deserved a little mental break. "I need to go talk to Rhea, wanna come?"

"By talk you mean yell, right?"

I nodded, "Yeah, I don't want to, but someone needs to tell her she was stupid."

He cocked his head, unsure if he wanted to see me chew out the gentlest of our group, but I knew he would come with me. I was starting to realize that Jason was on my side, and perhaps only my side.

"Yeah, I'm coming. Need to say sorry to Zack anyway."

I laughed, "Can't believe you slammed the door in his face."

Jason chuckled along with me, and I led the way back to our waiting group. I re-entered the kitchen to find everyone except for Eva, Anne and Sophie there. I knew they were probably in the basement, Eva unconscious, and the other two attempting to help her. I was actually surprised to see Rhea there, but I supposed she had already spent the last hour trying everything, and now it was the other girls turn to give it a shot.

My eyes fixed on Rhea's as soon as I walked in, and I cornered her quite purposefully against a wall. Her blue eyes were wide with fright, and I felt bad for scaring her, but she needed to learn.

"You almost died today, Rhea!" I said softly, "And all because you were afraid of a gun that could have saved your life! They aren't people anymore, and you need to learn to accept that."

"Sorry." Her voice was meek and guilt rushed through me, but I knew she would do the same thing again given the chance.

"Sorry changes nothing!" I yelled, "You nearly died! And not only that, you nearly got Eva killed!"

Her eyes didn't leave mine, but her apology got quieter, "I'm sorry, Sandy."

I shoved her back, into the wall. "Don't say sorry, fix it! Your weakness could hurt us all! In fact, how did Eva get hurt anyway?"

She started to cry, tears rolling out of her big blue eyes. Obviously she felt bad for getting the other girl hurt, and if she felt guilty enough to cry, Eva's injury was probably her fault.

I was about to start in on her again, when suddenly I was yanked away and thrown against the wall, the same thing I had just done to Rhea. Only this time, John had me, and he had me by the throat.

In that moment, I was going to die.

Zack lunged forward, "Let her go!" Before he got close enough to attempt to free me Jason yanked him back forcibly by his arm. I appreciated Zack's effort, but Jason was right. John would kill Zack if he so much as spoke to him wrong.

"Stay the hell out of her face, Sandra." John snarled. It was probably the most emotion I had ever heard him use.

"John." I didn't touch him; no one did if they wanted to live, "Let me go. You know as well as I do that Rhea broke the rules, and we could have all been killed." My voice was a choking gasp, and I knew I'd have bruises.

He let go of me with a shake, "But we weren't."

"Because you were quick enough with your knife!" I snapped, "She has to learn to fight, or she'll die!"

Harsh words that stung my heart, though my friends would never see it on my face. Rhea was my friend, I wanted her to live!

Rhea's clear voice cut through the tension, "I don't want to learn to fight if it means becoming a killer. I would rather die. I respect your strength for survival, Sandy, but the thought of killing just doesn't sit well with me."

Her words stung, and all I could do was snap: "You will die, Rhea."

Instantly, John's fingers were once more biting around my neck, and each word was punctuated by a harsh squeeze.

"She. Will. Not. Die."

Rhea's body was suddenly between us and she was pushing John back with her hands on his chest. She was *touching* him! Anyone who touched John died, he despised contact. That was the one thing I had learned in the last ten days. He was going to kill her; but instead, the hands that I had seen kill dozens of animals, and pull the trigger of a gun, and throw knives at bulls-eyes at twenty metres, the hands that had just been around my throat, snapped reflexively closed around Rhea's own on his chest.

John was holding Rhea's hand to him.

Everything became clear in that moment, totally obvious. John cared about Rhea.

"Your responsibility." I stated this, my voice hard. I turned to walk away but John's vicious words stopped me.

"My **only** responsibility."

His voice was devoid of any warmth, and without a second thought he released Rhea's hand and turned to walk away. I knew that John meant more by his words than Rhea would ever imagine.

She was his only loyalty, and he would kill all of us without blinking if it meant keeping her safe.

I left to the basement, his words still ringing in my ears. They had forced me to make a decision about this house, and about the group that was now too big to keep alive. We needed to move on, or split up, or something.

Before I called that meeting, though, before I dealt with everyone that would oppose me on it, I needed to see my friend.

Eva was on the pallet that Sophie had been on the day we arrived. Her wound had obviously already been cleaned with real rubbing alcohol this time, and instead of stitches with sewing string, we used medical glue and tape. Like the kind real doctors used for real wounds.

Anne had taped her all up, and she was now wrapping bandages on the cut. I knew it was worse than Sophie's injury because her normally dark skin was sallow and sweaty. Obviously she had lost a lot of blood.

Anne glanced up at me, and for the first time since I had killed her mom, her sapphire gaze held gratitude and appreciation.

"Thank you for bringing him home. He told me what you did."

I didn't reply, but I was so intensely grateful that my instincts had told me to save Andrew. I was so grateful Anne wouldn't turn into an unstable wreck. Like Sophie.

Speaking of Sophie, she was crushing pills in a little bowl, and I tossed some iron pills at her. She caught them reflexively.

"She's anemic, and if she's lost this much blood already she'll need all she can get."

Sophie dropped six into her mixture and went back to crushing them. Eventually she put them in a glass with some condensed milk from a can. Milk covered the flavour of pills better, and all we had was warm cans of it.

They forced it down Eva's throat, which wasn't hard considering she was still unconscious.

"Will she live?" I asked.

Sophie laughed, "Hopefully, and she might even thank you. That'd be nice, to have a patient that actually wanted to survive."

I ignored her and turned my attention to Gabrielle, who was holding Dana and feeding her some warm soup. Dana was snuggled down in her lap, and looking at me with huge trusting green eyes.

"Hey Dana, how old are you?"

She answered without hesitation, "Six."

I had thought she was younger, she was small for her age, but her eyes were large and wiser than her time. I wondered how much she had seen, things that no child should even have to contemplate.

"How long were you hiding in that food store?"

"Not long." She shrugged, "I used to live near it, but when my mom killed my dad I ran away. She told me to, said she couldn't help it. I've been hiding in different houses, and stores. I slept by the pond for a while."

I didn't think my heart could take much more breaking, between all the killing I was doing, and the way this tiny girl told me of her father's death. Her mother must have loved her to stop herself from attacking and let her run away. I knelt down near Gabby and looked Dana straight in her face.

"We are going to take care of you now. You'll be safe with us."

She crawled out of Gabrielle's lap and into mine and hugged me, "Thank you."

I realized then she didn't even know our names, except for Gabby.

"Dana, I'm going to go introduce you to everyone in our group. They won't hurt you." *I won't let them.* The words were unspoken, but I realized that I would kill anyone who threatened the little girl who clutched me tight with skinny arms.

"What's your name?" Her voice was curious, and she finally pulled away long enough to look at me.

I laughed, "Sandra. You can call me Sandy if you want. You've met Gabby," I gestured to my best friend, "this is Sophie, and the girl who is hurt is Eva."

Dana studied the tape on Eva's stomach, and the droplets of blood seeping from it, making my stomach twist. "She'll be okay, right?"

Sophie nodded grimly, "That's the hope."

I stood with Dana in my arms and decided to leave the basement, and Sophie's morbid presence with it. Gabby handed me the soup bowl and turned to Eva, going to help Sophie with mending her friend.

Clutching Dana and the bowl to me I headed up the stairs. John was nowhere near the door, his usual post, and I figured he would be explaining some things to Rhea, or else working off some anger by shooting dinner for tonight.

I ran into Andrew first while holding Dana, and for that I was grateful. As much as I knew Jason would never hurt her, I knew she had been frightened by his anger towards me.

"Dana, you met Andrew in the car. Andrew, this is Dana." I introduced.

Dana waved shyly, her head buried in my neck. Andrew waved back with a huge grin on his face.

"Hi Dana. You met Anne right?" He asked.

Dana smiled, "Yes, she was helping Eva."

Andrew nodded, "Yeah, Anne is my girlfriend and she makes the most wonderful cupcakes ever. I bet if you asked her really nicely she would make you one!"

Dana giggled at Andrew's theatrics as he whispered out Anne's skill with baking as though it was a national secret. Despite the fact that we probably didn't have the ingredients for that type of treat, I was glad that Andrew had picked something from the time before, something a little girl would understand, and miss. Dana would be quick to trust him, and once more I was thankful that I had gone back for him.

"Really? I love cupcakes!" Dana whispered conspiratorially back.

Andrew grinned, "Good, because if you didn't like cupcakes I would have thought you were some strange alien! Everyone loves cupcakes."

Andrew continued on his way and left Dana still laughing in my arms. I toured around the house for a while longer, looking for others. I found Rhea first, and her eyes were troubled, but she smiled for Dana as I knew she would. Rhea was always predictable in her kindness, she never failed to be the most compassionate.

"Rhea." My voice was apologetic, but I would hand out no words to go along with it. I would not apologize for what I believed to be the truth.

She smiled softly, and I knew I was forgiven, "Sandy. And you must be Dana, of course, we met in the car but I was busy with Eva."

Dana nodded, "I think she will get better."

Rhea laughed, "I think so, too."

"Do you know where any of the others are? I wanted to introduce them properly to Dana so she isn't scared if she runs into someone she doesn't recognize."

Rhea shrugged, "I have no idea where Jason is, last I saw he was with you. He'll turn up eventually for you, he always does."

I didn't know what she meant by that, by Jason always turning up for me. She didn't speak of John, and I wondered if I should ask. In the end, I didn't need to.

"What about the other man, the one in the car?" Dana's shy voice was curious.

Rhea frowned, "John disappeared. He'll be back, but he was very angry. He told me to go away when I went to ask if he was okay, and he's never mean to me."

Her words spoke volumes to me, because as far as I knew John was harsh with everyone. So if Rhea thought John was pleasant, obviously he was dramatically different for her.

He was angry though, and not only with me, but with Rhea. I couldn't have him be angry at Rhea, so I needed to find him after this.

"That's okay, we'll catch him at dinner, and Jason too. Don't worry, nobody here will ever hurt you Dana." I promised softly.

Rhea grinned, "Everyone here is very kind, even the ones who seem scary at first." She looked up at me, "Sandy, I put some colouring books I found in the basement in your room, I thought Dana might like them."

I thanked her and headed to my room that I shared with Eva. She wouldn't be there for the next while so there was no need for me to find another blanket for Dana, she could just sleep with me.

We ran into Zack on the way there, and I tensed at his black expression. I knew he would never threaten Dana, or anyone in the group for that matter -perhaps, excluding John?- but his anger would definitely scare her.

"Zack!" I smiled, "This is Dana."

His anger melted away and he grinned at the little girl in my arms. I had never seen the type of softness and gentility that Zack now exuded before; his whole face lit up for Dana.

"Super-girl! The one that Sandy saved, right?"

Dana giggled, "Yeah, she saved me."

He winked at her conspiratorially, "I think she's saved all of us a time or two. Gotta go though, see you later super-girl!"

He continued down the stairs, and Dana laughed softly after him. She grinned up at me, twining her brown freckled hands around my neck.

"I like him." she declared, "He's funny."

I rolled my eyes, wondering if the reason Zack seemed so fond of kids was because of how loving they were to him. Dana was probably his biggest fan now, and he had said maybe three sentences to her.

"He's a nice guy, don't you worry. Anyone here will help you if you just ask."

"Will I really be safe here?" Dana asked softly.

I swallowed the lump in my throat, because I knew I couldn't truly promise that in these times, but I would do my damnedest.

"You will be the safest little girl in the whole wide world." I swore, and I knew I could promise this, because there probably weren't very many little girls left, and I would protect this one to the death.

The biggest, most trusting eyes I had ever seen stared up at me, and in a solemn voice Dana thanked me. I had never heard a six year old be so serious, and I wondered if she had always been this way, or perhaps the chaos of this new world had created her.

I handed her a colouring book and some crayons I had, and let her play. As I exited the room, I looked back to watch her scribble all over the pages. I wondered how long it had been since she had been allowed to just relax and enjoy herself.

Probably as long as it had been for me.

Chapter Ten

I found John sitting against the house outside. I knew him to be in a terrible mood because recently I had learned to judge his moods by his actions, and the best mood I had seen was when he was eating, and the worst was when he was playing with knives.

Today, he was playing with a knife across his knuckles and staring angrily into the forest far away. His whole body was tense and I realized that he wanted to be anywhere but there, and with anyone but me.

Abruptly he stuck the knife in the ground and pierced me with his ice blue eyes.

"Sandra," he said my name angrily, though his expression was controlled, "what do you want?"

I was grateful that John always got straight to the point, "John, when I said that Rhea would die..." He narrowed his eyes at me, but I persisted, "When I said that, I didn't mean I wanted her to die. I didn't mean I wouldn't continue trying to protect her, or let her stay with us. I just want her to fight, I don't want her to be helpless! I want... I want to make sure that..." My voice died before I could force the words out.

"They can survive if you die." John finished.

I nodded, "Yes. And you know that she can't."

He glared again, but I stared back and we both knew the truth.

He nodded, "Yes. She would die."

My stomach sank at the words; saying them myself was one thing, but hearing from John was even worse.

John stood slowly, languidly, his huge body uncoiling as if there wasn't a threat to the human existence, "She would die if you weren't here or I wasn't here, Sandra, but she won't die because we are here. Neither of us will let anything happen to Rhea."

I was distracted momentarily by the way he said my name distastefully and said Rhea's name like a prayer; my thoughts scattered once more as I took in the rest of his words.

"Yes, but what happens when we die, John?" I asked softly.

John lifted a blonde eyebrow, and my blood turned to ice at his devil-may-care expression, "I'd like to see what could kill *us,* Sandra."

He picked his knife up and walked away from me: as he left he tossed the knife, end over end, always catching it on the handle.

Never once dropping it.

***

"Sandra." John's voice, instantly stopping me on my way to the kitchen. He looked haggard, his eyes weary from lack of sleep. I probably looked the same, seeing as for almost a week we had all suffered along with Eva as she started to heal. The painkillers we had found were helpful, but they weren't strong enough; her moans woke me almost nightly, and the similarity they had to the sounds the Hungry made sometimes terrified me.

"What's up?"

He scrubbed a hand down his face, "I killed two Hungry last night. They've found this place, we need to move."

I was speechless, and more than that, frightened. This had been safe, this tiny little house had become a sanctuary to us! Now we were going to leave it, and with Eva down for the count it would be no easy task.

"We'll need to move Eva to do that." I told him softly.

He shrugged, "She's doing much better. Even if all we can do is move her it will be better."

"She'll be in pain."

His eyes hardened, the sympathy fleeing quickly, "Better than dead. She won't complain."

I sighed, "Stall as long as possible. Eva's awake this morning, I haven't talked to her yet, I'll see how she is."

I turned towards the basement, where Eva was still situated. She hadn't been completely lucid yet, and I was so excited to see her, despite the bad news John had now relayed.

Everyone in the house had worried desperately that she would never wake up, that even after all of our efforts we would lose her anyway. The household had been tense, despite the fact that Rhea had forgiven me, and John was back to being barely civil and Jason had won over Dana (a feat that had taken him the same amount of time as his brother) despite her original fear of him. A pallor had hung above our heads, speaking of the first human death of our party, and it wasn't a death by infection, or a Hungry One. It was the lack of skill that would be the death of Eva if we couldn't fix her.

No one in our group was a doctor, none of us had even graduated yet, except for maybe John, who had yet to reveal his age or past to us. How could a group of nine teenagers and a six year old hope to heal a bad wound, let alone stay alive?

I was eager to see the calm brown eyes of my friend, and I took the stairs down two at a time to find Rhea, Anne and Gabby were already down there. They were already trying to help, putting some sort of antibiotic we had on the cut, and re-bandaging it. For nearly three days they had held the coldest things we could find on the wound, trying to reduce the swelling, and it seemed like it had helped.

I dropped to my knees beside Eva's pallet, and was overjoyed to see the eyes I had so hoped for. Her skin was still a sickly shade of taupe still, although the iron pills had been a good idea, and though she looked like she was in pain, she was awake, and she sent me the weakest, most beautiful smile in the whole galaxy.

Then for the most absurd reason, I burst into tears. I had forced myself to stop crying at least a week ago when I realized it only made me feel worse, and everyone around me feel bad, and didn't help a thing.

Yet for the first time since this all started, my tears were ones of relief and joy.

"Sandy, you're... crazy. Stop... crying..., I'm - I'm fine." Eva's voice was weak and she took long breaks in between words, but she still said I was crazy in the same exasperated tone that she always had.

"I missed you." My words were barely distinguishable from my sobs, and I choked back my ridiculous display of emotion.

"Sorry." I cleared my throat, "I missed you. I am glad you're better."

Eva smirked, "You're still... emotionally... stunted."

I burst into laughter at her joke from another time. I had always been considered incapable of normal emotions, when it was a happy time: I cried; when it was sad: I was angry or didn't care. Eva and I used to try and work out what caused me to be this way, and we would laugh about it.

"I know," I giggled, "But you love me anyway."

She nodded almost imperceptibly, and I realized how much of her strength I must have sapped, and before everyone else even got to greet her! I grasped her hand strongly for a moment.

"I'll let you rest, you need to get strong again." I looked at her bandages again, "You're gonna have a mean scar —the guys'll dig it."

She rolled her eyes at me, and I stood to leave; every bit of the strength I could feel in my own body I willed into her to get better.

Because when Eva was better, we would have to leave.

If John had already killed two of the Hungry, more would be coming. They had found us.

So if they could find us, others could too.

***

It wasn't until Eva had recuperated enough for us to at least move her without extensive bleeding, and four more Hungry had found us that it became obvious to everyone what we had to do. We had a large group; probably one of the largest surviving groups in the area, if there *were* any other surviving groups in the area. Gabrielle, Eva, John, Zack, Rhea, Andrew, Anne, Jason and I had sat down to eat some of the cans of soup we'd scavenged. It was beef vegetable; I had decided to get over my dislike of meat very quickly after starting to run for our lives. If I wanted to survive, I had to eat, simple as that.

"We have to separate, at least to travel." It was Andrew's suggestion, and I had known it was coming for days now. I also agreed, of course, because Andrew and I thought so alike. Instantly, everyone was objecting and angry.

For the first time I missed Sophie, who had finally gotten her stitches taken out and had been disappearing for a few days at a time, always returning more haggard than before. I missed her because she was always enthusiastic about anything controversial, or anything dangerous which could get her killed. I needed someone to be predictable and fully with me on this decision.

I looked helplessly to Jason, which I seemed to do more and more often every day. He was staring at me, dark eyes asking me to do something, but I also knew no matter what I did he would support me.

"Hey, quiet!" I demanded, "We've been safe here so far, but you all know better than to make that much noise. It draws the Hungry." We had unanimously decided the official name for the zombie-like creatures would be the Hungry, or the Hungry Ones. It sounded better than the infected, "Now, Andrew is right."

"Of *course* he is, because Andrew is constantly right! That's what you always say. Do you ever actually disagree with him?!" Gabby's voice was harsh, and immediately I was shocked.

Before I had time to defend myself, Jason was already there, "Andrew hasn't been wrong yet Gabby, if he had, we'd be dead. We're all alive, aren't we? We're all just doing the best we can okay?"

Jason merged straight back into the background after this, as if he had never been there. It occurred to me, not for the first time, that maybe he should be leading this group, not Andrew or I. Too bad he had no interest in leading.

Gabby apologized after a moment, and I gratefully accepted it; I was happy not to have strain on my friends, and it was understandable when we got angry; we were, after all, fighting for our lives.

"We do need to split up." Andrew continued, "Right now there are too many of us, and eventually we might make a mistake, and then we're all dead."

The reality of it hit us very hard in that moment and I knew we all agreed finally when Anne gripped Andrew's arm as if to stop him from coming to my side. I understood why they wanted to stay together, they were in love, and I also understood that Anne didn't really want to be near me. I was a good fighter, but I had killed her mother. It pained me to see the way Andrew wanted to be beside me, but wouldn't leave Anne, but I understood at least.

"Not smart to have some of the best fighters together." Anne lied for my sake. I knew she didn't want to be near me, but at least she was trying to be gentle with me. "Andrew, myself, Zack, Gabrielle and John?"

"I go where Jason goes." Zack's objection was quick, and I couldn't blame him for it. They were brothers, they stuck together.

I couldn't give them John though, despite Anne's suggestion, I knew Andrew did *not* want him on his team. I couldn't give them Rhea, since they already had Anne. They didn't need both the weak links. Eva could go with them, but I knew she would rather stay with me.

The last thing I wanted to do was send Jason, who was at my back, to Andrew's team, but I could also see no other acceptable course of action. Sending Jason would mean Zack would go with them too, and therefore their group would be much stronger. Andrew wouldn't want Zack, but he would deal if it meant he got Jason.

Truly, it was selfish of me either way; I could keep Jason and Zack to help us survive, they were both incredibly tough, and generally followed orders. Or I could send the brothers with Andrew, solely for the purpose of protecting that group without me there. It was silly, but the thought of anyone else being hurt made my heart pound, and my skin grow clammy. Just remembering how I felt when Eva was down was enough to imagine my feelings if Gabby or Rhea were to be hurt like that. Jason and Zack would protect the group in my stead, and I needed it safe to be able to function.

Besides, John was the best fighter I had ever seen, and he would be able to keep Eva, Rhea and I safe. If he wanted to keep us safe, at least. All of us were smart, and none of us were slackers in a battle either. We would be okay without Jason and Zack.

I didn't exactly know how I would hold it together without Jason though; he was my rock, my foundation.

"Jason, Zack, go with Andrew." I said. John and Eva didn't flinch, and I knew that they had already expected this. Gabby, Rhea and Anne gaped at me, probably wondering why I would give up a huge asset to my group. Andrew was frowning, but he understood my reasoning, as he always had.

I looked to Jason, positive he would support this latest decision or mine, as he had all my other decisions, but all I could see was black anger clouding on his face.

"No." He snapped. Every face showed shock; I apparently wasn't the only one who counted on Jason being my solid supporter. Even Zack seemed surprised by Jason's answer.

"Jason…" I murmured. His face softened slightly.

"No, Sandra. I'm going with this group, we barely know John, and Andrew is more than capable of keeping those three safe. Zack's my brother so we stay together. It's only fair."

John nodded, as though it was true that we couldn't trust him to stay with us and keep us safe. If John left Eva, Rhea and I alone, we wouldn't survive long. I was a good fighter and merciless, and Eva was tough, but she was injured and we were no match for more than a few of the Hungry.

I knew there was more to it than just *fair*. Jason had never before questioned me, and I couldn't see why he would start now. I also knew he would never tell me with everyone else around, it was just the way he was.

"This isn't over, Jason." I warned. "But for now, we will say you're both coming with me. We will stay here one more night, as a full group. We'll divvy up our supplies and decide on our next meeting places."

Jason nodded easily, and the tension lessened in the room. Everyone could sense I wanted to talk to Jason alone, so Gabby and Rhea quickly headed off to their room, helping Eva slowly hobble towards the room where Dana was sleeping. Andrew and Anne left shortly after, and John slipped silently into the living room, where he slept on the couch. In only a few minutes, the room was silent, and only myself, Zack and Jason stood there, alone in the kitchen.

"Jason, Zack, you *have* to go with them." I pleaded.

Zack shrugged, "Honestly, I'd rather go with you, Sandra, but I'll go wherever Jason thinks is best, and he wants to be here. This isn't our fight. I do want to stay near John, mostly cause I want to knock the smug look off his face."

I glared at Zack momentarily, "The last thing I need is you fighting with John. That can only end with one or both of you dead."

He rolled his eyes, "*Like* he could hurt me." Apparently he had forgotten the little knife-to-the-throat incident.

"Zack!" Dana's voice clouded the room, and I turned to the door to see her grinning.

Zack's annoyance melted into a smile, "Super-girl, what's up?"

"I wanted you to play with me, and Eva said you would if I asked nicely."

He shrugged at me, "Super-girl's calling, you gotta decide, Sandy."

Dana skipped out of the room with her tiny hand engulfed in his huge one, and I sighed heavily. My eyes turned to meet Jason's, and I knew that I was not getting away with my decision that easily with this brother.

"Jason, *please*."

"No, Sandra. I don't care if you don't want me here; I am staying with you, John, Rhea and Eva."

I stopped abruptly, "Of course I want you to come with me! I just can't *have* you come with me!"

"Why not?" Jason asked, I could now see the hurt in his face. I had offended him when I told him to leave; God, he thought I didn't *want* him by my side!

I could feel my eyes filling with tears, and I desperately wished they would go away, "Because I can't let anyone get hurt, and I love Andrew like a brother, but you are the only one I trust to keep them all safe."

Jason's anger left him with a sigh, and he shook his head gently.

"Sandra, you know I would do almost anything for you, but I *cannot* do this."

"Why?" I whined, and it was almost a nice change to be the complainer instead of the leader.

"I just can't protect her while I'm wishing I was with you guys. Zack wants to be with your group, too."

"But I need to know they are safe. I need to know *Gabby's* safe. I love her Jason; she's my family!" It was a low blow, making her out to be my only family left, and Jason would never say no to me now. I almost felt guilty, and he obviously did, because his midnight eyes were tormented.

"I love her, too, Sandy, and she *will* be safe. Andrew will protect her, you know he will, he's too good to do anything less than the best. But I'm still going with *you*."

I stopped and stared at him for a moment, sensing the determination radiating from him. I knew then that I had accepted his choice, mostly because I realized he had stopped talking about me as if I was just the group, and started just talking about me. *Just* me. Alone. He had also called me Sandy. He only did that when he was trying to communicate something important.

My heart raced painfully, "What if she gets hurt? I can't let her get hurt, Jason."

Jason stepped forward, closer to me than I expected him to come. He swallowed.

"What if you got hurt, Sandy?" He whispered. "I can't let *you* get hurt."

I knew it, then, Jason cared about me. He wasn't concerned about which group was going to survive; he was determined to help me survive. Did he love me?

I didn't know what to say at this revelation, so I forced out some words, "I won't. I swear."

Jason nodded, "Let me come with you."

I nodded, barely able to do that much. Jason smiled though, a soft smile of triumph, and I knew that he would have eventually have gotten me to give in anyway. He reached out and grabbed my hand, squeezing it gently. Fire burned where he touched me, and I resisted the temptation to walk straight into his arms.

"Thank you." He said softly, letting my hand drop to my side. Then he disappeared to his bedroom, leaving me alone in the kitchen, too full of words and feelings to even want to be sleeping.

I would send Rhea with Andrew. She wasn't a good fighter, but she was always calm in the face of danger and would hold the group together. She was the best with any injuries, too. It was the only solution.

I walked out of the kitchen and straight into the rock hard body of John. His blond hair was shorn close to his head and I could see the warning in his icy blue eyes. I immediately stepped away from him, coming too close to John was like having a brush with death; he was gorgeous, in a dangerous way, and I always felt I had been electrocuted when I came into contact with him.

He hated when people touched him.

"John, I thought you went to bed." I said breathlessly. To be honest, John had terrified me ever since he had me by my throat and I had felt the strength in his hands and saw the insanity in his eyes.

He stared at me emotionlessly. The one thing about John's stare is that I couldn't distinguish it from a normal person to one of the infected. He always looked cold, cruel and hungry for something.

"I wanted to tell you something."

My breath caught, "What?" I prayed it wasn't him kicking us out of his house after all this time. Or him trying to take over my group. I knew I would probably let him.

"If you send Rhea with Andrew, I'm going with him. I go where she goes."

He didn't explain any more than that, and I remembered when he had declared that he was only loyal to her. I wondered if Rhea knew he felt that way. It was a strange thought, actually, because John respected only strength and violence, and Rhea was gentle and soft. His complete opposite.

"Then who am I supposed to send, John?" My voice was harsh, mostly because I was too frustrated with the world.

John shrugged, "Sophie might be back by tomorrow, she said she would. Send her. Or else keep the groups together."

My eyes narrowed, "I don't trust Sophie's will to survive. Do you think it's a better idea to stay together? My van won't fit us."

"It will fit us well enough, we can leave a seat. If you want to stay together, it's your only option." His voice became icy, "I wouldn't doubt Sophie if I was you, she's unbelievably tough and fearless."

"Only because she wants to die. It's not fearlessness, its apathy." I corrected. I then brushed by, close enough to feel the heat and rage that always exuded from John. I stopped; the thought of his anger and hatred coming too close to Rhea scaring me.

"John."

He didn't move, "Yes, Sandra?"

My voice was wintry, and full of threatening violence, "Don't you dare hurt her."

I didn't let him respond, I just headed towards the bedroom Eva and I shared, my mind still swimming in terrifying images of the cruel John twisting Rhea's beautiful soul into something evil.

I stopped outside the bedroom door, hearing soft breathing that I easily recognized as Dana's. Eva was in there as well, but I knew she wasn't asleep yet. She wasn't a very good sleeper. I didn't want to go inside, I didn't want to crawl into bed and stare at the ceiling feeling the weight of the world sitting on me, and the warmth of Dana in my side.

I loved her, but she frightened me. It was frightening being a mother figure, being the protector of a child. I had barely had enough time with my own mother to even know what the hell I was doing with Dana.

I wanted to be sheltered, and held, and consoled.

I wanted Jason.

My body turned to the right without a conscious thought from me, and before I knew it I had walked into Jason and Zack's room, seeing the inside of it for the first time. He had boarded the windows and piled some blankets in each corner. I hadn't realized there was no real bed in this room.

It was dark in the room, but I could still see Jason by a candle he had lit beside his bed. He was sitting up, fully clothed and by all appearances, it looked as though he was reading a book.

I glanced at Zack's corner, surprised to find it empty. I was simultaneously glad he wasn't witnessing this moment, and annoyed that he wasn't there to make me return to my own room in shame. I faced Jason again, intending to ask him where his brother was.

Jason's eyes shot to me, and embarrassment flooded my body, followed closely by anger. I hated feeling weak and Jason's eyes made me feel more exposed than anything ever had before.

"Sandra?" His voice was surprised more than anything, and I took it as an invitation to come in. I shut the door, forgetting all about Zack, and let myself walk to his makeshift bed, flopping down beside him. I was beyond exhausted.

"John likes Rhea." It sounded stupid, but it was the first thing that came out, and I realized I wanted to talk to Jason about it.

"I know." He responded softly, "I've known since pretty much our first night here."

"How?" I asked, "Am I that dense?!"

Jason chuckled softly, a dark and seductive sound that sent my mind into overdrive, "Yes, I do believe you are. I knew because he just kept staring at her. She shocked the hell out of him, jumping between you two that first night, and since then it's like she's a puzzle he's determined to solve."

"I don't think anyone's ever stood up for him before." I said softly, my voice filled with sadness. I could say whatever I wanted about my life, about how I had lost everything, and yet, I had never lacked love, or friendship.

"I don't think so either." Jason confirmed. He fell silent, and I sat there thinking for a few moments.

"I threatened him." I told him.

Jason sighed, "John? Jesus, Sandra, you would do that, too. How are you still breathing?"

"I'm not sure, actually!" I laughed. "I told him not to hurt Rhea."

Jason was quiet for a long while before he said, "I don't know if it's possible for him to hurt Rhea."

"Of course it is, look at the size of him! He could kill her in one hit." I scoffed.

Jason rolled his eyes, "No, I mean, I don't think he could hurt her. You know, how when you love someone you could never harm them."

I was dead silent, "No. I didn't know that."

Images of Dara, and Mrs. Hines, and how I had instinctively known I would kill Eva if she had been infected.

Did I not love them?

Jason's hand grasped mine, "I didn't mean that, Sandy, I meant that you would never harm them given the choice. You would have given your life to prevent that pain."

I looked away, letting the tears that were starting to sting my eyes disappear. Jason's words did make me feel better, but certain hurts were never going to leave me.

His fingers were gentle on my chin, and he turned my head to face him again. I twisted slightly, attempting to turn away, hiding my glossy eyes.

Jason held me firm, but he blew out the candle. Darkness surrounded us, making everything surreal. The only thing I knew for certain was that Jason's hand was still on my cheek.

"Jay?" I whispered, scared and exhilarated.

His other hand came up and held my face steady, "You're gonna be fine. You're safe here."

It meant the world to me, that he had said those words. That he had turned out the light and made me feel so safe. I threw myself into him and let myself cry. I was crying for every reason under the sun: I was crying for Dara, for myself, for my mother and my father. I was crying because I was afraid of this newness I had within my arms, of these feelings that were rushing through me for Jason. I let the soft kisses I felt on my hair soothe me, and the gentle rubbing on my back heal my pain.

"You've never called me Jay before." Jason murmured into my ear after I had fallen silent.

I laughed thinly, "You've never held me like this before, either."

"Be serious, Sandra," Jason said, "would you have let me?"

I pulled back and stared at him, unsure about how to answer. No, perhaps not, because I would have been scared and unsure and afraid, but then again, I was all of those things now and yet I was in his room.

"No." I decided, "But not because I didn't want you to. I was afraid before."

"You're not afraid now?"

"I'm always afraid these days." I smiled softly, "But I'm not afraid of you."

"You shouldn't be." he said, and then he kissed me. It was gentle at first, and my skin felt too small for my body; my heart pounded in my chest. I felt more alive than I had since my mother had died.

He pulled away, only to kiss my cheeks, my nose, my eyelids. I sniffed as delicately as possible and opened my wet eyes. I knew he could feel their wetness, and he probably wondered if he hurt me, or if this was too overwhelming.

"I am so glad I have you with me." I whispered. My heart hurt a little bit at the truth of that statement, because I knew that I was distracted by him, and everyone could be in a little more danger because of my selfishness. I couldn't bring myself to regret Jason though, he was everything now.

Calloused fingers wiped my tears away, probably leaving dirty marks on Jason's hand, but he didn't notice. He wouldn't care, even if he had. "Don't cry."

I smiled at his words, "Sorry." I cleared my throat. "Where's Zack?" I asked suddenly.

Jason shrugged, "He's been staying downstairs with Sophie, he feels bad that she's alone now."

"She's going to get herself killed, you know."

Jason sighed, "I know, and that will hurt Zack. He needs to learn though, he needs to see it. This is all a game to him; it's just a survival scenario that will be over next week. He doesn't get it yet, doesn't get that people get hurt."

"I'm sorry that he needs to understand." I whispered.

He held me for a long time after that, another immortal moment in my mind. As we sat together, I realized I was going to have to tell Eva that I would no longer be sharing a room with her, she would be alone with Dana; and I would be with Jason.

It was this thought that made me think that there was absolutely no reason to be afraid, ever again, because why would there be? Why would I ever need to be afraid again when Jason was there, Jason was all around me.

For the first time in maybe my entire life, I was absolutely fearless.

John

You can only be civil for so long. I didn't know this for most of my life; I was pampered to be in the thin veneer of diplomatic society. But a society is really just another kingdom of animals, and the stronger animal wins. Now that I know the true nature of humans is animalistic, and that deep down we are all beasts, I will be the stronger human. Always.

Chapter Eleven

The group came together for the meeting the next day, this time in the basement. Eva was back on her pallet, awake and lucid, and able to move around slowly, but in more pain because of it. I knew Sandra's decision would cause more anger and chaos. I did respect her for her strength, in my own way, but I also disliked her because she didn't understand her temper. Strength always lay in those who could control their emotions, and the ones who got angry lost reason. To lose your reasoning in this day and age was to die.

"Okay, as you all know, yesterday we decided we should split the group up and we were deciding on who should go on which team." Sandra's voice was tired, accentuating the smudges that were accumulating under her brown eyes, and for a moment I pitied her. I supposed it was difficult to be the leader.

"So is Jason coming with us?" Anne asked, all innocence and copper curls.

Jason scowled, "No, I'm not."

Sandra quelled him with a fierce glare although underneath it I could see a tenderness, a softness that hadn't been there yesterday, "No, I've decided that we shouldn't split up."

This was where the chaos came in; Andrew was in disagreement, Anne was on his side, of course, and Eva was also annoyed. I knew Eva's anger stemmed from the fact that Sandra had changed her mind just when Eva had accepted the idea.

"Sandra, you know as well as I do that we need to split up." Andrew's voice was determined.

Sandra shook her head, her fall of chestnut hair following her movements over her shoulders, "No, I thought about it, and Jason wants to stay on my side, Zack won't leave his brother, and Rhea isn't the best fighter to send to your team. Eva is weak right now, and this type of injury will take a while to heal, and I don't trust Sophie. This leaves only one option."

The anger fizzled out at the mention of Sophie. She had disappeared again on one of her two or three day trips. Her promise to return last night had been broken, because she hadn't come home yet. Everyone thought she was dead.

I didn't, because I had gotten to know Sophie well enough to understand that she was tough and smart. She wanted to die, but she wasn't enough of a coward to just let herself be killed. She was hunting down a challenge, and she would be hard pressed to find something that challenged or outsmarted her.

Andrew sighed, "We'll take Rhea, that's fine."

Instantly my body tensed, expecting a fight. I knew that if Andrew wanted Rhea, he would have to deal with me, and Andrew hated me enough not to bother. There was no way I was letting Rhea wander off without me, especially since I had gone and declared myself her protector on a stupid whim. I still wasn't clear on why it had been so important for me to challenge Sandra over her, but I knew that my instincts had called for it. So far, my instincts had kept me alive, so I followed them.

She shrugged, her delicate shoulders looking like they would break with the movement, "I'd go with you, but I don't think we should go without another fighter. Neither Anne nor I can fight at all, and Gabrielle's strong but she hasn't really been taught to fight. And I know you can fight Andrew, but your attention will be divided on Anne. Don't deny it."

I almost smiled at her perceptive words, but I held myself back at the show of emotion. Rhea knew that she had amused me, however, when her dark blue eyes caught mine and showed her own laughter, and I hated that she had read my emotions without my permission. My almost-smile turned into a scowl.

Andrew scowled, "You're probably right, Rhea."

She giggled, "I know I am. I could go with you, but we would have to take Jason, who doesn't want to go, or John."

Rhea knew she had Andrew when he let out a furious sigh. There was no way he would force Jason to go with him, and he hated me.

"Fine, we'll stay together. But it's more dangerous, we draw more Hungry and we're easy to track."

Sandra let loose a rare grin, "It's okay, we'll be really careful! But the real question is: where are we going to go, when we leave the house?"

I could almost feel the sadness in the room at the thought. Everyone had come to look upon the house as a safe place, a permanent place.

"North." I said this before I could stop myself. I hated drawing attention to myself, and I was pretty good and staying in the background, despite my size. I was a far cry from Andrew's lanky, skinny form. He just barely trumped me in height, but he would probably never have the type of shoulder breadth I had gathered from a life of hard exercise. The closest to me in size was probably Zack, though I still had him beat.

Sandra frowned, "North? Farther north and we'll end up in Nunavut, or the Hudson Bay. We'll freeze."

"That's the point. Not only will we be freezing, so will any Hungry. We just have to dress better and survive better than them."

Andrew's slow smile told me I had hit the jackpot with my latest idea, "That is brilliant."

Sandra grinned, "John, you're a genius. We're pretty used to the cold, but this will be a whole different cold. No Hungry with a brain would go there, and the ones that do will die."

Anne's soft voice broke the spell, "That is a good idea, I only have one objection."

"What?" Andrew questioned, his gaze turning tender as he faced the woman at his side. Weakness, the way he hinged his happiness and life upon her trivial emotions.

"We didn't bring much winter wear. Hunting in snow is harder. Blizzards are deadly and happen often. Most importantly, we have no shelter."

"That is more than one objection." Zack's joke drew a few laughs, but Anne's concerns were all appropriate.

I could put at least one of those fears to rest, "I can hunt in winter. I have before."

I had been hunting since the time I could hold a gun, and if at first I had hated it, if I had at first despised my father for forcing me to do something that caused me such grief, I was now grateful because I was the ultimate survivor. Besides, I had eventually gotten over the fact that I was unwillingly killing animals that I didn't want to harm, and decided to become the best at it that I could be.

He had taught me to survive, and how to kill any emotion that may distract me. As much as I had hated my father, he had created me. I was the top predator.

"Good, so we have a food source." Sandra said, "Shelter won't be that difficult, because most houses are probably abandoned up there, we just have to find a well insulated one that is far away from any towns. Blizzards are a chance we will have to take, but we will make sure to get some sort of rope to connect us in case visibility gets bad."

Anne sighed, "Okay, good. But what about the fact that we have no winter wear? We barely have clothes enough to change daily."

To my extreme surprise it was Rhea who answered this. She had been pretty quiet during the whole exchange, but at this last point she brightened, her smile spreading over her face.

"Oh, I know where some winter clothes are!" She exclaimed, "Zack and I found the attic the other day, and there's tons of clothes in there, and lots of coats and scarves and such."

Zack grinned at her, "That's right, it's even pretty good stuff, although we'll need better when we get farther north. We could always raid a ski shop though."

Why in the world had Rhea been exploring the attic, and how did she even manage to do it without me noticing? And with Zack, of all people! Although Rhea managed to get along with everyone, Zack was probably the one she had the least in common with. I was disappointed in myself for not already knowing they had done this, usually I noticed everything that went on this house; more than that, I saw everything Rhea did, always. I watched her constantly.

I realized how bad that sounded in my head immediately after I thought it, but I didn't have it in me to take it back. It was the truth, and I refused to lie to myself. I always watched Rhea because I had promised to be responsible for her, and as much as it irked me to be accountable for another person there was no way she would get hurt under my watch.

"So we go north, and we go together!" Sandra's words were proclaimed with a huge smile, and in her happiness I could see the girl she probably had been before she had learned of death. She was beautiful, and innocent, and full of joy.

I hated her for that, and the meeting was concluded. I stalked away from all of them, leaving them to their laughter and planning. I was going to scan the house and the surrounding area again to make sure it was still clear. Then I was going to throw my knives and shoot my bow until my head cleared of these ridiculous people, and their plans.

Chapter Twelve

We hadn't left yet, and it was all because of Sophie. It had been two days since the decision to go North; the van was packed, the route was decided and everyone was itching to go. Yet no one wanted to leave Sophie for dead, and even if she was alive, to leave without her was to abandon her. So we had all decided to give her three days to return, and if she wasn't home then, we would leave the house with a note and forget the poor woman who had already lost everything.

Sophie only had today and tonight to come home, we would leave tomorrow morning come rain or come shine. I didn't like the thought of leaving without her because she was such a good fighter to have around and I knew in my gut that she still lived, but I also hated sitting around waiting for her.

I hadn't spoken to anyone since the meeting when my anger had caused me to storm away. Zack was angry with me, too, and it probably stemmed from the fact that I had spent every waking moment glaring at him. I knew Rhea thought I was in some sort of 'mood', and it puzzled me that she wasn't fearful of me or avoiding me when she knew I was mad. She just smiled whenever I went by and waved if she saw me.

The thought of Rhea made me infuriated and confused so I grabbed my knives and headed out the door. I was tossing them into my target angrily when I felt her presence behind me. I always knew when Rhea was near me because it was though the world was lit up with warmth. She exuded peace and gentility.

"John, why are you so mad?" She asked softly, and I thought I could hear sadness in her tone, "Did I do something?"

I whirled on her in surprise: Rhea? Do something wrong? As if. She was practically an angel, and the difference between us was glaring in my eyes.

"No." I answered.

She chewed her lower lip nervously, "Then why are you so mad at me?"

Her standing there, nervous that I was angry with her, had a strange effect on me. I wanted to reassure her. She was so tiny in my eyes, so fragile, and yet so very terrifying to me.

I dropped the knife I still had in my hand, and stepped closer to her, knowing that she was probably the one person I had ever willingly come close to. I reasoned that I trusted her because she was so predictably kind, she could never hurt me.

"I'm not mad at you." I told her forcefully, "I'm never mad at you."

This was the truth, because who could truly get mad at Rhea? Sure, she was useless as a teammate, but she was generous, and good at fixing injuries. She could practically do no wrong.

She smiled at my words, and the whole world glowed for a second, "Ever? Sandra thinks you're always mad and grumpy, but I told her you never were mean to me, and then suddenly you were glaring at me when I said hi, and you haven't said a word to me in three days."

I cursed myself fiercely for a second for drawing her attention. I shouldn't have made her think that I was mad at her. I would probably never be mad at Rhea, because she was the only person I had ever met in my life who was truly kind. I didn't even know if she had it in her to be mean or angry. The closest she had ever come to anger was when Sophie wanted to take her stitches out early, and Rhea had refused quite forcefully. I had been surprised, because she always seemed quite meek, but the show of backbone had pleased me, it showed she had a shot of surviving.

She obviously was passionate about healing people. I was passionate about killing.

The irony was ridiculous.

"Sandra makes me angry. I'm not mad at you though." I repeated, and the fact that I was explaining myself to some slip of a woman irked me, "I wasn't trying to glare, I was just in a bad mood."

She frowned for a second, "Why does Sandra make you mad?"

A flashback to when Sandra had told me not to hurt Rhea played in my mind. I had been so furious at her words I had barely restrained myself from strangling her... again. The rational part of my mind restrained me for two reasons: one; Sandra had every right to worry about Rhea, she was her friend, and two; I hurt everyone, willingly or not.

I tried to explain as best I could without telling Rhea of her words, "She thinks I'm a monster and she looks at me like she's planning her uses for me. I hate that."

Rhea's frown turned into a scowl, "You're not a monster." Her voice was firm, "And I won't let her use you, ever."

I almost laughed at the thought of this wisp of a girl trying to protect me, when I could kill her in a thousand ways bare handed before she could move. What could she possibly do that I couldn't do myself? Rhea eyed me like she knew what I was thinking and her scowl stayed firmly planted on her face.

"What? You don't think I can be tough?"

I raised my eyebrow, "Rhea, you're afraid of a gun."

"I will give you that." She conceded, "But be very afraid when I have a scalpel and all the medication, mister."

The very thought of Rhea's adept hands wielding a scalpel made me slightly worried. She was so good with needle, thread, blood, and wounds that I was sad for a moment that I had lost a great warrior in her. Then I was grateful that she hated violence and only believed in helping, otherwise she would be very dangerous, and I preferred her meek and harmless.

"If I ever have a scratch, I'll be sure to come to you." She giggled at my words, and it occurred to me that she had understood my sarcasm and she had *laughed*!

She laughed harder, "John, you look like you've never heard a person laugh in their life. What's wrong now?"

I couldn't answer, I was too stunned by her warmth towards me. I could count on one hand the amount of people who had ever been this tolerant of me, and I had never before had anyone laugh at my humour.

Her face grew solemn, "John, seriously, what's wrong? You look like someone died!"

"Nothing." I managed to say, "I just... you laughed, and I was surprised."

I almost hit myself as her serious face melted into more laughter. She was laughing at me again, and I hadn't joked this time.

"Oh John, you're hilarious." She stepped forward and looped her arm in mine, "You always make me smile."

I pulled my arm out of hers, but for the first time I almost regretted doing so. I despised when people touched me, but with Rhea it wasn't so bad.

"I'm glad." For the first time I could understand the happiness that Sandra had so easily displayed a few nights ago; a happiness at the most inane of things.

Or the most amazing, depending on whose point of view it was taken in on.

"By the way, John, I have a question for you." Rhea didn't seem hurt that I had rejected her touch, if anything a patient smile was playing on her lips.

The way the sun hit her hair made it glow gold, and I knew that I would answer her question. She was a beautiful woman, and I wasn't immune to her, despite the fact that normally I wouldn't have even noticed. Yet Rhea was nothing if not extraordinary.

"Okay."

She stepped closer again and just the warmth from her skin made me jittery. I stepped back. "Why did you say I was your only responsibility that day? Why did you stop Sandy from getting mad at me? Why does Sandy now look at me as though I am some sort of bargaining chip?"

"That's more than one." My throat was dry at these inquiries, they were harder for me to answer than I had predicted. I didn't know the answer to some of them, and I hated myself for some of my actions.

"Seriously, John." She admonished. I had never been told I needed to be more serious in my life, and her doing so now, at one of my most important moments was almost laughable. Except I never laughed.

"I stopped Sandra from getting angry with you because I didn't like how she talked to you, and my instincts..." I sighed, "My instinct was to protect you. That's why I said you were my responsibility, because Sandra never would have let it drop unless she knew you were under my wing. She knows I would kill anyone who touched you."

Rhea's blush was almost instantaneous and the redness in her normally pale face was endearing, "You didn't have to... protect me."

I wanted to deny it, I wanted to tell her I had to protect her because she the only person who had ever looked at me like I was a human being, and she was the only one who had ever touched me without fear. She was the first weak link I had ever had in my armour, and I simultaneously hated her and liked her for that fact; I had to protect her.

I was much too afraid to try and explain these things to her without giving away the fact that she was the only one who could ever control me. I had too long been free of anyone else to relinquish myself over to her now.

I shrugged, "Well, I did. Sandra now looks on you as a bargaining piece probably because if she has your friendship, she has my allegiance."

Suddenly Rhea's blushing complexion turned white and she gasped, "Oh John, I'm so sorry."

"What?" I said, "Why are you sorry?"

Her blue eyes turned watery, "I promised that I would never let Sandy use you in any way, and now I am the reason she's able to do so! I'm the bargaining chip! I'm so sorry."

I was so shocked I didn't reply for a second, "Rhea, I willingly made you my bargaining chip, it's not your fault."

"So you aren't mad at me?" She asked in a small voice.

I scowled at her, angry that she obviously hadn't listened to me earlier when I said I was never mad at her. I hated when people ignored me.

"No." I said shortly.

"Promise?"

"Yes." I attempted to grasp at patience, something I had never bothered to do for anyone else. I ignored this fact and the many questions that would accompany it, because I wasn't ready to face Rhea's impact on me yet.

She giggled, and my heart was lightened with the fact that I had made her smile again, although I didn't know how my not being angry with her was a cause for smiling. Maybe because if I wasn't angry she wasn't going to die. "Thank you, John."

"You're welcome." Sandra probably would have had a heart attack seeing me have a full conversation with Rhea, and not even get angry during it. I had even let her touch me briefly and hadn't stormed away or yelled at her. Sandra's earlier words echoed once more, but I didn't let it deter me.

I knew now, I would never hurt Rhea. I had sworn to protect her, and I would not break my word.

"Come on, I'll make you some lunch." Rhea offered. I nodded and jogged to my target to grab my knives. I returned quickly to where Rhea was waiting for me, and together we walked towards the house.

Just as we reached the door, I heard something and threw myself in front of Rhea, scanning the area.

"John," she whispered, "is there something there?"

I didn't answer, and I couldn't see what had caught my attention. I just knew in my heart that there was something watching us, and I prayed it wasn't any Hungry. I readied my knives just in case.

It wasn't a Hungry that walked out of the woods, it was Sophie. A bedraggled, dirty Sophie, who was waving at us.

"Sophie." I gasped.

Rhea pushed me aside to see for herself, and her whole face lit up, "She's alive!"

Instantly she turned and opened the door to the house, yelling for everyone to come, that Sophie was back, Sophie was alive!!

Sophie reached the porch as everyone came streaming out of the house, eager to see the girl we had almost left for dead. Sandra's face was torn between joy and resignation. I knew that Sandra didn't trust Sophie because she knew Sophie wanted to die, but I also knew that she pitied her because she had lost her husband, Alex.

"Hey guys." Sophie greeted us. Her face was scratched up, like she had been running through brambles, but otherwise she seemed whole and healthy. Her hair was matted and so dirty it had lost its sheen, and I could understand now why she had cut off the long curly locks she had worn before.

"Sophie! I'm so glad you're okay." Rhea's voice was ecstatic. She was still hovering close to my side, and I realized I had frightened her when I had put her behind me. She had probably thought the Hungry were about to kill us all.

"Come in, come in." Sandra prompted, "We'll get some lunch and explain to you what we are planning to do next."

Sophie didn't have the heart to ask about what our plans would be, and she didn't object when we all escorted her into the kitchen. Rhea left my side to start heating the soup, and for once, it wasn't the canned soup we had been trying to save forever. I had found some leaves and berries I knew to be edible, and I had taken down a rabbit last night, and Rhea had quickly put everything into a pot to create one of the best soups I had ever tasted. I would have tried to patent it if the world hadn't gone to hell.

Sophie started eating like a madwoman, as if she hadn't been fed since she had last been with us.

"This soup is fantastic." She complimented before asking for another bowl.

"Thank you." Rhea said. I could see she was shocked that Sophie was eating as much as she was. She wasn't a big woman, but she was eating as if she was making up for lost time.

Sandra seemed distracted by this too, but she managed to start up on explaining anyway, "Okay, Sophie we're glad you're back. We've decided to go North, as far as we can go. We'll head back towards Alberta, try and get on a secondary highway into the Northwest Territories. I didn't realize we were as close to the border as we are. We're going to find shelter and stay up there for as long as possible."

Sophie nodded, "Sounds good, the Hungry will be way less up there. It's safer, but we don't have the gear."

Rhea grinned, "We do! Zack and I found a bunch of winter stuff in the attic, and we've cleared out as much as we can to bring with us. We'll have to pick up stuff as we go too, but we all have big coats and mittens and scarves and boots at least."

Sophie smiled at Zack, "Good one."

He shrugged, "We'll get you outfitted soon, we all have our stuff."

I remembered how everyone had snatched coats and boots, thanking Rhea and Zack for their discovery. She herself had been wearing the most ridiculous pink parka I had ever seen, and black and orange work boots that were about five sizes too big. Her mittens had been tiny green ones, with a strap connecting them, like the ones children had.

I had barely been able to hold back rare amusement at her outfit, but I didn't want to hurt her feelings, because she had been so delighted by the colours. The memory both pleased and annoyed me, because I had never before cared about anyone else's feelings.

Sophie's voice brought me back to reality, "Okay, when do we start?"

Sandra laughed under her breath, "Figures you'd be gung-ho. We leave tomorrow morning."

"Cool, I'll be ready." Sophie declared, "Now, may I have more soup?"

Rhea dished out another bowl, and Andrew and Anne disappeared to get ready, and probably to spend more time together. They never left each other's side when Sophie was around. It stemmed from the way Sophie stared at them longingly, as if she was imagining her life if Alex had survived.

Dana, the tiny kid Sandra had rescued was sitting beside a newly moved Eva, who had a fresh pallet in the eating area of the kitchen now, and both were enjoying their soup. Even I had to admit she was a cute kid, and well behaved too. She never complained about this lifestyle she was now leading, or the people who now surrounded her. In fact, the only thing I had ever heard her complain about was that Sandra had cut her hair.

Before we had rescued her Dana's hair had been dark brown and to her shoulders, and Sandra had decided it was too much trouble to wash and brush everyday so she had shorn it off. Dana now had hair that spiked off in every direction. She was still sweet, and her big brown eyes still begged you to give her the whole world if she asked it of you.

In all honesty, I didn't mind the kid, because she was tough for a little girl, and she wasn't afraid of me either. I think it had something to do with Sandra promising never to let anything hurt her, and 'something' included me. Either way, she wasn't shy around me, and that pleased me. If she managed to survive long enough to grow up, she would be a fantastic fighter.

As if she had heard my thoughts, Dana's eyes met mine and she smiled, "John, may I ask you a question?"

I glanced around, only Sandra and Rhea were paying attention to this exchange. I wanted to keep it that way, because if suddenly I had the eyes of Gabby, Jason, Sophie and Eva I would probably become angry and leave.

I nodded.

She grinned, "Will you teach me to use a knife?"

Sandra's eyes widened, but I knew that she thought it might be a good idea to let Dana learn to defend herself. While I agreed that Dana should know how to fight, I thought it might be a little early. I knew what it was like to learn to kill at a young age, and I didn't want anyone else to feel that.

I looked to see what Rhea thought, and her wide eyes and horrified expression told me everything I needed to know. She obviously thought no child should know how to kill, or ever need to know how to fight at such a young age. Children should be protected and sheltered.

"Dana, it's good to know how to fight, but you are young." I said softly, "We'll protect you until you're older, and then I'll teach you how to use a knife."

Dana frowned, but I could see that Rhea was smiling and thanking me with her blue eyes. Sandra was also pleased with this conclusion, I could tell by her grateful expression.

"But what if I have to help fight with you guys?" Dana asked, her eyes frightened.

"You won't have to, super-girl." Zack told her, and for once I was grateful he had spoken. "We are going to be careful and strong."

Dana thought for a moment and nodded decisively, "Alright. Thanks."

I decided that I had done quite enough conversing today, and headed towards the living room where the couch I slept on sat. Most of my gear was beside the couch and I thought I might take a nap while others were watching the house and making sure we were safe.

I had barely laid down on my couch when Rhea came in. She sat down on the floor in front of me and eyed me.

"Thank you, John, for what you did in there." she whispered, "I know you did it for me, because I was so against her learning to fight."

"No, I didn't," I denied grumpily, "I didn't want her to know how to kill at such a young age." I turned over, and gave her my back, knowing it would hurt her. I felt bad for a moment but I stomped out my guilt because she had been dead accurate with her thanks. I had said no to Dana because Rhea had wanted me to.

For an instant Rhea's small hand rested on my back and her words showed me I hadn't insulted her at all, "Well, thank you anyway." I could almost hear her smile, and her hand still burned against my shirt, "Now get some sleep. I know you spend all hours of the night patrolling the house to make sure we are all safe."

Her hand left me, and I heard her walk away. I thought perhaps I should be mad, but instead I wondered how she knew that I often stayed up all night.

Chapter Thirteen

In the morning we cleared out everything we wanted from the house and got into the van. It was a tight fit, with all the cans of food, alcohol and containers of gas, weapons and winter wear. Ten people in a van that normally would fit seven, and one of whom needed more space to heal.

We had decided to take one of the seats out, and leave the longer one in. Eva, Gabby and Sophie sat on the seat, Eva's head and feet propped on the other girls. She had managed to walk to the car herself that morning, and despite feeling pain she had done so without tearing her cut open again.

Sandra drove with Andrew directing her. Anne had sat herself where the console had once been, her form slender enough to fit. Her head was lying against Andrew's leg, and his hand rested gently upon her hair. He didn't seem to mind that her curly red hair was matted, and it's lustre had been lost with our struggles.

I wondered if that was what love was.

The thought was stupid, and I shook my head lightly, ridding myself of the foolishness that seemed to be infectious around this group. I focused myself again on the position of my newest comrades; Dana curled up with Rhea beside me, while Jason and Zack leaned against the side door. We were all sitting on coats and blankets to make it more comfortable, but it was still squished.

However, if I thought this was bad, I just imagined what it would be like when we all had to go to sleep, and crowded together on the floor. I hated to have people that close to me, and I just knew that the night would be a million times worse than the drive was.

I cursed the fact that I had resigned myself to staying with this group. It was Rhea that had solidified my decision, and I knew that I wouldn't leave while she stayed with them.

We drove away from the house that had sheltered all of us in silence. We mourned the loss of our haven, for a while, but eventually excitement filled the air about our newest adventure.

"We're going to be like real live Eskimos!" Gabby exclaimed.

Sandra laughed, "Yeah, and hopefully we'll get used to eating polar bear and fish!"

Dana made the most disgusted face I had ever seen, "Ew, I hate fish."

Rhea laughed, "That will be a problem, I have a feeling we are going to be eating a lot of it! I'm going to make snowshoes!"

Jason snorted, "And just what will you make them out of, Rhea?"

She shrugged, "John can make a bow, I'm sure he can make the frame for me, then I'll use some twine to make the net part!"

Sandra eyed me from the rearview mirror, "You think John's going to make snowshoe frames for you?"

Rhea asked me with her eyes and I couldn't say no, especially since snowshoes were practical. "If she wants."

Sandra's shocked expression was worth it, and Jason snickered at her. She glared at him, golden-brown eyes afire, and I was thankful that for the moment her anger wasn't directed at me. I wondered how Jason managed to keep breathing, and not sleeping on the couch.

We were back in Alberta, heading North. We had debated for a long time to continue North from where we had been in Saskatchewan, but the way was practically blocked with waterways. So we had returned to Alberta, to seek a safer route into the far North.

We stopped driving four hours later when Dana had declared quite firmly that she had to use the washroom, and Sandra had finally pulled over at a rest stop. The rest stop was near Fort McMurray, although we had no desire to go anywhere near the once populated area.

There was a convenience store there, but the washrooms weren't attached. This made them safer, but I still wanted to check out the store. While everyone was taking their 'breaks' I grabbed a couple knives and a bag and went through the back entrance of the store.

It was silent in there, and dusty, as though no one had been inside in a long time. I snuck through the employee area, seeing nothing I wanted to take from there. I entered the actual store behind the counter. The till was open and I could see hundreds of dollars sitting there.

Once upon a time that would have been long stolen, but these days, it was worthless. I moved on, taking some chocolate bars for treats. I could see that all the food that could be kept over time had been looted but I wasn't here for that.

Ice cream, chocolate bars, slur-pees. I was here only to get some much needed junk food to cheer everyone and keep us awake. I also wanted to see if they had any books, tape or string.

The bell over the front door jingled and I spun on my heels and brought my knife up.

Instead of a Hungry, I saw Rhea.

I spun back towards the shelves to see if the bell over the door had drawn anything, but luckily nothing had popped up.

"What are you doing here?" I hissed. Rhea looked a bit taken aback at my venomous tone, and I realized that I had obviously never been harsh with her before. That was a feat, because I was mean to everyone else.

"I came to see if you were here." She answered, blue eyes concerned.

I waved her over to my side, knowing that if she was going to be in the store I might as well keep her close and protected. I kept grabbing things; I had finally found the books.

"You shouldn't have come, what if it hadn't been me when you opened the door but a Hungry?" I was infuriated now, but as promised, my wrath wasn't aimed at her, it was all for me. I should have told her where I was going, or better yet, I should have never left her side.

"You're very irritated." She observed mildly.

"You think?" I snarled.

She stiffened, "You said you wouldn't get angry with me."

"I know." I retorted, "And I'm not angry with you, I'm angry with me."

Finally, she reached out and slowed my hands from their actions. We didn't need that many books.

"John, you shouldn't be mad, especially not with yourself. I knew you had to be in here, you would never stray too far from the group when we aren't in a safe place, and I knew you would keep me safe. Plus, if it's anyone's fault, it's mine. I give you full permission to be furious with me."

My rage dissipated after that and I sighed, "I'm not mad anymore. Come on, let's finish up here."

I led her to the section of the shelves where I had seen tape and various other hardware objects. I was grabbing more string and twine, and tapes and oil for the van when Rhea gasped and grabbed my arm. I didn't even pull away from her touch I reacted so fast to danger.

My knife came out and I searched for what had startled her.

In the hallway to the storage room was a thin man, and he was staring at us.

I handed the bag to Rhea and stepped back so that I had her completely behind me. The man didn't move, and that unnerved me. Every Hungry I had encountered had launched themselves at me immediately.

"Looters?" His voice was low and gravelly, and as soon as he spoke I knew the truth.

This man was not Hungry, he was normal.

"Not intentionally." I responded, "I thought it was deserted and decided to get supplies."

The man shrugged, "Not much left anymore."

"Enough for us." I frowned, "You live here?"

The man's eyes were sharp as he watched me, "Maybe."

I nodded, I had expected this. Rhea was shaking behind me, I could feel her tremors through the hand she had pressed to my back. I rationalized letting her touch me and not pushing her away with the thought that she was frightened and it was easy to protect her when she was practically glued to my back.

"I'm not here to rob you." I told him, "I'm travelling with a large group of survivors. I would rather trade information than food."

The man nodded, "You can take the food, I don't need it."

My suspicions were confirmed with his words, he must have an underground shelter or something, because he obviously wasn't worried about food. I wondered why he stayed here, it was obviously not a prime location.

"Why do you stay here?" My question was asked, but not by my mouth. Rhea's head had poked around my frame to ask the man this.

The man laughed at her meekness, and told me, "You travel with a very frightened girl. I stay here because my wife is here. She has a degenerative muscle disease, and I can't move her. I refuse to leave her, this is our home."

I realized I respected this man very much, especially as he told us of his weakness, and let us know without as many words that he had food. He was obviously well prepared to fight anyone and anything off.

"Do you have any information on the rest of Canada, or the world?" I asked.

He laughed sadly, "Some; I know Toronto went to hell shortly after Edmonton did. British Columbia held out the longest because the mountains slowed infiltration of the disease."

"Disease?" Rhea asked.

"Yeah, that's what they were calling it before the radio stations went quiet. They thought it was biological warfare but nobody knows who started it. The U.S broke off all connection with us, and refused to help when our military asked for it. Their northernmost States had a touch of it, but from what I hear they are still safe. The only problem with that is that no one can get in. They shoot on sight, infected or not."

So South hadn't been an option, the States was on complete lockdown. They weren't taking any chances.

"What about Europe? Africa? Asia? Australia? South America?" I was hungry for answers.

He shrugged, "Africa had it bad, it somehow got in there. They think it was through the soldiers in the Middle East, and it spread from there. Most of Europe went on lock down fast enough. Russia seems to be safe. Australia is okay, probably because the surrounding waters. For some reason the infected don't like water. Even if you throw it on them, they hate it. Like cats."

I hadn't known that, and it pleased me to hear they had another weakness. I was going to use it to my full advantage next time I ran into a Hungry.

"I haven't heard anything about South America, but I assume it's probably okay considering the States was blocking it from Canada, and Canada seemed to be where the infection started."

"Where did you learn all of this!?" Rhea's voice was incredulous, and heartbroken.

"I have a brother in the States, and he still has all the comforts of home. That includes Internet."

"Internet still works!?"

The man shrugged, "Yeah, it's faster than ever before. A lot of sites are down, but my email account is working. I don't know how long it will be, probably until the provider finally cuts everyone off. For now, I'm still connected."

This amazed me, but I suppose that the rest of the world hadn't just stopped because our world had been torn apart; and the internet would always be there, as long as satellites and modems were around to pick it up. Or at least, that's what I thought with my limited knowledge.

"What about Asia, you didn't mention Asia?"

For the first time the man's voice wavered, "It's off the map. As far as my brother knows, everyone is either dead or hiding like we are."

"Thank you for telling us this." I said, and I was barely aware of Rhea's face buried in my back. I thought she might have been crying, and her emotions frightened me more than any Hungry ever could.

"You kids going North?" The man asked.

I nodded blankly.

He sighed, "That's a good idea. I have something for you though."

He disappeared and I turned to see if Rhea was okay and to force her to stop any silly emotional displays. I had been right, she was crying, and her red rimmed navy eyes were puffy. The instant I turned around she dropped the bag and wrapped her arms around me, crying into my chest.

I didn't know what to do with myself, having her so close to me. Usually I hated when people touched me, but Rhea was another case. I did hate that she was crying though, and I wanted her to quit.

"Stop crying." I ordered.

She lifted her face from my now wet shirt and sniffed. I knew she was trying to curb her tears for my benefit, and I felt bad that I was so socially inept that I couldn't comfort her, and was barely tolerating her arms wrapped around me.

"Oh John," Her voice cracked, "why did this happen?"

"I don't know." I replied. "At least most of the world is okay."

"But Asia was decimated..." Her voice was barely audible.

The man came back with a device with what looked like a corkscrew on it. It wasn't big, and it ran on a hand crank, about the same size as a hand drill. I knew immediately what it was, though I had never seen one quite so compact and manual. I thought that perhaps this man had saved us in his own way.

"For ice fishing!" I said, completely amazed. I hadn't even thought about the fact that drilling a hole for fishing was going to be very difficult in the dead of winter.

The man nodded and eyed Rhea, once more buried in my chest. He gave me a small smile.

"You two better get out of here, I don't want to meet the rest of your friends. I've gotta get back to my wife. Try to survive, and keep the shy one outta trouble too."

I pushed Rhea away from me and handed her the bag to keep her that way. I snatched the strange corkscrew device from the man and thanked him once more. I tugged Rhea along with my other arm and left the shop, the entrance bells jingling as we left the man and his poor wife.

Rhea was still sniffling sadly, and I wished I could brighten her mood more than I wished for another day of life. Only because I hated nothing more than her pathetic emotions. Unfortunately, I could think of nothing that would make this better, nothing that would ever make her smile again.

"Rhea." I stopped her and reached into the bag, bringing out a giant chocolate bar.

Her eyes brightened slightly, "For me?!"

"Yes, and it's not even expired."

She giggled, and I knew that I had not fixed all the problems of the world, but I had made her stop her crying.

"You shouldn't have come in there." I repeated, "You didn't have to hear that. I could have done it alone."

She shook her head determinedly, "No, I had to. Someone has to have your back, John, and I know I'm not the best fighter, but I'm on your side."

My heart felt very strange at her words, and I wanted to smile at her. I didn't, because smiles weren't something I ever did, but I was tempted, "Thank you."

She giggled again, "I noticed that I'm the only person in this entire entourage that is allowed to touch you. Without you getting angry, that is."

I glowered at the thought of anyone touching me, and I knew that had it been anyone else who had decided to cry into my shirt I would have mercilessly killed them for it. I supposed that, in a way, Rhea was the only one I would allow to touch me without fear of retaliation. "I suppose." I said distastefully.

She laughed loudly, "There you go again, making me smile."

I shrugged self-consciously.

"There you two are!" Sandra's voice cut in. "We were worried! Come on, we're all ready."

I lead Rhea to the van, and upon entering I handed out the contents of the bag, garnering thanks from everyone for the ice cream and chocolates. We had all missed junk food.

No one questioned the machinery I tossed in the back, or the way both Rhea and I were subdued as we drove away from the tiny convenience store, watching it as it faded into the distance as if we would never see it again.

"Gabby?" Rhea said softly.

"Yes? Gabrielle answered without hesitation, eyes clear and curious.

Rhea smiled, "You said when we started all of this that your parents were in the States, right?"

Gabby frowned, sadness coming to haunt her, "Yeah, they were in Florida, for their anniversary."

Rhea nodded, "The States is on lockdown. It's safe." Gabby gaped at her, "Your parents are alive, Gabby, they're okay."

She started to cry, huge tears of relief streaming down her cheeks, only emphasizing the beauty that dirt and sadness had tried to conceal. Slowly Rhea explained to the group the man we had met, and the stories he had told us. Tears flew freely, whether from the sadness of losing half the world, or the gratitude of knowing that we were not the only ones left.

The world was still out there.

Chapter Fourteen

Everyone was sick of driving, and we had used up all our gas twice, each time finding another supply to re-fill the jerry cans. We were unsure where we were once more, mostly because none of us were familiar with the towns that appeared on the signs we passed, and the last thing we had recognized had been two days ago. We had been unbelievably lucky so far, other than the fact that Dana apparently got car sick.

"Please, please, Sandy, stop! We need to sleep a single night without moving." Dana had long finished whining, and was now pleading with everything she had. I actually felt bad for the kid, she had to be in pain to complain this much.

"I agree, and we will stop tonight but we need to find somewhere safe to stop driving and rest." Sandra consoled her from the driver's seat.

I remembered the words of the man in the gas station, and how he had told me that the Hungry hated water. An idea formed in my head, and I watched out the window to search for any signs that might have a creek nearby. We were in luck once more; an hour later we drove over a bridge that stood above a shallow river.

"Sandra, take this turn off road." I ordered. She obeyed, mostly cause she was curious as to what I was going to say. The van easily drove down the gravelly path and Sandra came to a stop before the water.

"How deep do you think that is?" I asked.

She shrugged, "I can see the bottom, I doubt it's more than a foot or two."

"Drive in, make sure water is on all sides of the van."

She did as I said, and for a second we feared we were wrong about the depth, but she came to a stop with the water covering half the tires. We were in no danger of slipping, or flooding the bottom.

"This is perfect, the bridge hides us, and we're in the middle of nowhere."

Rhea laughed, "And the Hungry hate water!"

In sharing our story of the man in the gas station we had also shared this knowledge. Sandra had wanted to try and help the man, but we wouldn't let her turn around. She thought herself evil, but she truly wasn't. As much as she annoyed me, she was a great leader, and a kind person.

"This is exactly what we need." Jason said. Jason rarely said anything, and he was strong, which made him one of the few people I actually liked. His brother, Zack, was unfortunately the opposite, and I couldn't stand him. It didn't help that he was constantly cracking jokes and making everyone —Rhea— laugh. Still, the biggest fault in Jason was that he was obviously terribly in love with Sandra; it was the kind of love nothing would fix.

"Yeah." Zack replied, "I haven't slept properly since the house."

Everyone agreed, we were pleased with the thought of sleeping without motion. Dana wasn't the only one who hated being so nomadic. It wasn't in human nature, we liked to settle, and have a safe place to sleep at night; a familiar place.

"Perfect. Dana, you have your sleeping spot." Sandra turned in her driver's seat to look at the little girl, but she was already dead asleep in Jason's arms.

Sandra laughed and turned the van off, locking all the doors. She left the key in the ignition and laid the seat as far back as it would go. Eva, who had long since claimed the passenger seat for herself did the same, wincing as she laid back. Andrew and Anne stretched out, twining their limbs together, on the backseat, with Zack behind the backseat in the trunk, basically on top of all of our gear. Sophie grabbed a blanket to curl herself on the floor with Gabrielle. Jason arranged himself and Dana into a better position beside Sophie under the driver's chair. I sat against the door, my legs crossed. I watched out the window, determined to protect the people while they slept.

An hour later everyone was dead asleep, and I contented myself with the fact that I had no trouble sleeping in a moving car and decided not to wake anyone else for the watch. I settled more comfortably into my seated position.

My movement woke Rhea, who was curled beside me, her back sometimes brushing me knee. I hadn't moved away from her because then I would be touching Sophie or Jason, and that thought was less than appealing to me. At my small shift Rhea sat up, her eyes wide and fearful once more.

"John?" she immediately asked, her body coiled for action.

"Yes," I whispered back, "We're safe, go back to sleep."

She sighed, "John you shouldn't have to watch over us all the time. Wake up Andrew or Jason, they'll gladly take watch."

I eyed Andrew, who was wrapped around Anne and sleeping so soundly I feared a foghorn wouldn't wake him up. Jason was equally asleep, and I didn't want to disturb Dana who was snuggled in his arms. She had fought hard for her rest.

"No, I'm not tired." I told her, "But you are."

She had been yawning as I said this, and promptly closed her mouth in embarrassment, "Okay, but only if you promise to sleep once we're driving again."

I nodded and instantly she was placated. However instead of laying back down on the floor beside me, she cozied herself into my side and set her head on my arm. For a moment I was going to toss her back where she came from, but she was warm and soft, and already drifting off to sleep. I moved my arm briefly to see if it would cause her to move away, but instead she came closer, settling straight into my chest. There was no good way for me to get her away, and I wasn't really angered by her proximity since she was obviously not a threat, and perhaps only staying so close to me because she was scared.

I held my breath while she sat there, fearing that any movement I made would bring her closer, or make her leave me, both of which would cause me pain. As soon as I heard her soft, even breathing I knew I was safe.

Rhea was once more asleep, and this time she was beside me, touching me. I had never had anyone this close to me before, unless I had been fighting them, and I decided to take the opportunity to study her.

She was still as pale as ivory, and I knew that beneath her eyelids lay the faded navy eyes that reminded me of the comfort of blue jeans and summer. Her lashes were thick and cast charcoal shadows on her cheek bones, and a pert nose led the way down to her soft lips.

I quickly moved on from her tempting mouth; her hair was the next object of my gaze, and I hesitantly let my cheek rest on the top of it. It was soft and honey blond, a warmer shade than my own short blonde hair. It grew in straight sheaths to her shoulder blades, and I found myself finding a strange wish to bury my head in it and inhale.

I did so, deciding that the opportunity would never arise again while I lived and breathed, because as soon as she woke up I would never allow her in my arms again.

She smelled like spring mornings full of flowers and sunshine, and I knew the instant I inhaled that I was irrevocably lost to her. She would always control a piece of me now, because there was nothing in the world that had ever smelled so wonderful, and I never wanted to smell anything else ever again.

She was beautiful and warm, and I had never had anyone as lovely as her be this close to me. In fact, I think the last woman who had gotten this close to me had been my mother, and I had been a child. I didn't even remember her, so it barely counted.

I raised my head again, understanding that if I spent my watch mesmerized in Rhea I wasn't doing a very good job of protecting. My raised gaze met Sandra's, and I realized she had heard mine and Rhea's entire conversation and was now watching me hold her gently.

She didn't speak, but she did nod at me gravely as though she finally understood that Rhea was my responsibility, and I would never hurt her. I think it made her sad, seeing the way she had lost a friend to me, a man she disliked and perhaps feared.

At least she wasn't afraid I would harm Rhea anymore; Sandra had discovered that I counted my vow as my personal law, and nothing would touch Rhea while I lived and breathed.

Sandra sighed sadly as she rolled over, her back to me. "John, go to sleep. I'm watching."

I frowned at her, even though she couldn't see me, but I realized that I had given her mind too many things to think about for her to go back to sleep.

Maybe she hadn't ever been asleep, her mind full of all the fears mine had been full of. Fears of leaders and protectors.

I finally had an excuse to move away from Rhea and I did so, feeling a strange pain in my chest that felt like remorse. I lay down beside Andrew and Anne, focusing on not touching them at all. For the first time I wished Rhea was beside me, because I would rather have her than anyone else. Instead, Rhea was still sitting up, and I felt bad for leaving her there so I shook her knee until she woke up startled again.

Her fear faded once more and she lay down in between Anne and I, as if knowing that I would prefer to have her on my one side, and the door on my other.

For a second, I let myself mourn the loss of her at my side, and wish that Sandra hadn't spoken, because now we lay beside one another without touching. I only let this regret continue for a second because it was a new and unknown feeling and nursing it would probably be a bad idea.

The minutes dragged by and with each passing second I feared that perhaps I had imagined her warmth and her smell and her closeness. As if hearing my thoughts she shifted and brought herself closer and I turned my head to stare at her once more.

I was trying to intimidate her with my gaze and make her go back to her own side but it didn't seem to work. Nothing ever worked with her the way I wanted it to.

"What's wrong?" I finally murmured.

"I hate that..." she breathed back, "I just hate..."

Instead of finishing, she shook her head and buried her face in the coat she was using as a pillow. Her hair spread over her shoulders like sunlight, and I desperately wanted to hear what she was going to say, because it was my job to kill anything she hated or feared, and I found myself rolling onto my side to reach to her shoulder and turn her.

"You hate what?" I asked. My voice was nearly inaudible, mostly because I knew Sandra was awake and listening. I prayed she could not hear our almost silent whispers.

Instead of speaking Rhea came very close to me again and pulled her body flush against mine. Her face was smashed into my chest, and one dainty hand was resting above, over my heart.

I was too shocked to move, until I heard the tiniest of whispers from her, "I hate that I wake up afraid when you aren't there."

I wondered if she would wake up without fear if I let her sleep this close to me. I supposed that I had already let too much weakness in tonight and a little more wouldn't hurt, and so I could let her stay near me. Besides, it was my job to make her feel safe.

Hesitantly, I placed my arm around her body and tugged her with me as I lay once more on my back.

She lifted her head from me and smiled, "Thank you." Her hand once more curled on my chest, and her head rested on my shoulder, close to my face. I wondered if she could hear how my heart was thundering. I pulled the blanket at my feet over us and swore at myself in every language I knew, and in many different creative ways. As often as I told myself I was an idiot and I should just shove her away as soon as she was asleep I knew I couldn't do it.

This stupid, weak girl had made me a joke.

I brought my free hand up to rub my face in anger and frustration and misery, but Rhea's left hand raised at the same time and clasped mine and brought it down to my chest with hers. I stared down at our intertwined hands resting over my heart.

She fell asleep quickly, and it didn't take me long to join her.

I was woken by the engine starting, and Dana's low miserable moan. Rhea wasn't resting on my chest anymore, but I could feel a hand stroking my hair and a softness under my head that hadn't been there before.

I sat up instantly on edge, wondering what in the world was happening. Never had I let myself be so vulnerable in front of other people and it worried me. I glanced behind me and saw that Rhea had been letting me rest in her lap, and talking to Dana at the same time.

Everyone else who sat in the back was staring at me as though I had grown another head. I knew it was because Rhea had been touching me, and I hadn't yelled at her or pushed her away yet. They had probably woken up to us coiled together and been trying to work it out ever since.

I hated when people stared at me. I sent my glare of death around the room and wrapped the blanket over my head and rolled away from Rhea. It had felt wonderful in her lap, but I refused to show a stupid weakness in front of anyone.

I knew that even though I had moved away and couldn't see the faces of my companions anymore, they were still staring; murderous intentions filled my brain and I prayed for the strength not to slaughter these stupid people I had gotten myself saddled with.

I felt a push at my back and I realized Rhea had shoved at me with her foot. I thought I should probably hit her, but I didn't move. Perhaps patience did come with age.

"John, come out from the blanket!" Her voice was bright and unafraid and I was pleased that I had made her brave with my protection. I was also furious that she was calling me a coward by hiding under my blanket.

I stuck my hand out and flipped her off, intending it to be vicious and cruel, but her giggles mocked me as I pulled my hand back under the safety of the blanket.

Obviously the girl had a warped sense of humour. I comforted myself and my ego with this fact as I stayed hidden under my blanket.

What felt like hours of sleeping, pretending to sleep and praying that eventually everyone else in the car would either mysteriously die, or go to sleep and forget the entire event had happened went by before anything happened. I was still wrapped in my blanket, but now once more aware of everything surrounding me.

My invitation back into the real world came as another soft kick to my back, and once more I thought that perhaps I should kill Rhea so she would cause me less trouble, but once more I withheld my instincts and did nothing.

"What?" I practically spat the word out, and I knew my fury was palpable in the air.

"John, everyone's asleep, except for Jason, who is driving." Rhea's words were murmured, and I was grateful she was at least intelligent enough to keep our conversations semi-private.

I rolled myself out of the blanket and sat up. My glare was still firmly planted on my face and I scanned the van to discover Rhea had been correct, and everyone was taking a nap except for Jason, who I was surprisingly comfortable around as he wasn't a big talker.

I transferred my scowl to Rhea and I sat and glowered at her for a long time, long enough that she started fidgeting, and I had finally, finally gotten under the skin of the calmest of the group. She even looked close to tears.

"John..." Her voice was uncertain, and it emerged closer to a whisper.

"I *hate* when people stare at me." I told her. I injected as much poison as I could in my words and shot them at her, hoping against all reason that maybe she would finally get the hint and stay away from me.

Instead, my words had the opposite effect, and she moved towards me carefully, as though she was approaching a sleeping bear. She avoiding the sleeping bodies once more piled around us and I had absolutely nowhere to run, locked inside this van. I was cornered and she came so close to me that I could almost smell the sunshine and flowers she brought with her everywhere she went.

"I'm sorry." She murmured, "And I'll tell them not to stare, if that will make you feel better. I don't want to hurt you, John, I only ever want to-"

I was suddenly too tired to feel confused, and too tired to hold Rhea and too tired to even convince myself that I needed to survive. I could feel exhaustion seep into my bones, and I realized it was because I was fighting a losing battle against Rhea and my own heart. Eventually, I would have to give in, but it would not be tonight, and it would not be to this brainless woman who just didn't know when to *give up*.

"Forget it, Rhea, okay." I snapped, "Just, leave me alone."

I couldn't run from her, but I could ignore her, and I turned my head away from her. Eventually, she once more moved away from me, back to where it was safe, back to where sunshine and happiness belonged.

Once more I was alone, and it was comforting and familiar and *lonely*. I was where I belonged as well.

Chapter Fifteen

"I would have been happier being eaten." Dana's loud six-year old voice proclaimed this fact two days later. It was no longer a joke, because nearly everyone in the van agreed with her sentiments. We were sick to death of the van, and the movement, and the cold fruit we were eating out of cans because we had no heater or stove. The lack of privacy was terrible, and even worse was the smell. Rest stops had started to become far and few between and no one had showered in a while. It wasn't a point that we brought up, but it was always present, especially when Sandra would open a window despite the air that was growing steadily colder.

"Dana." Sandra admonished tiredly, "I know, everyone hates this van and travelling. We're sick to death of it. But we can't stop until we find a safe place."

"We have to be far enough north now." Zack reasoned. I wasn't so sure, there wasn't very much snow yet, and all the still water we had seen wasn't fully frozen. Still, I was as ready as anyone to stop moving for a while.

Sandra shrugged, "Yeah I think we are, but I haven't seen a house in a while, and even then they are usually in towns that had once been populated. That would be a hotspot for Hungry."

With the argument once more settled Dana nestled back into Sophie's arms. It had been strange the first time Sophie had cuddled Dana, but now it was becoming a common sight. It turned out that before the world had gone to shit, Sophie had been a teacher.

Everyone had stopped staring at me, thankfully, because I had gone back to normal. Rhea and I didn't speak, or even look at each other, and I didn't bother to answer anyone else. I was always distanced nowadays, and I slept alone against the door as far as I could go. I guessed that my bout of insanity had been something to do with cabin fever, except in a van.

With this thought my eyes strayed to Rhea, and I noted how tired she looked, with dark smudges underneath her eyes. I hoped this wasn't because she was afraid of sleeping again, just because I wouldn't allow her anywhere near me. She was barely eating enough either, and I worried that my distancing myself from her for her safety had in fact harmed her.

It was her own fault if she made herself sick though, I had only vowed to protect her from Hungry and death! Sickness and hunger was not my problem.

Still it didn't sit well with me that the kindest and most exuberant of our group was now reserved and sad. I felt as though I had destroyed something precious, and the one thing I hadn't wanted to do was hurt Rhea.

"Rest stop!" Sandra's excited yell brought everyone scrambling to attention. We had all been dying for a bathroom, but it looked as though this rest stop even had a showering area.

"Thank god." Anne said, half laughing. Andrew squeezed her hand and I could tell that this bathroom and shower break was the highlight of everyone's day.

Sandra pulled over and killed the engine. We had been getting more confident as every day went by because the sightings of the Hungry were getting fewer and fewer. Still, everyone was subdued as we got out of the van, and I saw Andrew grab a gun as I snatched my knives. We were still too low on weapons for my tastes, but at least we were proficient in what we had.

Rhea was beside Eva and Gabby, helping Eva along. Eva was recovering nicely, and she probably could have walked on her own, but we didn't chance it. I shadowed them all as they headed towards the ladies washrooms. I knew it annoyed Rhea that I had spoken so harshly to her and ignored her until danger might be present, and now I wouldn't leave her alone. However, Rhea's feelings were not my problem, only her safety was.

Finally, she spun on me, and for the second time I saw anger on her face. It was truly difficult to make Rhea angry, and I was almost proud I had done so. Eva and Gabrielle saw what was about to happen and continued on to the washroom where Sandra was waiting. I appreciated their sense of privacy, and for the first time I thought maybe these people weren't so bad.

"John, go away. I am perfectly safe with Eva and Gabby, and Sandra is just over there. You don't need to follow me around." She was stunning in her fury, icy eyes glinting and pale cheeks now rosy. Her chest heaved in ire, and she struggled to control her tone.

"I'm keeping you safe." I replied, unfazed by her anger.

She glared, "I don't want your protection."

"Too bad."

Finally, her controlled voice cracked, "You are the one who told me to leave you alone! You can't just ignore me for days and then suddenly hover around when there is danger."

"Why not?"

"It's unfair to me." Her words made absolutely no sense to me, since by all accounts my actions were simply to protect her, and if anything, they were unfair to me! I was the one who had to protect a weak imbecile, and I was the one who had to torture himself by hanging around but not being allowed to talk, or touch, or care!

"How is this unfair to you?" I growled.

"You're toying with me!" She cried, "I hate trying to be your friend and never knowing if you hate me or like me. I'm tired of waiting for you to snap on me like you did two days ago, and I don't want to deal with your hurtful words."

"I don't need any friends." I told her cruelly, even though the thought of having Rhea as a friend was surprisingly pleasing. She would be a good friend, always loyal and generous; betrayal probably wasn't even in her vocabulary.

"Everyone needs a friend." She admonished, "And I would have been happy to be yours if you wanted me to!"

"I don't want you to." I snarled.

Her eyes filled with tears, and she sagged as if her anger had been the only thing holding her up. For a second I almost lunged forward to catch her against me and shield her from the world that was hurting her, but then I remembered that it was me who was hurting her. It was my words that had made her cry. A feeling I had never really experienced before flooded through me, making me shudder, and my own heart pounded in pain; it was guilt, strong and shocking and so damn powerful I was frightened for a moment.

She shoved me then, and caught me completely off guard. Her push barely moved me back a few steps, but it was more shocking to me than if Sandra had stabbed me with one of my own knives. Rhea hated violence. She had once jumped in front of me to protect me from her friend, even though she hadn't known me and I had held a knife to her other friend's throat.

To push me was probably the greatest show of hatred Rhea had ever put on.

"I *hate* you." She said, glancing between my face and the hands that had betrayed her by trying to hurt another person. Then, as if it was to too much for her, she turned back towards the bathrooms and ran.

I didn't follow.

***

I had finished my showering before the girls had exited the bathroom, mostly because I was still trying to watch out for Rhea. Her words had shocked me, and I supposed that they had hurt me. If Rhea, the kindest and most compassionate of our group couldn't stand me, no one would ever be able to.

I set the hurt aside, because I had always known that I would never be liked. I had long ago accepted this fact, and even liked it.

I despised that I was upset now, and only because Rhea was loving and beautiful and I realized too late that I wanted to be kind to her. Even if I didn't know how to do that.

It was too late now, but I would still protect her, because I had vowed it. There would never be another being on this planet that I would value more than Rhea, and I knew that I would go to my grave willingly if she was safe.

That made her a huge weakness, but I would be damned if I suddenly proved Sandra right and got Rhea killed.

I heard her before I saw her, she was laughing. As much as the sound pleased me, it also wounded me. We had just argued, and it infuriated me to no end that I was affected and she wasn't. How dare she be so free and happy while I brooded?

When I saw her though, I could make out the sadness lining her face. The toll that the fight had taken on her made her look weary and much older; the looming fear of Hungry had never had this much of an impact on her before.

She also was smiling, if sad, and I knew that she had reached some sort of conclusion where I was concerned, and I only prayed it wasn't that she hated me any longer. I could deal with sleeping beside her without touching, as long as I could smell her floral fragrance and pretend to ignore her. I could deal with not talking, as long as she smiled and laughed again.

"You're staring." The voice came from my left, startling me. I realized I had been so wrapped up in Rhea I hadn't even noticed Jason come to my side. I bristled at his nearness and my own obliviousness, but if anyone wanted to have a chat with me, Jason was the one I trusted the most, if only because of his strong-but-silent attitude.

"So are you." I retorted, seeing the way his eyes were all over Sandra from across the parking lane. He frowned, but I noticed he didn't move his gaze to glare at me.

"If you care, don't treat her like dirt."

I growled low in my chest, hating the way he said 'dirt' as if Rhea was now associated with that. I knew that he wasn't insinuating it, he was telling me I was the jerk in this situation, but I still wanted to rip his throat out.

"She likes you." Jason finally glared at me, "So stop being a stubborn ass."

I lunged at him but he moved too quickly for me to get any contact. The only reason a fight didn't erupt was his unshakable calm, because I was itching for him to even try it. Jason smiled a slow, smug grin; I wanted to knock it off his face.

"She's staring." He mocked, and saluted me. I spun on my heels to see Rhea watching me with the same intensity I had paid her. It pleased me that she wasn't ignoring me, but I didn't like that she had seen me go for Jason's throat. He had probably planned that out, just so I would now have something to talk to her about.

Almost immediately she started towards me, piercing me with a gimlet stare and frowning. I cursed Jason in every language I could manage in my head, and reigned in my temper so I wouldn't lash out at Rhea anymore. That had been what had started this whole thing: my temper.

Distasteful as it was, this whole stupid fight was my fault. Rhea had played a part by being stubborn, but if I was honest with myself, and I always was, it was my fault. Therefore, I would have to apologize.

My throat almost closed with the thought, and I wondered if I would manage to even choke out the words. I didn't think I could do it, not even for Rhea.

"John," She started, "don't you dare start taking out your anger at me on Jason. It's not his fault you-"

"I'm sorry." I blurted.

We both paused, as if unsure what to make of this new development. I don't think I had ever said those words to anyone in the world, I wasn't even sure if I had ever been taught them. Rhea seemed as shocked as I was, because she hadn't recovered and her mouth still hung open in a tiny oval.

"I beg your pardon?" She whispered.

I scowled deeply, there was no way I was ever going to repeat that phrase for her, or anyone ever again.

"You heard me." I muttered.

"No," she challenged, "I don't think I did hear you, John."

I once more wanted to hit her, but I remembered my temper, and the fact that a bruise marring her face would forever guilt me, even after it faded. I would hate a mark on her even if I hadn't caused it. If I had been the cause, I would never have been able to live with it. No, I wouldn't hit Rhea, as much as she may have deserved it.

"I'm sorry." My words came out as a growl, but her deep blue eyes still lit up like the sun.

"Why?" she asked, "Why are you sorry?"

I tensed, I hadn't expected this question, "Because I lost my temper on you."

"And?" She was pushing me again, and I was going to either get used to the fact that Rhea had a surprising amount of backbone and bravery, even if she couldn't use a gun, or else sink to the low of hitting girls. Since I had already established that I would never hurt Rhea, I had to learn to live with her insubordination.

"And," I gritted my teeth, "I was wrong."

She giggled, "I think those words would have given Sandra a heart attack. I was just talking to her in the bathroom and she told me that you would never apologize. You apparently always have to be right."

Anger was infusing my limbs again, and I prayed for the patience to deal with this infuriating and addicting creature. I wished I would have gone to anger management long before I had ever run into Rhea, the only person who I had ever tried to manage my anger with.

"It would seem I'm not always right." I retorted.

Finally, her smug satisfaction with my apology melted away, and she was back to being my meek Rhea. Her eyes were liquid, and she stepped closer to me once more.

I had missed her closeness, and the thought of that shocked me so much I stumbled back a step.

My movement made her eyes narrow, and she pinned me with her gaze so I wouldn't move while she stepped forward once more.

"John, I'm sorry, too." Her apology caught me off guard. I had always thought the point of a fight was to win, and I had given her that victory with my concession that she was right, and now she was putting us back on equal ground?

"Why?" I asked her, but unlike her question mine was full of shock, and hers had been hunting for reasons.

She laughed, "Because I was cruel as well, and I pressured you. I know you don't like it when people touch you, or stare at you, and yet I was persistent. I also yelled and pushed you."

Her stare dropped to her hands as if she was reliving some horrible nightmare. I knew she was only thinking about how she had shoved me, and it was haunting her.

"It's okay. It's not the first time someone's pushed me, and it probably won't be the last." It wasn't meant as a joke, because I thought it was true, but she laughed, and that was all that mattered.

"That's the most violent thing I've ever done." She confided.

"Then you are still a saint in most people's eyes."

Her smile grew, and all the weariness that I had previously put on her face with my anger dissipated and once more she was young and free and fearless.

"I don't hate you."

I nodded at her and gestured towards the van where I could see people were starting to gather. Dana was napping already, taking every advantage of the not moving vehicle. She looked adorable cuddled in the corner, and I wished that her childhood hadn't been snatched away the way that it was. It was probably the most unselfish wish I had ever had in my life, and I knew that Rhea had started this change in me.

I wasn't sure if I liked it yet, or if it would help or hinder me, all I knew was that it was there, and it wasn't going to leave me with Rhea looking at me with such hope.

We reached the van, and I held my hand out to help Rhea up. I knew that this would cause everyone to stare, because I was about to willingly touch Rhea and help someone weaker than myself. It was basically against everything I had ever believed in to help the weak.

She grinned from ear to ear and took my hand.

We clambered into the van, and I could see Jason's pleased expression and Sandra's shock. Smug satisfaction swept through me at proving Sandra wrong and it made it easier to deal with Sophie, Anne and Andrew's open-mouthed stares at me to know that I had at least won a battle against Sandra in this. Zack was glaring, and I glared straight back, unsure why he would become so angry at my helping Rhea. Still, I didn't like him, and he didn't like me, so perhaps that was reason enough.

Rhea sat beside me against the door, the place that was our usual spot before I had been an idiot. Dana woke up the instant the van started moving and groaned as if in physical pain. I pitied her, I knew she could barely stomach the moving of the vehicle, and yet she didn't voice a complaint.

"Will we stop to sleep tonight again, Sandy?" Dana asked. I knew she looked back on the night stationed in the river fondly.

Sandra frowned, "I suppose. I'd rather find a house, but if not, I promise we can stop tonight."

Dana grinned and clambered over to Rhea to sit with her. Rhea opened her arms and clasped the little girl to her chest.

"Try to go back to sleep, Dana." Rhea whispered softly. Dana nodded and settled closer to Rhea, closing her eyes. I hoped she would find the sleep that usually eluded her when the van was moving.

Rhea leaned closer to me about an hour later, and smiled.

"Look, she's asleep." She murmured, "She told me once it's easier to sleep in someone's arms because then she can pretend the van's movement is just them rocking her."

After Rhea's words I noticed that she was rocking Dana, and despite the fact that Dana was small, she was still a heavy thing to rock for an hour.

"That's good." I said, lost for words. I wanted to help Rhea, especially since I was trying to stay in her good books, but I desperately didn't want to take Dana from her. The last thing in the world I would be good at would be holding a child and putting her to sleep. It was more likely I'd frighten them to death.

"Sandra, I can drive if you want." Andrew offered from the back. Anne was curled beside him. I had forgotten that Sandra had driven all morning before our rest stop, and had now resumed.

I knew that for once it wasn't her desire to be in control that had caused Sandra's need to drive most of the time. It was because she wanted everyone to sleep and rest as much as possible before we got to wherever we were going.

I also knew that no matter how hard she tried, Sandra rarely ever slept more than a few hours at a time. I wasn't sure what haunted her, but I knew it was terrible, because I had seen her wake up in a cold sweat and search the van to make sure we were all still alive and well many times.

This time, Sandra listened to reason and pulled over. We were all on the lookout as she climbed into the back next to Jason, and Andrew took the driver's seat. Gabby had long ago curled up in the passenger's seat, and Sophie and Eva were napping on the very back seat. Anne didn't move from where she had been curled around Andrew, which was surprising, because usually the two were connected at the hips.

Andrew had settled into the seat when I saw the foliage moving in the ditch.

"Andrew, get ready to go. There's something moving down there." I told him. I grabbed the gun from behind the backseat and opened the door, shifting Rhea aside. If it was a deer, I wanted it to eat. If it was a Hungry, I wanted to kill it before it could hunt us down.

She lunged out of the brush faster than I could track her with my eyes. She was Hungry, it was obvious from the crazed movements.

I had finally locked onto her when I noticed she was holding a gun and aiming it at us.

"Andrew, go!" I yelled, realizing a second too late the kind of danger we were in. I knew the Hungry could think and remember things they had learned in their lives. They weren't truly Zombies, they were just infected with an irrational hunger that they couldn't satiate.

I threw myself in front of Rhea and the now-awake Dana. The burning in my shoulder reached my brain a split second before the crack of the gun did. Zack had scrambled to shut the door, so the quick moving Hungry couldn't get in, and Andrew squealed away from the threat.

Rubber burned as he zoomed down the highway, and I lifted myself off of Rhea and Dana, my one hand clamped down tightly on my right shoulder. If I hadn't moved as fast as I had, the bullet that had embedded itself in my muscle would have hit Rhea through the heart.

As it was, she looked as though she had been shot. Her skin was sallow and white with shock and Dana was crying. Rhea pushed her into Eva's arms and made me sit down.

"Give me the first aid kit!" Rhea yelled, "Now!"

Sophie handed her the white tin with the giant red cross and clambered to face me. I felt her cut my shirt off and I was grateful that the one person in the whole van who probably wasn't afraid of me or didn't want me dead was the one person who was trying to fix me.

"John, take your hand off the wound, I'm going to put the alcohol on it. It's going to hurt." She warned, her voice in control despite the situation, "Then I'm going to dig out the bullet."

I nodded and pulled away my blood soaked hand. The cool alcohol hit my skin and I hissed as it sank into my wound. My vision blurred and I nearly passed out when Rhea started digging around for the bullet.

"Dammit woman, it's not a treasure hunt." I swore at Rhea.

Her giggle was shaky, but the small clink on the floor that told me the bullet was out rewarded me.

The worst unfortunately was not over. I thought it had been bad with the tongs in me, but the prick of the needle as Rhea threaded my flesh back together nearly made me throw up. I had never thought of myself as weak stomached, but the stitches were my undoing. I was soaked in sweat, and my abdominal muscles hurt from clenching them.

It was a cool washcloth wiping my forehead that brought me out of my tense state. Rhea was leaning around me and wiping me with a facecloth. I was so grateful for the feeling I could have kissed her.

"Thank you." I breathed, barely coherent. She laughed at my state, and I thought perhaps I should be affronted, but instead I forced my eyes open to survey the area.

My shirt was in tatters, and stained with blood. A new one was set out for me, and I grabbed it to pull it on only to find I could not move my arm.

"This is going to be a problem." I said angrily.

Rhea took the shirt from my hands and gently slipped it on over my head. The feeling of uselessness consumed me, and I realized I couldn't shoot my gun with a lame right arm, the kickback would tear my stitches out. It was a left handed knife fight for me until I healed, and I didn't like my chances with that.

"Damn!" I exclaimed suddenly, grabbing the bloodstained shirt. My eyes roamed the van interior and I saw that Rhea had managed to contain the blood to my dirty shirt and some bandages. I took everything and threw it out the window.

"Why?" Rhea asked. Her eyes were red-rimmed, and I felt bad that I had fought with her, nearly got her killed, and then made her perform surgery all in one day.

"The Hungry that attacked us." I explained, finally turning to face the other people in the group, "Was not just a regular person. She was a cop. Special Forces probably, the way she moved. She shot that gun like a pro, aimed it straight at Rhea's heart."

Rhea's hand flew to her chest and then eyed my shoulder again. An expression I knew to be guilt crossed her face, and then gratitude so fierce I was slightly embarrassed.

Anne shrugged, "So? I don't want to run into her again, but what does it matter?"

I frowned, "It matters because she's smarter and tougher than us, even with being Hungry. If she hadn't been consumed with the need for food, she would have thought before shooting at Rhea and aimed for the van tire. She would have hit it, and we would have a seriously bloody battle on our hands."

"There is ten of us, and only one of her. How bad could it be?" Gabby's voice was confused.

Sandra was pale, "None of you get it! Did you see how fast that thing moved!? It would have taken out Rhea like a pro, the only thing that stopped it was John. Normally, John could have shot it down before it even got close to us."

I nodded, "It's true. I couldn't lock on it. She was dangerous, and I bet my other arm that she can track us." I frowned, "So that's why I threw the bloodstained stuff out."

"She'll already be after us." Jason said.

Eva grinned wickedly, "I think we should set a trap."

"I agree with Eva." I added. "I can't shoot a gun or a bow, so it would be better to get rid of her early so we don't get caught off guard later."

Rhea laughed, "I think I have an idea!"

It was everyone's turn to be surprised that Rhea was ready to suggest an idea that would lead to the death of something. Rhea's eyes were glinting with something like malice, and I wondered if perhaps I was corrupting her without meaning to.

"We find a river and park in it, just like last time." She said, "But we don't stay in the van, because she's going to find it and wait at the banks to get at it. We should hide in the trees, or anywhere downwind. Anyone who can aim can shoot, and if we miss, she won't run. She's too hungry."

"She might sense a trap." Gabby said.

"We have to put someone in the van." I said. I instantly regretted my words, because I instantly knew I would be relegated to it.

Sandra smiled, "That's easy. Anne, Rhea and Dana get to go in the van, cause they won't be any use in the fight, and John gets to stay with them, because he can't shoot. Plus, I'd like to leave at least one fighter with them in case she's Hungry enough to go through the water."

"What about Eva?" Rhea asked softly. She was nearly better, but it was still risky to have her out fighting, she was slow moving these days.

Eva shrugged, "I'll stay in the tree, I'll be very careful."

"I don't want to be in a tree. I want to be on the ground." Jason's voice was deadly serious.

Zack laughed, "Good luck making him get in a tree, he hates climbing them."

"But, Jason the trees are safer! And better for aiming! Plus, you can't be the only one on the ground." Sandra's arguments fell on deaf ears.

"He won't be. I'm staying on the ground too." Gabby said, "I would be immobilized in the trees, you know how afraid of heights I am."

Sandra's voice died, and I knew that it was because the thought of Jason or Gabby getting hurt destroyed her.

"Sandra, this is better. This way I can look after Gabby, and we can knock the gun off the Hungry before she can shoot the car." Jason reasoned.

Sandra nodded, she knew she would lose the battle, but I could see her mind was still clicking for a different answer. There was no way she would let Gabby be in harm's way.

"I don't want to be in the van." I said. "I know that my shooting arm won't work, but I'm still the best knife thrower here. Even with my left arm."

Andrew glared, "You will stay in the van, or none of this will work."

"Why not?" I growled. I hated Andrew, but not nearly as much as he hated me. His loathing of me was deserved, because I had once held a knife to Anne's throat, and Andrew adored Anne. But I had needed a hostage if I wanted to find out if the people who had invaded my house were dangerous or not.

"Because if you aren't in the van, I refuse to leave Anne there. I don't even want her there with you!" Andrew's voice was rising.

"And you don't want to leave Dana or Rhea unprotected!" Eva said.

"I won't." I said, "Because Gabrielle and Jason can be in the van."

I knew instantly Sandra agreed with me, because this put Gabrielle out of harm's reach, and Andrew couldn't argue, because Jason was a good fighter, and Gabrielle had the makings of one if Sandy would let her out once in a while.

Andrew also hated me and the thought of Anne and I alone together.

"But we're losing a fighter." Eva said, unsure.

I scowled, "And gaining the best shot in the group."

"You'll rip your stitches if you shoot." Rhea scolded. I frowned at her, mostly because she had just told me off in front of the group.

"I'll use my left arm." I said.

"Fine." Andrew gave in, "Who's going to be the throwers or shooters?"

"John and I with knives." Sandra said. I agreed, she was a shaky shot with a gun, but she had learned quickly when I had been showing her how to throw knives back at the house.

"Andrew and I with guns." Sophie demanded.

"Can you shoot?" Andrew asked warily. None of them had ever seen Sophie in action, but I knew she was a good shot.

"Yes."

"I want the other gun, the rifle." Zack said.

"What about us in the van?" Gabby asked.

Jason shrugged, "We'll use knives. They can cover us better from the trees anyway."

"Now all we need is a river." Zack muttered.

Dusk was falling and still no opportunity had arisen. I had been sleeping, a rare thing for me to do, but I knew I would need the rest, and the blood loss of the afternoon had taken it out of me.

Rhea's leg was near me, and I could almost sense the nervousness exuding off of her. I sat up gently so as not to scare her, and saw that Gabby was driving. Andrew and Anne were curled together in the passenger seat, and Jason and Sandy were talking, Dana sitting in her lap. Eva was sleeping next to Sophie and Zack, and I was pleased to see I had a free moment to talk to Rhea.

"Don't worry." I whispered, once more sitting straight beside Rhea against the driver's door, our shoulders barely brushing. "I won't let anything hurt you."

She sighed, "I know, that's what worries me." Her hand slowly moved from her lap to my hands and clasped onto one of them. I treasured her warmth, and for the first time, didn't try to extricate myself from her grasp.

"Don't worry about me." My muttered command barely phased her.

"I'm worried you'll do something stupid to protect me, and I don't want you to get hurt for me. I also don't want you to rip your stitches."

I shook my head at her, "I promise I won't rip my stitches unless absolutely necessary. I don't want you to have to sew them up again."

"Did it hurt?" She asked softly, her voice shaky. I thought I had made her cry again, and rushed to reassure her.

"No, not as bad as the tongs. I just don't like needles."

She squeezed my hand and leaned into me, snuggling as close as possible. I wondered if the fight this morning had been my imagination.

"I missed you." Rhea's gentle whisper informed me otherwise, and I clasped her hand tighter. There was no way I was going to tell her I missed her too, the words probably wouldn't have come out anyways. She would have to understand that by letting her close to me, and by apologizing,

I was showing the most tenderness I had ever shown anyone. Probably the most I would ever show.

I wondered if I would ever outgrow this stunt in my social skills, and if Rhea would ever understand if I didn't.

"Don't die on me." She asked suddenly, her voice muffled from my arm. The shoulder throbbed, but she was careful around it.

"I won't." I said.

"Don't leave me."

I cocked my head at this and looked down at her wide blue eyes. There was nothing I could say, I was completely flabbergasted at this. Rhea actually wanted me to stay around her!? Just this morning she had told me to leave her alone!

"But, this morning-"

She interrupted, "I didn't mean, don't leave me without your protection, I meant, don't leave me. Ever. I can't sleep without you."

Her cheeks went rosy at having to explain this, and she buried herself once more in my side. I didn't know how to respond, or if I even wanted to respond to that. Rhea didn't know what she was asking for if she wanted to stay with me.

"Go to sleep. I'll be here when you wake up." I said. It was the closest I could come to promising her not to leave her. I didn't know if I could do forever.

The only thing I knew was that I was terrified of spending more than a week with Rhea, but I wanted to try it.

She seemed to understand because she let herself lie down on my leg, and I stroked her golden hair as she had once done to me, the morning I had rolled away from her as everyone stared. She dozed off quickly, and I prayed that I would be there to see her fall asleep again the next night.

Chapter Sixteen

It was three hours later and the dead of night when I woke Rhea up. Sandra had found a perfect spot for the ambush, a shallow river, but wide, with plenty of high trees surrounding it.

"What?" Rhea jumped when I shook her shoulder. She was sitting in an instant, her cheeks white with fear.

"Don't worry." I said softly, "It's just time."

If possible she went even paler, "I don't want to do this, we should just keep running from it."

I frowned, "We can't, she's hunting us. I know it, I can feel it." I didn't know how I could explain to her that I knew we were now hunted people. I knew Jason, Zack, and Sandra could feel it, and Sophie and Andrew. They all had the same wide eyed and fierce look I was sporting. The others looked terrified, even Eva who was usually strong in the face of danger.

Sandra pulled the van into the shallow river and turned it off. The silence was ominous, and I realized that I would also rather be running away with Rhea than fighting, something that never would have normally even occurred to me. I had always been a fighter.

"Okay, grab your weapons." I commanded. "And grab your winter gear we found, it's cold this north at night."

Everyone clambered into their coats, and the scarves and mittens we had found. It would be cold, but we would warm with the fight and hopefully finish off the Hungry quickly.

"Rhea, put on your jacket." I muttered to her.

"But I'm staying in the van." She replied, confused by my request.

I sighed, reaching for patience. "Please, just do it. I just want to be prepared in case anything happens. Also, it's going to be cold in here once we turn the motor off."

She eyed me strangely but did as I asked, reaching for her ridiculous pink parka. I was always amused by Rhea's winter wear, she looked like a giant pink marshmallow, and it was endearing.

"Okay, knives." I handed three to Sandra, and took three for myself. I left the other two with Jason, just in case. The three guns we had collected were left with Andrew, Sophie and Zack.

"Is this a sword?" I asked, surprised as I pulled a sheath from the cargo we were carrying in the back of the van.

Sandra laughed half-heartedly, "Yeah, it was my grandfather's, from the war. I killed my first Hungry with that thing."

Her laughter died quickly, and she stared at the sword with her brown eyes sad, as though she was mourning. I realized I knew nothing about Sandra, and while I wasn't truly interested, I figured her story would probably be amazing. Everyone who was still alive in this day and age probably had a remarkable story.

She shook her head slightly as though clearing out those thoughts and hardened her expression. The Sandra I knew and hated was back.

"Okay, we are on a limited time schedule, so everyone get in your trees." Andrew ordered and opened the van door. The forest was silent except for leaves rustling in the forest. It was icy cold, and I knew we were heading into winter, and must be very far north by now. I was glad I had thought to put on a jacket.

Andrew leaned back in the van and kissed Anne softly, letting his lips linger on her pale skin, whispering into her ear. I looked away, but I knew exactly what he was doing. He was preparing, in case everything didn't go as planned. He needed to let Anne know he loved her.

His last words. Just in case.

I had nothing I could say, even though I knew exactly who I would say them to if I had them. I would tell Rhea my last words, although I couldn't even think of what they would be. I had already told her I would be there when she woke up, and I would never break a promise to Rhea. I had a feeling that even if I became Hungry I would show up just to be there, and I wouldn't hurt her.

I'd probably kill the entire group, but I would never hurt her.

I looked at her, her pale face stark in the moonlight. Dana was snuggled in her arms, looking terrified. I wondered what other six year old had ever gone through something like this and not cried. She was an astonishing child, one who needed to be treasured and coddled. Protected.

I frowned, "I'll be back."

It was all I could say before I turned and led the way through the icy water that came to our shins. Ice floated at the edges, and I hardened myself against the stinging cold. Andrew, Eva, Sandra and Sophie followed me, looking for all intents and purposes like they were going to war. In a way we were; surviving was always a battle.

The shore was a relief from the water, and I glanced back to see that the van door was shut and the tinted windows hid Rhea's face from view. I was grateful for this, because I didn't need the distraction.

Andrew shimmied up a tall tree faster than anyone I had ever seen. It was impressive, and I found myself wondering how we could ever use that as a tactical advantage at another time. I boosted Eva onto a low hanging branch of another tree and watched her climb higher and higher till she was out of sight. It was slow going, but she didn't make any noises of pain, so I figured her injury was okay.

Zack had no trouble with his tree, apparently not sharing the dislike of heights his brother had.

Sophie grinned at me when I held my hands out to boost her, "Getting okay with human contact, eh John?"

I scowled, "Not even a little bit. But if we want to live, I have to do this."

Her grin grew, "We weren't in a dangerous situation when you helped the girl into the van today."

I stepped threateningly towards her and gave her my iciest glare. Her grin fell a little, but Sophie was almost as crazy as I was, "You keep talking and I'll leave you down here to deal with the Hungry yourself."

Sophie laughed softly, insanely, "Oh please do, I'd love to get my bare hands on that bitch."

Her eyes dropped to my shoulder, and I saw the calculating look enter her face. I was in serious trouble. Sophie wanted something, and Sophie always got what she wanted. She had no respect for anything since Alex died; life and death didn't concern her.

Her hand reached up and traced my gunshot wound softly. She bit her plump lip and stared up at me through her eyelashes. I assumed Sophie was attempting to manipulate me. I disliked it immediately, and the urge to toss her in the cold river consumed me.

"John, you and I are the strongest here by far. We would do well...alone." Her voice was sultry, and I knew immediately what she was doing. Sophie was good at seduction, but I was better at mind games than she ever would be.

I slapped her hand away from me and lunged forward, cornering her against the tree trunk.

"Don't you ever touch me." I hissed, "I don't have time to waste on the likes of you."

She wasn't phased in the slightest, and the thought that Rhea was watching this scene unfold from the van was lingering in the back of my mind. Sophie stepped forward and I backed off, because I wanted her nowhere near me.

"John, we could do it. Leave them, live and save this wretched world." She giggled, "Or let it burn."

I snarled, and used the only thing I knew would work on her, "If only your Alex could see you now."

Her hand whipped towards my face so fast I almost didn't see it, but I knew it would be coming. I had brought up Alex once before to Sophie when I had first saved her from her leg wound, and I had never seen fury that thick before or since. I stopped her slap before it came near my face and I glared at her.

"You know better than to touch me. Or to toy with me. Get up in the tree." My voice was deadly and I twisted her around so I could lift her into the tree. She didn't respond, but I knew that her anger wasn't going to fade for a while yet.

Sandra was already in place and I nodded at her before I pulled myself into my own spot. We all had a strategic place to be, and we were covering all angles of the van, which was the most important part to me.

My mind wandered while I scoped the area. Sophie was becoming a menace, and as good as she was for fighting, she was unstable. She would do anything to get her way, and she had no desire to live. If she was willing to try and seduce me, she obviously wanted to leave the group.

The Hungry came to our ambush only a few hours after we had placed ourselves in the trees. We were all numb to the bone with cold, and exhausted from lack of sleep, but we were ready to end this.

I was right, she was a different sort of Hungry, she was wearing a bulletproof vest, and her hair was buzzed to her head. I wondered if perhaps she had been in the military. All I knew was she moved like the wind and barely made a noise as she advanced towards us. If we hadn't had the strategic advantage of the height of the trees I never would have seen her.

I had a clear shot on her with my knives, but I didn't know if I had the range for it. I wished mightily at that moment that she hadn't shot me and that I had a gun in my hands, because if I did, the Hungry that was now threatening the only thing I cared about would be dead.

It was almost lucky however that I didn't have a gun, and was unsure of my throw, because it was barely minutes later another three Hungry emerged from the trees and met with the military one. They didn't talk, and they stared at each other as though they wondered what the other might taste like, but apparently the fresh meat the military Hungry had promised was enough to hold them off.

She had brought friends.

I palmed a knife, and made eye contact with Sandra between the branches of our trees. I saw her turn slightly to show the others we were all ready, and then return to my gaze. She nodded slightly, and then the true chaos started.

The first shot was Andrew's, and it went straight into one of them, a short squat man who I would have assumed was a harmless lawyer or businessman in another life. He went down easily, but I knew it wasn't over because he thrashed on the ground, struggling to gain his feet.

Sophie was fast after Andrew, and she hit another one in the arm with her knife, another woman, but one who had perhaps once been a soccer mom. Exactly the type of woman who would have coveted and sheltered a little girl like Dana, and was now starving for her flesh.

The Hungry were angry, and they knew we were there now. The three that had met the main threat were staring into the trees and growling like rabid animals. The one on the ground had almost lifted himself to his knees.

I had to take action, but I didn't think I could hit them at this range. I slid down a few branches and watched as Andrew and Zack repeatedly shot at them, not quite as successfully as I had hoped, but well enough that the one still struggling finally hit the ground and stayed there. They were both surprisingly good shots for people who hadn't been raised on death and violence like I had been.

We were down to three Hungry, and no one was in danger yet, although I couldn't see where the military Hungry female had gone, and she was the one I worried about the most.

Everything changed in an instant when Andrew hit the ground. His face was stark with rage and fear, and he raced towards where the van was, the opposite direction we wanted the fight to go. He shot the soccer mom Hungry on his way, straight in the forehead. I was impressed with his aim until I realized why he was so panicked that he was going against the plan.

When I looked at the van I felt the same sinking terror Andrew must have been feeling, because the military Hungry, the only one that had managed to intimidate me since this whole damn apocalypse had started, was standing on the edge of the river, grinning.

There was a flare gun in her hand.

I was scrambling down the tree with no thought in my head except for that I needed to get Rhea out of that van. There was enough gasoline and alcohol in there to send everyone even near the vehicle straight to hell. Rhea could not die. Not while I still lived and breathed.

I tossed my knife ferociously at the last Hungry that was standing. It embedded itself in his chest, and I noticed that I had completely missed anything vital.

Didn't matter. It would slow it down. I didn't care if it was at my back, not if Rhea was in danger.

I heard branches shaking as the others tried to follow Andrew and I, finally understanding why we were fleeing.

The van door opened up to Jason standing there, a knife in hand. For a moment I was grateful that he was willing to stand and fight the Hungry that was threatening Rhea, but then I realized how stupid it was for him to open the doors, baring the jerry cans of gas to the flare gun.

"Get out of the van!" Andrew yelled, his face red with exertion and his gun held shakily toward the Hungry. I knew he wanted to take the shot, but he was afraid of how quickly she could pull the trigger on her weapon. I was as well, whoever this Hungry had been in her previous life, she had been damn dangerous and well trained. I'd bet my life she could shoot a gun faster than we could blink.

We had to get everyone out of the van, we had to get far away, or else we had to kill her before she massacred us. The only option was me to throw my knife. She wouldn't expect that, most people didn't toss knives willingly, and her eyes and concentration would be on Andrew's gun and the movement in the van.

I had only taken one step forward when the Hungry I hadn't finished off launched itself at Andrew, throwing both of them into the river. The Hungry reacted badly, hissing and pulling his teeth away from Andrew's neck. Andrew had been saved by the Hungry's stupidity and fear of water, and I had no time to act anymore, because the military Hungry was using the fallen enemies as a stepping stone. I threw my knife as hard as I could, but it missed her by inches. I cursed at my own ineptitude.

She launched herself into the van, knocking Jason over. I saw the knife fall out of his hand into the water. The only hope they had, glinting up from the one thing we had prayed would save us.

A strange buzzing was sounding in my ears, and my throat felt raw. I realized that the noise was me yelling and I knew that the scream I heard was Dana's.

It was the last straw for me. I couldn't stand here and watch a child die, and I had sworn on my life that Rhea would never be harmed. I could hear Eva, Sandra and Sophie running up behind me, and finally, finally my legs moved.

I threw myself into the river, scrambling to reach the van in time. I heard a shot, and was baffled as to why Eva would shoot at me. She was a poor shot, it completely missed me. I heard another one, and then realized they were trying to finish the Hungry that still held Andrew in its grasp.

If Andrew had been bitten, we would have to kill him. Then we would have to deal with Anne in all of her misery.

Anne. She was in the van. The last thing she had heard were Andrew's last words, but she had never given him hers. We had thought they were safe, but they had no chance with the military woman in there.

I would never talk to Rhea again. Dana would never find a family. Gabby would die and Sandra would never function properly again. Andrew, if he lived, would never know what Anne's last words would be.

I had to save them.

I threw the van doors open, taking in the scene in front of me with both horror and a sort of detached rage. Rhea and Gabby were standing in front of Dana and Anne, and Anne was wrapped around Dana, the last defense for a defenseless child. Rhea was holding her arms as open as they could get in the cramped space, as if she was hoping to catch the Hungry before it could hurt anyone else and hold it still. Gabrielle was white and determined, her hands morphed into claws.

Jason was grappling with the Hungry, her teeth snapping at anything within reach, and his arms blocking her every time. I wondered if he had been bitten, but I decided he hadn't, because he was concentrating so hard on avoiding her mouth. A man who had already been infected wouldn't have been so concerned.

I launched myself at the Hungry, not caring that I had no knives left, and only my bare hands to finish this fight and an injured shoulder. I would end this, even if it meant my life.

It was Rhea that saved my life, I saw her fly by Jason and I as we struggled with the Hungry. She dove into the water, face first, scrambling for something. I knew it was the knife she wanted, the knife Jason had been given and dropped.

The Hungry was the strongest woman I had ever encountered. She was kicking and scratching, employing moves I had only ever seen on movies. She elbowed Jason in the jaw and for a moment I thought she had shattered it. She took every advantage and snapped her teeth straight towards Jason as he wheeled backwards with her blow. I snatched her short hair and yanked it, hard enough that clumps came out in my hand. I had never pulled a woman's hair before, and I normally wouldn't have felt satisfaction at fighting so dirty, but the rage that clouded her face after my hair pull was so gratifying I almost grinned.

She threw herself on me, ignoring the stunned Jason for the moment and struggling to take a chunk out of me.

Rhea, soaking wet and holding a knife in a bloodied hand appeared back in the doorway. She threw the knife toward me, as gently as she could. It landed near my head, and I knew I could finish this if I could get a free hand to grab it. I let go of the Hungry for a brief instant, and knew I had made a mistake as it used my distraction to launch itself towards Gabby, Dana and Anne, still huddled in the back. I saw that they were both sneaking towards the door, avoiding the fight, and I knew exactly what was about to happen.

The Hungry flew over me, and I grabbed her bulletproof vest, feeling myself being dragged over vehicle carpet as I tried to slow her momentum. It wasn't enough, I knew it as soon as I heard the impact of body on body, and heard Anne screaming.

I hadn't saved Anne.

I threw the Hungry off me, and dislodged it from its prey. I spun round to inspect the damage, and realized I had been wrong.

It wasn't Anne who had been attacked.

It was Dana.

Anne was holding the bloodied child, cradling her as she cried. Dana was curled around her arm, clasping it to her chest. I knew that she wasn't in much pain, the Hungry hadn't injured her badly.

It had gotten close enough though. Dana was bitten. I could see it in Anne's eyes, and in the way Dana's eyes were closed as though she didn't know how to face the world now that we weren't protecting her from monsters anymore. Now that she was the monster.

Now that we had to protect the world from her.

It was Sophie who broke the immeasurable moment in time when we all stared at Dana. She cried out and pulled Rhea out of the van's doorway, throwing herself in.

I wheeled around, seeing that the Hungry had once more grabbed her flare gun and was grinning at us, as though it wasn't about food anymore, it was about revenge.

She didn't want to eat us anymore. She wanted to kill us.

Andrew appeared in the doorway, soaking wet and bloody to drag Gabby, Anne and Dana out, they went scrambling, Anne holding Dana to her chest. Gabby grabbed a backpack that was on the floor on her way out, the backpack that held the a few clothes, the first aid kit, the small ice drill and the rest of the weapons. She must have thought she could fix Dana, but no bandage could fix this.

Then it was only Sophie, Jason and I crowded into the van, facing off the Hungry that had just destroyed our spirit.

How could we have let this happen to a child?

How could I?

"Get out of the van." Sophie was smiling, a maniacal grin to rival the one on the Hungry's face. I knew instantly what she was planning.

"Sophie, we need this van."

She turned to me, and sobered, "Go John. There's more coming. You know it's true, she's calm. She has backup. You have to run, they'll never stop looking."

Jason was getting out of the van, snatching up the packs he could reach, and then gesturing me to follow. I did, unwillingly, but also gratefully.

Sophie moved like lightning after we left, and I knew the fight had begun. Jason and I were sprinting through the water, the cold and the weariness holding us back. We reached the shore that held our rag tag dirty group of survivors and pulled them back into the trees with us.

Sophie needed to come on top of this fight, or we were done. It would be basic suicide.

We were hidden in the trees when I saw our downfall. It hadn't truly occurred to me that Sophie was right, and that the military Hungry had informed more of her kind that we were here. They would hunt us forever if they survived. Five of them had come from the other side of the river, eyeing the water as though it was acid. They quickly saw the body of the Hungry we had killed, so conveniently placed to make a good bridge from land to van.

Sophie's fight with the Hungry had been contained to the van, and I wondered what was taking her so long. We would have to go out and save her from the five more Hungry that had arrived. We had no chance, we were all tired and missing weapons and heartbroken.

Then I realized what she was really doing when she opened the door and panic I knew to be fake filled her face. She was acting. Cuts that hadn't been there before lined her arms, and I knew she was drawing them in with the scent of blood and fear.

She was going to save us all, and kill us in the process.

The Hungry entered the van as eagerly as ants flooding into their nest after someone stomped on it. I could hear her screaming and crying and laughing as they bit her, and I knew that this was the greatest thing we could ever ask of her.

The only true way Sophie would sacrifice her life. She wanted to die, but she was no coward. She would never have just given up.

She wanted to take as many of the bastards that had stolen Alex from her as she could.

"Turn away." I said softly to the group, "Shut your eyes."

We weren't truly far enough away, but none of us could have moved if we tried. Sophie's face appeared one last time in the open doorway of the van as she threw it shut. She was smiling; not insanely, not cruelly or with some sort of smug satisfaction. She was just smiling, beaming as though she had finally been given the type of peace everyone always raved about.

She was going to see Alex again. She was going to be rewarded for her sacrifice.

The door shut, and the gun shot was almost inaudible from inside the van. Seconds later it felt as though the world had exploded. The amount of heat that ravaged our skin shocked us, and I had a feeling that those of us who had stayed dry from the creek took the worst of it.

The van that had sheltered us and saved us many times was covered in flames, flames that were tinged with the blue of gasoline and alcohol. I knew that we had lost most of our food, all of our gas, and our safe place. We had survived though, and we would continue to do so.

"She's dead." Sandra's voice was empty, and I glanced at her to see she was looking at the van, and holding Dana. Dana was crying still, softly into Sandra's neck. I wanted to tell her to kill the child now, before it was too late, but I couldn't bring myself to say it.

Zack was squatting, his hands on his face. "I didn't think... I didn't know--" His voice cracked and broke off. I wondered if that was the first bit of death he had seen since the beginning.

"Sophie's gone. We have to leave here, that explosion would have drawn more of them." Andrew's voice was tired, and his arms were wrapped around a crying Anne. I was pleased for a moment that they were both alive and well.

"Come on." Jason's voice was strong in the face of everything that happened, and we started to follow without even thinking about it. I wondered if Sandra knew that Jason was a natural leader, or if she was as blinded by his strong and silent nature as the rest of us.

Rhea was shaking violently, but she said nothing as she followed Jason through the brush. We were making too much noise, but I didn't have the heart to say anything.

"I'm hungry, Sandy." Dana's weak and broken voice broke the mournful silence. Sandra's next exhalation was more of a whine than anything, and I knew she was beyond tortured by the child that had won all of our hearts.

Dana was infected, and she was hungry. It was too late. We had to do something.

"We could just leave her here." Andrew's voice was soft, only audible to myself and Jason. I shook my head and shrugged.

"She knows a lot about us, but it's Sandra's choice." It was the kindest and cruelest thing I could do. I had given my blessing if Sandra wanted to leave Dana a Hungry and be relieved of the task of killing her, but I also knew her need to protect the group of survivors would force her hand. She was going to kill Dana, and I had placed the duty on her shoulders.

"Sandy." Dana whined. It was the first time I had truly heard her complain, and I knew that for her to do so meant she was truly starving.

Sandra kneeled down and set Dana on the dirt in front of her. Dana's face was twisted with fear and pain. Sandra was breathing heavily, but she wasn't crying.

"Dana, do you want to see your parents again?" She asked gently.

Dana's eyes widened, "No, they're bad. You told me so, they tried to hurt me."

Sandra shook her head, "No, your parents are good. But they got sick, which is what made them go mean. But your real parents are still around and you can go back and see them! When they were still nice."

Dana's eyes welled with tears, "They got sick? I can see them again?"

Sandra's voice cracked, "Yes. They were very sick, and then they went somewhere that only certain people can go. Sick people." Sandra cleared her throat, "Only sick people, who were once good people can go there."

Rhea's face pressed into my spine, and I knew she was trying not to watch, and trying not to cry, but she could still hear. I didn't want to watch either.

Dana looked down at her arm, which had teeth marks and dried blood, but otherwise didn't look too bad.

"Am I sick, Sandy?"

Sandra nodded, too overwhelmed to speak.

"Is that why I'm hungry?" Dana asked, "All the people we hurt, they were just sick?"

Sandra nodded once more.

Dana started shaking and more tears rolled down her dirty face, "Am I going to get mean?"

Sandra shook her head and pulled Dana in for a hug. She squeezed her so tightly I thought she might break her, but no one was willing to pull her away.

"You will never be mean. I won't let you." Sandra promised, tears finally falling from her eyes, "I'm going to let you see your parents."

Dana's eyes flickered to the knife on Sandra's belt, and she shook her head violently, the black curls Sandra had tried so valiantly to tame bouncing.

"I'm scared." She said.

Sandra nodded, "Me too. But I'll see you soon, I'm sure of it."

Dana's eyes were wide and terrified, and I knew she was torn between running away from us, and staying near us. We had sheltered her, and coddled her, and now we were going to kill her.

It was too much for a six year old.

It was too much for anyone.

Dana spun around and started running, back to the van, back to the last place she was safe.

I didn't want to see, so I turned to Rhea and put my arms around her, not sure if I was doing so for my own comfort or to shield her. Andrew and Anne were faced away. I saw Zack hand Sandra his gun and shut his eyes for a brief moment.

Eva stood with Gabby, watching. They both had tears falling from their chin, and their hands were clasped so tightly they were white.

Rhea was shaking in my arms, and I concentrated on looking at the top of her blond head.

We both jumped with the gun shot, and as the forest fell silent after the noise, all we heard was Sandra keening in the background. I had never heard her cry like that, as though the world had ended, and I wondered if this had broken her and we had lost our leader.

I wanted to give them time to mourn, but we had to move, now. Hungry would be racing towards us, especially with the earlier explosion and now the gun shot and fresh blood. We needed to push forward.

"We need to move." I said, letting go of Rhea and spinning to face reality. Dana's body was fallen on the ground, Sandra on her knees beside it.

She looked like nothing more than a bird that had fallen from the nest too soon. Too fragile and broken for this world. Blood stained her clothes, and the ground beneath her, and I wanted nothing more than to change everything that had happened from this morning.

This day had been it's own hell.

Sandra didn't move, even after my words, but Andrew gave me a nod. I wondered why he was being so civil. He gathered the group, and picked the gun up from the ground where Sandra had probably dropped it.

Jason went to get Sandra and as he pulled her up she fought him, fought him with everything she had. He took it, letting her hit his arms and thrash around, and did nothing more but pull her closer. I knew that he loved her, loved her more than anything on this planet, and she loved him too. Yet she hurt him, hurt him with her own pain. This world was turning her into someone unrecognizable. Jason took this though, this pain, because for now, this was all he had. Sandra's violence and fury and heart wrenching sadness in the face of all of his love.

She gave in, eventually, and just collapsed into his chest. I had never seen anyone so defeated, and Sandra was one of the strongest people I had ever met. I respected her, despite my dislike for her. Now she let herself be held up, sobbing into the chest of the one person she was probably hurting most with her indifference, the body of a child she had shot in the back lying at her feet.

I walked to Dana, unsure what I was going to do, but knowing that I had to do something. I pulled my winter jacket off and slipped the long sleeved white t shirt I had underneath over my head. I put the jacket back on and set the shirt over her. It was big enough to cover the entirety of her tiny body.

Rhea walked up beside me and set a fresh set of pine needles beside her, the only flower-like thing we could find in this cold. We both stood there for a moment, hearing Sandra cry and the rest mourn.

"Let's move." I said, my voice heavy. I turned to Rhea and saw she was pale as a ghost and her lips were blue. I realized she was still wearing her wet jacket and pants, and that at this rate she would get hypothermia before long. I also recalled at that moment the way her hand has been so bloody when she had thrown me the knife.

"Gabby, can you get Rhea a bandage?" I asked.

I yanked my jacket off again and unzipped her. She didn't fight it; her fingers probably couldn't even take the coat off on their own. I pulled her clenched fingers open to discover the long slice down her palm, it was clean and had stopped bleeding so I wasn't too worried about it.

"Does it hurt?"

She shook her head, teeth chattering, "No, can't feel it. Grabbed the knife by the blade.

"You saved my life." I said softly.

She shrugged and gave me a small smile, "You saved mine."

I nodded solemnly at her, thanking whatever god had allowed me to do that. "You have to get rid of the shirt too, Rhea, you'll freeze with all these wet clothes on." I murmured. I didn't want to draw attention to the fact that she was stripping.

Out of the corner of my eye I saw Andrew doing the same thing, taking off his wet clothes and sharing the inner jacket of Zack's coat. I was grateful I had put on sweats over my jeans, because now Rhea would have a full set of mostly dry clothes.

Andrew would have to live with wet jeans.

Rhea's face had gone red and she nodded. I pulled off my sweats and handed them to her.

"Pants too. Wear these and the coat." I ordered. She walked a few feet away behind some trees to block her from sight. I didn't like not being able to see her, but I wanted her to have her privacy.

"Can I have her shirt when she's done with it?" Eva's voice startled me. I didn't think I had ever said more than two words to her in my entire time with this group. I glanced over at her, and saw that her neck and chest had been burned badly from the explosion. The rest of her coat was singed, but had at least protected her skin.

"Yes." I said, pleased by the intelligence she had shown by asking for a cold shirt to put on the burns. Not only would the shirt dry faster near her body heat, but it would soothe the pain of her injury.

Rhea returned quickly, swimming in my much larger sweats and coat. I had only an undershirt and jeans on, and my skin was stinging from the cold, but it was worth it to see Rhea looking semi-warm again.

Gabby bandaged her hand swiftly and I took her wet clothes, handing the shirt to Eva. I turned back to see Sandra was no longer crying, but looked so calm she was almost comatose. We were ready to go, and we wouldn't stop moving until I felt we were safe once more.

Which might be never.

"John, you need a coat." Gabby said softly. I glanced at her and shrugged.

"Don't have one. Doesn't matter."

She shook her head and grabbed one of the surviving backpacks from the van, the one she had managed to salvage. The one that held the first aid kit that hadn't been able to save Dana. From inside she pulled a windbreaker, probably thinner than my shirt, but long sleeved.

"Here." She tossed it at me. I caught it and nodded at her gratefully. It fit snugly, but it stopped the biting wind, and I knew we would be alright for now.

We started walking, and I was grateful my watch held a compass on it, and hadn't gotten in the water. Our course was straight north until we could find somewhere safe to rest. We needed some sort of marshy island, or a house, or a cave where no one would ever look.

It was hours later, no one had said a word, and everyone was starving. It felt like we had become Hungry without even being infected. I needed to get us some food but the forest was silent around me. It worried me, to have the trees so quiet. I knew it meant that Hungry must be around, because normally animals would be everywhere. I wasn't surprised however, I knew that the noise and explosion would cause more to flock to the scene, hence why we had pushed on so quickly.

We had left Dana's body under my shirt. Not even a proper burial. I hoped she would forgive us. I knew that Sandra would never forgive herself.

A crash was heard behind me and I spun around, worry already filtering through me. I hadn't been watching Rhea as closely as I should have been, and I was already high strung from the day we had experienced.

She was fine, but sitting on the ground, her hands dirty from the fall. The bandage had come loose, and the knees of my sweats had dirt on them as well. It looked as though she was about to cry, but not from the pain of her impact. It was as though the entire day had caught up to her, and her feet couldn't hold her anymore, and her emotions were everywhere.

"I fell, John." Her voice was wavering, totally and utterly defeated. Part of me was disgusted by her weakness, and the other half, the stronger half, just wanted to carry her so she could rest. I couldn't decide, I didn't know what to think, except that I was too hungry and too tired to worry about such trivial things.

I knelt down and grabbed her hands gently, pulling her to her feet. I brushed her off and fixed her bandage, trying to warm her fingers with my movements. The others had stopped and I knew they watched us.

"Come on. You're fine." I said, "We're going to stop soon. We'll eat soon. You're fine."

I didn't understand comforting another person, but I knew that if I kept saying she was okay she might believe it. Rhea nodded, her eyes brimming with moisture.

We turned to keep walking, and I noticed that Sandra hadn't stopped with the rest. She was still plodding along, probably hadn't even noticed us pausing in our movements.

It was black in the darkness, the night finally catching up to us. The trees blocked all moonlight coming in, and we didn't have a flashlight. I probably could have made a torch, but it was too dangerous to have the light to draw attention to ourselves. We would have to struggle blindly in the dark, trying to be silent, and barely coherent enough to walk.

It was Andrew that saved us; one second he was beside Anne, practically holding her up, and the next second they had both disappeared.

"Andrew?" I whispered harshly, "Anne?" I didn't want to yell, but I also didn't want to lose another two people today. There had already been enough casualties to last a lifetime.

Andrew reappeared, his face drawn but pleased, "Come here guys, we found somewhere to hide out and sleep."

Eagerly, everyone rushed to him, even Sandra, as dead to the world as she was. We followed him through some brush to a huge pine tree, the low hanging coniferous branches brushing the ground.

He pulled them aside and we saw that underneath was a deep dug out section, leaving a dry spot to sleep. It was sheltered and out of sight at least. Not my first choice, but we didn't have any other option.

"We'll have to get close." Eva said, pushing Sandra in towards the trunk. Jason and Zack curled around her, probably both worried she would leave to do something stupid, and at the same time wanting to be there to comfort the woman who insisted she needed nobody.

Andrew and Anne went to the other side of the tree, Gabby and Eva following along. There was barely any room to sit, let alone lie down, but there was no way I was going to let Rhea miss this chance, and I knew she would never sleep alone.

"Lay down." I told her, watching as she settled herself between Jason's feet and the trunk, leaving a space I could squeeze myself into. I knew she had purposefully put herself as close to the trunk and other people as possible so I wouldn't have to, and probably for their warmth as well. I knew I had never been as cold in my life as I was at that moment.

The instant I hit the ground Rhea turned to me. I didn't move, I was still unsure what was happening to me, and between us. I barely understood emotions, I didn't know how I was ever going to deal with Rhea. I could feel her watching me.

I wanted more than anything to be like Andrew. It was something I had never thought would ever cross my mind, because Andrew and I had a long standing dislike of each other; but at this moment I wanted nothing more than to know what the right thing to say to Rhea was. The right thing to comfort her with.

My eyes met hers as I turned my head; it was almost unwilling, but magnetic, as though the pull of her gaze was strong enough to trick my brain into believing I wanted my neck to turn.

She was crying, silently, but tears were pouring out of her eyes. Confusion and anger hit me again, instantly. I wanted to send whatever was causing this in her straight into oblivion, but at the same time I knew it was because Dana had died and Sophie had sacrificed herself so we would live, and she was starving, and Sandra was never going to be the same again.

I brought my hand over my body, my muscles tensed with nervousness, as if I didn't know whether she would hit me or hug me. Both seemed like terrifying options. My hand reached her face, hovering over her wet cheeks for a moment, scared and unsure.

Rhea reached up and took the hand and pressed it to her cheek, covering her eye gently as if it would block the world from her. I was stunned, first by her willingness to touch me, as I always was whenever she allowed me near her, and secondly by the way she seemed to go to me for protection and comfort. I was easily the best fighter here, so I could almost comprehend why she would want my protection, but it was barely worth dealing with me for.

Why in the world would Rhea spend her precious time with me?

As if sensing my thoughts she let my hostage hand go and raised herself to press into my chest, her head resting in the crook of my neck. The warm breath on my skin bothered me at the same time it soothed me. I had never experienced anything even remotely like it. I wondered if Rhea would ever become boring to me, if anything she did would ever not surprise me. I doubted it. She was always shocking, and always wonderful, even if everything about her, right down to her tiny frame and big blue eyes would always frighten me.

She was still crying, I could tell from the moisture that was collecting on my skin and in my jacket. I didn't want to point it out, I wasn't used to sharing weakness and having weakness shared with me. I didn't know the protocol for this.

I gently brought the hand that lay limp under her up to rub her back, as slowly as I could. I made circles on her spine, inherently knowing that this would soothe her. It was something a mother did to a child, although I couldn't remember a time my mother had done that for me. I didn't remember my mother at all, I only had two items of hers to remember her by, and both of those I had received through my father, who was the last thing in the world from nurturing.

"Thank you." Rhea's murmur reached my ears. I decided not to acknowledge it, but almost ten minutes later I felt guilty for not saying anything back. I debated on what to say, torn between telling her about how difficult this was for me, and how much I wanted her, or, just shrugging it off.

In the end I went for simplicity, "I'll find you food tomorrow. I promise. I won't let you starve."

Her laugh was barely a whisper, and half strangled with pain, but still, I had made her laugh! When no one else could comfort her, when no one else could make her safe enough to sleep, I could! When she was crying, broken beyond repair, I was the one that made her laugh.

That had to be worth something.

"I know. You'd never let me starve." Her faith in me was surreal. I had never had anyone believe in me before, and the change was amazing. Suddenly, I had someone to take care of. Suddenly, someone was waiting around for me, making sure I was alright, and confident I would never hurt them.

She was amazing.

Emotions clouded in me in a way they hadn't done since I had been very young, and the only thing I knew with any certainty was that Rhea made me very happy and very afraid.

I was afraid of a number of things, such as being rejected, or hurting her, or not making her as happy as she was making me. Most of all I was terrified of losing her.

For the first time I had a reason to live and stay safe.

My hand snaked up to her hair and I brushed it through my fingers gently, as if to say *thank you, you mean everything to me.* She didn't stop me, she just snuggled closer, bringing her free hand up and knitting it with mine.

I thought for a moment I wouldn't sleep, so much elation and fright and confusion was inside me I felt I would burst. Yet I knew that we would be waking in the morning, downtrodden, hungry beyond measure and walking again. We still had farther to go. We weren't safe yet.

My eyes shut, listening for sounds of the forest around me. There was a bird chirping in the tree we were sleeping under, and the singing comforted me. I knew it would never share its song if there was Hungry around. I squeezed Rhea's hand gently, hoping she would understand I was saying we were safe, and let myself drift slowly into sleep.

For the first time, I had someone to watch my back. Someone who would never hurt me. Someone I wanted there.

Chapter Seventeen

It wasn't the morning sun that woke me, I had been awake for hours by then. It was the sound of muttering, of muted talking that was going on in secret underneath the tree. I knew it was Sandra and Jason, I would know her voice anywhere. The only difference was that her voice was broken in its sadness and despair, and I was too used to her obstinate and hard headed way of talking to not grasp that something was hurt deep inside her spirit that would never, ever be the same again.

I could hear what she was saying and I was grateful Rhea was sound asleep on my chest, because it would have broken her heart. I knew this, and shifted so that my arm covered her ear; there was nothing I wanted more than to shelter Rhea from the pain Sandra was going through; I wouldn't wish it upon my worst enemy, and I didn't want it for Sandra.

"I promised her Jason." Sandra half-sobbed, "I promised to protect her from anything. Everything!"

"I know. You did." Jason was probably as good at comforting a woman as I was, and I felt bad for him.

"No, I didn't!" Sandra whispered, "I killed her, Jason, I did it. I promised to protect her, and I was the one who killed her."

"Sandy, it's not your fault."

"I killed a child." Her whispers died down, and she just kept repeating this statement, over and over and over. It felt more real every time she said it, and I couldn't help hating her for her cruelty of pointing out what had happened. I knew why she was doing it of course, she wanted to feel the guilt, she wanted to know she was going to hell.

There was no place in heaven for any of us.

I corrected my thought after I glanced down to the angel facing me. Her face was peaceful in sleep, and the blonde hair, as dirty as it was, was beautiful. Her eyelids flickered, and I prayed she dreamt of a field of flowers far away where she could run and be safe without thought for tomorrow.

I realized I wanted that for her. I wanted this stupid war to be over, I wanted to go home, and it wasn't for me. I didn't care. I had no home, and I was good at battle. When the world went to hell it had barely phased me; but I wanted all these things now for Rhea, I wanted happiness for her.

It felt alien to want happiness for someone else, but I was doing it. The contentment I felt with that wish was enough, and I wondered if people who were good, people who did things like hope for others to be happy everyday felt like this constantly?

"John?" Rhea's worried voice caught my attention and I almost answered her instantly, completely by instinct, but she was still sound asleep.

"Rhea?" I asked, my voice barely a mutter. I was confused as to why she would ever say my name in her sleep, and I wondered if she was having a nightmare she wanted my protection from. I prepared to wake her.

"John." She sighed again, smiling slightly.

It hit me then; stronger than any punch, and more intense than any war or battle. Rhea was *dreaming* of me.

She was smiling. It baffled me. It terrified me.

She obviously wasn't scared of me, in her sleep or out of it. I didn't know how to feel. I was a child, a little boy again, too young for my father to influence me into cruelty, and all I wanted to do was run around screaming *she likes me*! She likes me!

I had never had that moment as a kid, so it must have been ingrained in me. I wondered if perhaps I had waited until this moment, waited for Rhea, just because I would never understand the feeling of complete and utter elation and excitement if it was with anyone else. My entire life had led to this moment, this moment underneath a tree, dirty, starving and sleeping next to a group of people who were borderline insane, it had all been in the journey to have this precise event happen to me.

Rhea was dreaming about me, and she was happy about it. It wasn't a nightmare, it was a good dream. I was an escape from the terrors of the day.

There had never been a more beautiful thing in the world than her small sleepy smile and blue eyes opening to meet my gaze. She probably thought I was crazy for staring at her as intensely as I was. For all the happiness that was bouncing around inside me, I still had not smiled. I never smiled, and it wasn't going to change.

Rhea knew something was different though, she knew me better than anyone ever could.

"What's happening?" She seemed satisfied, or well rested, because the enchanting grin was still placed on her lips.

"You said my name." I answered, my voice slightly hoarse. Perhaps my feelings were too much, and they were just about to burst from my throat; smile or not, my newly discovered emotions would find a way to throw themselves out of me.

Rhea frowned, "What?"

I coughed slightly, "While you were sleeping," My voice softened, "you said my name."

Her blush clouded her face, dropping her smile and making her hide herself in my windbreaker, "I'm sorry."

The last thing in the universe I wanted was for her to be sorry for what I had enjoyed so much, "It was... nice?"

A single blue eye appeared, crinkled around the sides with laughter.

"It was nice? You don't sound so sure." Rhea's voice was tinged with humour, and I knew I had made her laugh again. It was becoming a skill of mine, being humorous, and making her smile. Imagine that, I was the cause of someone else's happiness!

"What were you dreaming of?" I asked. Would she tell me?

Her eye disappeared again, her embarrassment hiding her from my view.

"Christmas. I was dreaming about putting up a tree, presents and all. You were there." She explained. "And then, I couldn't see you anymore, but I was holding all the lights, and you wouldn't come and help me. I kept calling and calling you, but you wouldn't appear. Then you said my name, and you were there, holding hot chocolate and smiling at me."

She brought her face back up, her blush gone and her amusement once more visible, "Can you believe that? You, John, smiling!"

Her dream made no sense to me, I had only ever seen Christmas on television, I had never experienced one. I had only ever had three gifts given to me over my life, the first was a knife my father had gotten me when I turned nine, the second was a gun, given to me for my thirteenth birthday, and the third and final gift was my father's death, which had both dealt me my freedom and money enough to enjoy it.

I supposed my mother's keepsakes, that I still carried everywhere with me counted as a gift, but seeing as she was never the one to give them to me, I didn't count them.

"Why would you dream about Christmas?" I questioned.

She smiled, "Because Christmas is coming up, it's almost the end of November, and it's my favourite holiday. I can't imagine not spending it with you."

Her favourite holiday and she would like to spend it with me? The desperate desire hit me instantly: I would do anything to make this happen, anything at all. I would give Rhea the Christmas I had always seen on T.V, the best Christmas ever. I would have a tree, and lights and presents!

Then I remembered that it would never truly happen. First of all, Christmas was about a month away, and who knew if we would even live to see another month. Also, where would I find these things, this tree, and lights and presents? Where would I set this up where we would be safe, where a Hungry wouldn't interrupt and ruin everything we had worked for?

I could lie though, I had always been a great liar.

"We will have Christmas then. I promise." I said softly, "With everything Christmas needs."

Rhea practically glowed, "Presents? Hot chocolate, carolling, lights? Stockings? Mistletoe?" The last word sent shock through me, and Rhea knew it because she snickered as soon as she said it. I felt faintly shamed by my reaction, and at the same time I couldn't see how I could have possibly reacted any differently. Mistletoe? Usually that meant kissing, and if Rhea was casually referring to kissing I was never going to recover.

I scowled at her to cover up how uncomfortable I was, "Yes, we will have gifts and all that. Now go to sleep, you could probably get another hour or so."

She smiled at me, gratefully, and I knew that my lies had meant the world to her, even if they were eating away at my heart right now. We fell silent, and all I could hear was her breathing steadily against my chest, my heart drumming under her head. Then Sandra's whispers started up again, and I felt blood rushing through my head. I didn't want Rhea to hear her.

"Rhea." I muttered, urgently, hoping my voice would cover up Sandra's continued chanting, "What was your family like?"

She looked at me, and I could tell she was confused as to why I would suddenly care. I had never asked before, I had never wanted to know, and it was strange for me to abruptly take an interest.

Despite this, she answered me, "It was pretty average: separated parents and three sisters. We all got along very well, loved each other more than anything." Her voice was sad, and I knew that I had brought this on for her, and yet now I was actually interested, "My oldest sister died before all this, in a car accident. Practically tore the family apart. Mom and Dad fought more than they had when they were married, and my second oldest sister moved out of Mom's house to live with him. I stayed with Mom, she needed me. But I was at Sandra's when all this happened, and I didn't go back for her. I couldn't. I was too afraid."

The laugh she gave was chilling, it was soft and quiet and full of sadness; the sort of laugh you would expect out of Sandra.

"Are you surprised?" She growled, "I'm such a coward. I couldn't go back and get her. I phoned and no one picked up, but I didn't have the guts to check. Nobody else knows that."

I was mad, not at her, but for everything that had been wrong in her life. She didn't deserve separated parents, nor a death of a sibling. She especially didn't deserve to feel as though she was a pathetic coward, she was about the farthest thing from that as one could get. Rhea wasn't a fighter, that was true, but she wasn't a coward.

"You aren't weak. You are no coward. You are strong, and brave. Did you see how quickly you reacted when I got shot? No pathetic weakling would ever have been able to do that. Or when you dove into the water to get me the knife?" I didn't know how to explain to her how amazing I thought she was, and I despised that she referred to herself as spineless, "You're very strong."

"My mother wouldn't agree."

I shook my head, "That's not true, she would. From what you've told me, she would have wanted you to live. Calling her was reasonable, but no one should have taken that chance to check if she was there. What if she had been Hungry? You wouldn't have lived through that."

Rhea smiled, weakly at first, but then stronger, "Thank you, John."

Sandra had gone quiet again, and I had a feeling I had Jason to thank for that. I had nothing left to say to Rhea, but I didn't truly want to stop talking to her. She needed more sleep though, especially since we would be walking all day today. I needed to hunt as well, if I didn't find us food right away we would all collapse from hunger.

"Sleep, Rhea." I ordered her, shutting my eyes forcefully so I would no longer be distracted by her face. They opened instantly when I felt Rhea sidle higher on me and her breath hit my face. I had finally gotten used to her getting closer to me, but this was a whole new level of proximity.

"What are you doing?" I asked, my voice harsh.

She smiled, "Thanking you, properly."

I was about to tell her to move away, go back to where she was before, where I had been comfortable having her, when she darted in, pressing her lips onto my cheek. Lust blazed through me, my skin on fire and my nerves vibrating through my body. Then it was cold fear, fright of what she was doing, where this put us, and how I could possibly even try to word how I felt when she did that.

I moved my head away, "Stop it."

She laughed, her soft giggles mocking me, "Okay, John. I'll stop."

Half of me was viciously glad she moved away, turning over and giving me her back, and the other half was cursing myself in every creative way possible. I was torn in two, as I always was whenever Rhea came along, because I could never be in harmony where she was concerned. She brought out the best in me, and the worst in me, all at the same time.

I should have killed her long ago.

I couldn't bring myself to truly regret not doing so.

I was so indebted to whatever god had stopped me from slaughtering this whole group, I owed him everything.

I owed him Rhea, the greatest gift I had ever been given.

She wasn't lying on my chest any longer, and I thought that perhaps I could sneak away for a bit, try and find something to fill our stomachs with. I didn't want to leave the group for long, it left them vulnerable, but I needed to make a new bow for hunting, especially if we were low on weapons. I was glad all the guns had made it out.

I gingerly tested my shoulder, it was healing well, despite all the dirt and fighting of the day before. Removing the stitches would be a blessing, because I could finally handle a gun and take out some real animal for food.

"Jason." I muttered, hoping to wake him. He opened his eyes and stared at me instantly, and I knew then that he hadn't slept a second, he was too busy watching and comforting Sandra. "I'm going for food, keep vigilant."

He nodded at my words, and closed his eyes once more. I was pleased that Jason was, if possible, even less of a talker than I was. He was also extremely reliable, and I was grateful to have him as an ally.

The tree branches parted under my hand, and I checked the two knives I had strapped to my belt. My hope was to startle a rabbit and throw the knife well, or else find something to make a snare with. The sun was out, brighter than I had originally thought, the branches must have blocked more than expected.

The forest was still too quiet, but it had the sounds of bird songs and squirrels scrambling in trees, and it comforted me to know that nature was not holding its breath on the next Hungry attack.

I set off at a brisk pace, the winter air a bit chilly on my face, but my mood considerably good. The kiss that Rhea had bestowed had thrown me off completely, but it was also a beautiful memory in my mind. I wasn't sure I would welcome a repeat, because it scared me, and I hated to be frightened, but I knew that I was glad it happened.

An hour later I was still without anything to show for my efforts, and exhausted. I decided that perhaps we would have to skip a meal with meat and just have some greens. There wasn't a lot to choose from, because the winter frost had killed off any berries that were edible, but luckily I knew which roots could be eaten, and I found a spruce tree and plucked the ends off the tree tips.

The group I had left sleeping was awake and packed once more, and I noticed Rhea had gone back to her now-dry clothes. I hastened to put on my jacket, and I gave Gabby back the windbreaker. We might need it again.

"Sorry, I couldn't find any game. I need a bow or a gun, and I can't shoot yet. But I got this." I handed each of them a fair share of plants, and watched as they all shoved them into their mouth, barely bothering to brush the dirt off. Everyone was still hungry, but there was nothing else I could do.

"They weren't half bad." Eva said, looking surprised.

"Get used to them, that's all the vegetables we will find in the winter. Although if I can get a moose or deer I can cure it and freeze the meat."

Sandra seemed disheveled, but perhaps slightly back to her normal self, because she stood straight and gave orders, "Okay, we're going to continue north, and pray we hit a town, because we really need to get more food, and maybe a car if we find one with gas and keys in it. We have to get to a house before it starts snowing in earnest. Or before anymore Hungry find us. We also need more weapons."

There were no objections, but that could have been because there were no other options. Everyone started trudging after Sandra and Jason, who had taken the lead. I waited for the end, because it was best to have me covering the back, and I also didn't like to have any of the others behind me. Rhea walked beside me, and I didn't talk to her, or look at her. I didn't know how to act.

"We're not going to be able to walk all day." Gabby said to Eva ahead of me. She was quiet, but I could make out the words.

Eva nodded, "I know, we're still starving, and it's too cold. Plus, look at the sky."

I glanced up instinctively, and saw that Eva was right. It was grey and menacing, and I knew that we would be in for snow and perhaps a good storm tonight. That was just our luck.

"Are you warm?" I muttered, the concern over the weather overshadowing me desire to ignore Rhea.

"Yes, thanks. I was lucky you made me put on all my winter gear." She smiled at me and tapped Gabby on the shoulder. Gabrielle spun around, and I realized that she was wearing just a dress winter coat, not meant for freezing temperature, meant for looking good in the city.

"Rhea?" Gabby asked, eyeing me briefly.

"Here Gabby, I know your coat is the coldest out of all of ours. Have my scarf." Rhea handed it to her, "Also, why don't you put the windbreaker John had on top of it. It might stop some of the bitter wind."

Gabby took the scarf, looking almost scared by it, "Thank you, Rhea."

She looked at me once more, more intently this time, and I realized she thought I wouldn't allow her to take the scarf away from Rhea.

"It's her scarf." I shrugged, turning to face the front fully, ignoring the women. It annoyed me to no end that everyone was afraid of me and thought I was controlling Rhea, like some sort of puppet. If anything, the damned woman was controlling me, and making me do all sorts of stupid unexpected things.

It was an hour later that something flickered in my vision enough to stop the entire group. I was worried, the forest was quiet, and everywhere I looked I saw phantom ghosts and enemies. This time though, it wasn't my imagination.

"Stay here." I ordered softly, leaving everyone to explore the bush a bit more. I walked briefly, scanning everywhere for whatever had alerted me. If it was an animal, I wanted to hunt it, if it was Hungry, I didn't want to be ambushed.

Kneeling to the ground made my knees damp, and I pushed aside the frost and snow and dead leaves that had gathered on the forest floor and looked around the dirt. It took a few minutes, but I found a footprint before long. The ground was riddled with animal prints, but they were old, the one I found was human, and it was fresh.

I didn't particularly like that fact until I looked up into the branches and saw what had moved enough to make me come over here. There was a fat rabbit, swinging from a snare, probably about five feet above me. I saw the cord attached to the tree, and thought perhaps our luck was turning around.

The Hungry couldn't set up snares, I didn't think, they weren't patient enough by far. Even if they had the knowledge, they were all about instant gratification, not planning the hunt out. They would chase a person for days, but never think to set a trap.

This rabbit had been hunted by other survivors.

Yet sometimes people were just as dangerous as Hungry.

I quickly cut the rope on the rabbit and snatched it, knowing we needed the meat, probably more than whoever had hunted it, considering they had the materials to make a snare. I kept the rope too, just so I could make a snare as well.

I jogged back to the group, holding the rabbit like a trophy.

"You got a rabbit!" Eva's voice was basically begging. I knew she was starving, I probably didn't even have to cook the rabbit to get anyone to eat it.

"Thank god." Anne smiled. I think it was the first time I had seen her smile ever, and I knew in that moment why Andrew loved her. She was radiant, and I couldn't even imagine her in happier times.

Rhea was smiling at me, and I couldn't understand for a moment what her expression was. It was almost smug, but I didn't think Rhea was capable of being conceited, and even if she was, what was there to brag about?

Then it occurred to me. Rhea wasn't boastful, she was proud. Of me.

I smirked, I couldn't help it. I couldn't remember the last time I had willingly smiled, and I had probably never smiled sincerely, only with arrogance, or hate. Yet this was a sort of smile, a half smile, straight at Rhea.

Her blue eyes went wide, and I knew that she had seen it. She hadn't expected it, I had surprised her! It was so rare that she was the one being shocked, usually I was blown over by her actions.

The return grin she sent me blinded me; it was beautiful, and so bright it rivalled the sun. I knew I had pleased her, not only with the rabbit, but with my happiness, and I never knew she would have this reaction. Every smile paled in comparison to Rhea's, I knew nothing would ever be the same for me. I would always throw the rest of the world into competition against Rhea, and they would never, ever win.

"I got a rabbit." I repeated, slightly awestruck, "But we have to move. Now."

Sandra frowned, "Why?"

"It's not mine." I explained quickly, "It was in a snare. Not a Hungry one! It has to be more survivors, but I don't really want to run into them."

"They might have food!" Anne objected.

Andrew scowled, "No, I hate to say it, but we don't want to meet them. They might be wonderful, but they might be bad too. We have a big group and a few supplies, in this type of world, they would want everything they could get. We should run, and if we want we can scout them out another time."

Eva nodded, "I think that's a better idea. Let's not get caught off guard."

"But..." Anne's voice died, and she looked sad once more, "What if they had soap?"

Her voice was so desperate, and it brought a few laughs out from the group. It was rare for everyone to have something to laugh about, and it was nice for once to do so. This time though, I could actually solve the problem.

"Did you know soap is made from ashes and oil? And you can press flowers, or leaves to put a scent in it." I said gently, "I know how to make soap, if you would like some."

Anne grinned sheepishly, but I saw that her eyes were moist, "Thank you. I'm being stupid, I know, but we lost it all with the van, and it was one of the only modern comforts of home we had left."

I nodded my head, and Anne smiled, "Alright, let's go."

We started walking again, faster this time, and I kept watching the sky, as if perhaps the glares I were sending were enough to keep the snow and storm at bay. I doubted even I could intimidate the sky, but it was worth a shot.

Chapter Eighteen

The weather was getting worse, and we were getting jumpier. I saw Jason scan the forest more than once, watching for threats, and Zack had his hand on the gun in his pocket. Sandy wasn't watching, but her knife was at the ready, and I knew she would spring into action in seconds if she needed to. My eyes were torn between our surroundings and Rhea, as it seemed they always were these days. I knew she was cold, and it was getting colder. I couldn't feel my hands, and they were shoved into my gloves. Snow had started to fall, tiny sparkles obscuring the vision of the world, and I knew it would only get worse from here on.

Everyone was starving, I could almost feel my stomach lining devouring itself, as the Hungry's did when they got infected. I knew I was not a Hungry, but I felt like one. I felt like a rabid monster, and at any moment I was going to bite down on the frozen, raw rabbit I was still carrying.

This continued on, this state of ravenous hunger and paranoia, until I felt I had gone mad with it. The girls were barely coherent, Eva was leaning heavily on Gabby, and I had a feeling Eva was only still walking out of sheer determination. Anne was walking, probably stronger than most of us, but I could see tears in her eyes, and I knew she was almost done.

My toes were numb, and the last thing we needed was someone to lose a toe to frostbite when we needed to keep on the move.

Rhea stumbled heavily, and this time I didn't let her fall as I had the day before, I threw my arm out and tugged her against me. She looped an arm around my hips and kept dragging her feet along. I wanted to stop, at that second, because I saw how her left foot wasn't lifting up anymore, but I also didn't want to stay here. We needed to hide, we needed to stay alive.

It was Zack who finally stopped us, and probably saved our lives.

"Enough." He said, his voice harsh, "We need to eat. This storm cover will hide our smoke for a while, and we can build a fire and warm ourselves. Then we can walk for another mile and hide to sleep. We can't walk through this storm, we have to wait it out."

Eva sighed, "It's true, but what about the other survivors? They must be out there."

Zack nodded, "I know, but they can't travel in the storm if we can't. Look at the sky."

It was grey, and angry, and the snow that had started just a while ago was falling heavier, and a soft new layer was upon the crust of the old.

"Let's move into the heavier bush." I said, gesturing left. It wasn't much denser than where we were, but it was more coverage. We all hobbled over and I quickly kneeled to the ground, dragging Rhea with me. She sat down on the ground, and I knew her jeans would get wet, but she didn't care.

"John, start the fire." Andrew said. I saw he was collecting wood, but I didn't want to heed his request just yet.

"Take off your boots." I asked Rhea, softly. She did as I asked, and when I pulled off her socks I was glad I had decided to check. Her three smallest toes on her left were blue, and I knew they would sting as soon as she regained feeling in them.

I clasped them tightly in my hands, rubbing furiously.

"John, fire!" Andrew repeated.

"Hold on." I snapped, "Everyone, check your toes, we don't want to lose any of them."

Andrew then finally looked at me, and saw that I was rubbing Rhea's feet, and I must have looked worried because his annoyance disappeared and he asked Zack to start the fire.

Eva, Gabby and Anne all surveyed each other's feet and hands, and made sure they could all feel everything.

"Is that better?" I questioned.

Rhea frowned, "Well, I can feel them, but they hurt now."

"That's good." I told her, "Another hour and you probably would have lost a toe."

I put her boots back on, and turned to the fire, which Jason and Zack were coaxing to light. I walked around our makeshift camp to get any kindling I could see to help them out, and found a few chunks of wood to make a spit.

The fire started in earnest when I threw the kindling on, and for a moment Jason and I sort of acknowledged each other with something a bit more than respect. I kind of liked Jason, which was surprising for me. I could rarely stand a person enough to be near them for more than a day! First, Rhea, now Jason? I felt like a man with many friends, and it was both weird and exhilarating.

I set up the spit and cleaned the rabbit as best I could with our knives. It went over the fire, and the scent of it cooking was possibly the greatest thing I had ever smelled.

"I'm so hungry!" Gabby exclaimed, "This rabbit will be amazing."

Sandra laughed, and it was so bizarre after her silence and sadness to hear it that we all stared. She didn't quiet herself either, even after seeing all of our shock, instead she kept giggling, and smiling.

"Oh, Gabby." She snickered. "I never thought I'd hear the day where a fire roasted rabbit we stole was a delicious meal."

Gabby laughed too, "It is a bit weird."

Rhea joined in, and soon everyone but me was laughing at a memory of a Gabrielle I had never met. It had never occurred to me that I was the only one left who hadn't started out with this group. I was still an outsider, albeit a borderline accepted one.

I didn't know this Gabby that they were laughing about, I didn't even know Rhea outside of a live or die situation. In truth, I didn't know any of these people, and they didn't know me, and usually, this would be exactly the way I liked it, but it wasn't that way with them all sharing a joke around me.

The sky had darkened more, whether with night or with the storm we weren't sure, but we were all warm, and the rabbit was finished. I had pulled it off the fire and was waiting for it to cool enough to cut, and everyone was talking. It hadn't been this relaxed since we had left our last house, and I felt like maybe we would survive after all.

"Do you remember high school?" Anne asked, her voice full of laughter and some yearning.

Andrew snorted, "I hated it, and yet I would love to be going there now."

Rhea smiled, "I can't believe the world went crazy the precise year of our graduation. Ugh, now I'll never have my high school diploma." I stared at her briefly, just realizing now how much younger she was than me. I didn't want to bring it up, but it had never occurred to me that I was travelling with high-school aged kids; though, I supposed they weren't kids anymore.

Gabby scowled, "And I will never wear my dress! It's so sad!"

Eva snickered, "Wow, don't make it sound like the end of the world..."

A new round of laughter issued from that remark, and it was a nice change, from fearing the end of the world that was upon us, to making light of it. I was glad our mood was light, and the rabbit was cut and we were safe.

I handed out slices to everyone, huge portions that I knew we would finish. I had gathered more roots and spruce needles and gave them out too. We all quieted with the food and started shoving it into our mouths as fast as possible.

As soon as we finished the meal, I hunted for a while for some water. We were parched, and I knew we hadn't had a decent drink in a day or so. The two bottles that were in the backpack were empty, and we had been so consumed with hunger that we hadn't even thought to be thirsty.

I found a pond, not far from where we had stopped and I filled the bottles. It wasn't a lot of water, and I didn't trust it, because it was from a stagnant pond that had been frozen on the top. I decided we weren't going to drink it, it would just put out the fire.

"What are you doing?" Eva exclaimed as soon as I tossed the water on the fire. A hiss sounded as the flames dissipated, and I could feel angry stares aimed straight at me.

"The water wasn't safe, and we don't have a pot to boil it. We aren't drinking any natural water unless it's running, and even then it's chancy." I explained, "We'll live."

Gabby swore and I shrugged at her. I didn't particularly care what expletive she called me, as long as she was alive enough to say them. It meant I was doing a good job of protecting this stupid group of survivors.

I leaned down and pulled Rhea to her feet, and instead of letting her go, I kept her tucked into my side. It was nice, and it felt like she was protecting me from the anger of the others, which was a total role reversal for me. She left her hand looped around my waist, and it sat there and burned my skin with it's heat. I wondered if anything would ever feel quite as remarkable as Rhea's arm around me.

"Let's go. We just have to keep walking till we find somewhere to sleep." Sandra's disgusted voice rang out, and I was glad she wasn't going to throw a fit about the water, she was going to give up. I knew I was right, and she knew it too, because we were both smart enough to realize that the water could make everyone sick, and dead was dead, whether by Hungry or infection.

The snow was starting to blow hard, stinging our skin as we walked, and visibility was getting worse. There was no chance of the survivors that were sharing this forest with us hunting us in these conditions.

Darkness had fully fallen by the time we had found somewhere to sleep. The snowfall had turned into a fully-fledged blizzard, and everyone had linked hands to make sure we didn't get lost. I was at the end of the chain, mostly because I didn't want to hold anyone's hand but Rhea's, and I was the best to have at everyone's backs.

Sandra had called a stop, and the wind was taking her words so we couldn't hear her. She seemed to realize this because she ended up gesturing upwards, pointing towards to a few different oak trees, giant ones, standing straight into the sky so far we couldn't see through the snow.

I understood fairly quickly, although we didn't have any rope to tie ourselves to the branches and we were taking a risk. It was the best option though, the snow would cover us from sight, the height would keep us safe and we wouldn't freeze from lying in the snow.

Both Gabby and Jason looked positively terrified and it amazed me that they could still have such trivial fears in this world. They seemed resigned though, and I wondered if they were just desperate enough to not care anymore.

Rhea went first into the tree to our left. I was pushing her high so she could grab a branch, and she quickly latched on. I could see Sandra and Jason helping Eva, Zack, and Gabby into a tree to our right, and Andrew and Anne clambering into the one across from us.

"Come on, John!" Rhea's voice was faint, and I knew that she had probably screamed to make herself heard. I launched myself into the air and grappled with the wide low branch to pull myself up, making my shoulder ache. Sometimes I would forget about my wound until it caused me pain. We both climbed higher and higher, losing sight of the ground, and all we could see was the branch beneath our feet and wild white snow around us.

"What about the others?!" Rhea asked, her eyes wide.

I shrugged, "Until the storm's gone, they're on their own."

She swallowed and nodded, and I pushed her farther, until we found a branch I deemed high and wide enough to hold us both. I sat against the trunk and took my belt off, wrapping it around my legs and our perch. I beckoned Rhea close to me, and she sat on my lap, her back pressed into my chest. The parka I was wearing was huge, I remembered the sight of it drowning Rhea, and I unzipped it quickly and pulled her against the shirt I had underneath. I zipped her into it, so that our body heat would keep us both warm, and I would feel her if she started to fall from the tree. I dug out the rope I had stolen from the snare and managed to tie it around our chests. My belt would keep us secure when we were aloft, and hopefully we would survive the night with little more than some sore muscles from our position.

"John?" Rhea had turned her head toward me, and I pressed my ear close.

"What?" I answered, nervous that I had been so close to her all day, and was still comfortable.

"Thank you for taking care of me." She said, "And thank you for smiling."

I coughed, "I didn't smile..."

She giggled and I remembered that I had hidden away some more food I had gathered from that morning. Rhea wasn't eating enough, and I knew it. As much as I wanted to feed everyone, Rhea was my priority. If the others wanted more food, they would have to get it for themselves.

"Here." I said, "Eat."

She smiled and did as I had asked, quickly finished off my offerings. As soon as she was done she looked horrorstruck.

"John! Was some of that for you? I didn't think, I was hungry!" She seemed worried, and I wondered if she thought I wasn't eating enough. I probably ate more than everyone else combined, seeing as how whenever I got the roots and needles, I sampled everything.

"I'm fine. I had lots today, that was all for you, I promise."

After a tense silence where she watched my face intently, waiting for any signs of lying, a soft smile broke out once more.

"Thanks." She whispered, her breath warm against my ear, "Again."

I shrugged, done with talking for the night. The wind was howling, and it was cold out. I pulled up my hood, and did the same with Rhea's. She had her big mittens on, so I put my hands in her pockets, warming them up.

Within minutes I could feel her breathing deeply, and I sat in complete contentment for a while, holding Rhea tightly to me, and wondering if the world would ever do us the favour of forgetting about us completely. It didn't seem unrealistic at the moment, with the bubble of winter that surrounded us, blocking all sight and sound of reality.

It was perfect, the most surreal and incredible moment of my life. I felt like I belonged, and nothing would ever get better than this. I drifted off, thinking only of Rhea's warmth, and the steady beating of my heart.

I awoke abruptly when I heard the voices, and I knew immediately that we were in serious trouble. The other survivors were around, I knew it, I could hear them speaking, way too normally and rationally for Hungry. Rhea was still tight to my chest, and I knew she was awake because her spine was rigid and her breathing harsh. I squeezed her hip through her pocket, hoping she would relax. We were more likely to fall if she was scared and stiff.

"Rhea, be still, they can't see us." I murmured, my voice barely audible. She immediately relaxed against me, and I took this time to glance around at the world that had morphed into a wonderland overnight. It was beautiful and cruel, all at the same time. The snow coated us, ice hanging off the branches and turning the world that had once been colourful and bright with autumn was cruel and cold with snow. I knew that if we moved the snow that sat upon our bodies would fall and tip us off.

"John?" Rhea whispered, "I'm so glad you're awake."
"Of course I am." I replied, "Now be still."

Their voices were only slight murmurs, and I knew that they were purposefully being quiet. I was thankful that the new snow had coated our footprints and any signs of life, but still, how had they found us so quickly?

It sounded like it was probably only three or four people, and there was definitely a woman among them, I could hear the higher pitched feminine voice.

"But we saw their smoke!" A man's voice, louder than the rest of them, tinged with anger. Our smoke had been a few miles back, and covered with cloud. They must have been close to even make it out. Then they would have followed our footprints until the blizzard forced them to a stop. We had kept going, foolishly, but it had probably saved our lives, because they must have stopped. They can't have been far behind if they had tracked us here so far.

I turned my head slightly, wishing only to see if any of the others were in my range of vision. As soon as I got Andrew and Anne's oak into view I heard the crack that spelled disaster for us. It had come from the tree I had just gotten into my view, and I knew that Andrew and Anne were in trouble.

Rhea's soft gasp frightened me, and I saw Andrew moving away from where he must have stowed Anne, probably trying to protect her with all his might. The three men and woman I could now see were circling the base of the tree, and I knew Andrew would have to go with them if he wanted to protect the rest of us. I knew he would do it, because he would never put this group in danger, and he loved Anne too much to ever cause her any pain.

"Come down from there!" One of the men shouted, drawing what looked like a crossbow. I yearned to have that weapon in my hand, I could have done serious damage, even with my injured shoulder. I could have taken all of those survivors out straight from my perch. If the man who had the crossbow was as good a shot as I was, we were all in trouble.

Andrew was jumping from branch to branch, getting lower as he went. He had pulled a knife, one of our smaller and weaker ones. I realized that he had left the gun with Anne so we wouldn't lose a valuable weapon. It wouldn't have mattered too much, we were almost out of bullets anyway. Each gun only had a few rounds left, and every other bullet we had had exploded with the van.

"Are you Hungry?" Andrew's voice rang out. It was a good act, I had to admit that. He played the part of a formidable but scrawny teenager who had survived this world alone well with only a single knife.

"Hungry?" One of the men asked.

The woman scoffed, "He means are we 'Vores."

The man who had asked the question laughed, "Do we look like 'Vores to him?"

Andrew seemed confused, "What are you talking about?"

The last man, brandishing a wicked looking machete stared up at him, "Come down here and find out." His voice was cold, and I could feel deep within me that both myself and machete man were cut from the same cloth. He was cold and cruel, and he probably knew how to use that weapon properly. He looked at Andrew as though he could already feel his beating heart in his hand. I wanted to kill him, because as much as I hated Andrew, he was a good man, and he didn't deserve whatever the machete man was planning for him.

"Okay, I'm coming down, but stay far away from me." Andrew dropped to the ground, his knife held tightly in his palm. I saw that he had left the toque and mittens he had been wearing since the van's blowup, and probably left them as well with Anne. I admired his willingness to sacrifice for her.

I wondered why she hadn't tried harder to save him. If it had been me I never would have let him go down to the ground, I would have fought them to the ends of the earth to save him.

Maybe I was just old fashioned that way.

"How could she let him go?" Rhea muttered, and I realized I wasn't the only one who was confused by Anne's apparent abandonment of Andrew.

"I don't know. Maybe she's scared?" I wondered. Perhaps fear had her glued to the branches.

"No, Anne doesn't like violence, but she is very serious when it comes to Andrew. I have a feeling she would rip someone's throat out if they even looked at Andrew the wrong way. She adores him, she lives for him."

I suddenly knew exactly what Andrew had done, and it made complete sense to me, because I would have done the exact same thing had it been me and Rhea. He had tied her up, maybe even knocked her out.

"Rhea, don't watch." I whispered. She didn't move, and I knew my words had made no difference. She was as glued to this as I was, and as badly as I wanted to save Andrew, I would not be leaving this tree. I would never put Rhea in danger, not for anyone or anything.

Andrew got to the ground, and was holding his knife, white knuckled. I could see the worry and concentration on his face from my height, and I knew he was praying that Anne didn't wake up before the men left.

"The things out here, the things that eat us, what do you call them?" The woman asked, her voice very casual.

Andrew frowned, "I call them the Hungry. I don't have a technical term." I was glad he had the sense to say 'I' not 'we'. Andrew was smart, and I trusted that no matter what these people did to him, he would never give us up. He wouldn't harm Anne. He wouldn't even chance it.

"Okay, we call them 'Vores. Cause they're carnivores." She explained, walking slowly toward him. Andrew was focused on her, fully, and I saw that there was another man, a new one, coming up behind him. There were at least five survivors with this group. Andrew didn't hear the man coming behind him, or if he did, he made no indication about it. I wondered if maybe he did know, and was just ignoring him to get out of there sooner. Get it over with.

The man hit him hard in the temple with a baseball bat. The crack it made when it hit his skull echoed in the trees, and Rhea jumped. I could feel her breathing, short and choppy, as if she was either in shock or crying. I didn't know what to do, and I just hoped she didn't make any noises.

The woman motioned for the men to pick Andrew up, and the one who carried the machete tossed him over his shoulder, no problem. I wouldn't want to fight the one that lifted him, he was a huge man, taller than I was, and I wasn't short. He was burly and cruel looking, the one I had assumed to be the fighter of the group.

They disappeared through the trees, and I waited silently to hear them leave. I thought they would take their time to be sure Andrew had been alone, but they didn't wait. I wondered if they were just sure of themselves, or if perhaps they didn't particularly care if others were here. If they weren't worried if we followed them.

They must be well weaponed not to worry about other survivors or the Hungry. Or they had a huge group of survivors.

We needed to get their weapons. We needed their supplies, or we were either going to freeze or starve out here. Especially now, with the new snow fall and every passing day. It was freezing, I could feel the cold permeating my flesh, even with Rhea and the coats surrounding me.

We needed somewhere to live this winter out.

I unzipped the coat, quickly and efficiently. We needed to get Anne out of the tree before she got herself out and ran foolishly after Andrew. Rhea moved away so I could unbelt myself.

"Come on, we have to move." I commanded, sliding down the tree, reaching up only when it became necessary to help Rhea down a really treacherous branch.

We reached the base of our tree just as Jason and Zack were descending from their own. It looked like they had left the others in the branches, coming to the ground by themselves.

"Watch Rhea, I'll go get her." I said, sprinting towards Andrew and Anne's tree. I easily climbed the boughs, scanning for any sign of Anne. It took me a while to find her, and my respect for Andrew went up another notch as I saw where he had hidden her. She was shoved into a crook of a bow, tied on by Andrew's belt and winter wear. I saw that he had shoved a mitten in her mouth, and there was a bruise forming on her temple. I wondered how guilty Andrew felt now, for hitting Anne and leaving a bruise. It would destroy me to see Rhea hurt, especially by my own hand. But to save her life? I would probably do the same.

Anne's eyes were open however, and confused. I quickly untied her, snatching the mitt out of her mouth so I could explain.

"Andrew!" She gasped, the second she could speak, "Where is he?! Did they get him?"

"Yes, come on, everyone's waiting. What happened?" I asked her only to keep her preoccupied while we climbed down so she didn't go into hysterics.

"The branch cracked, I don't know if it was because of the added weight of the snow... I just don't know! But a lot of the snow fell and Andrew knew that the other survivors, the ones hunting us, they saw it. He turned to me, I knew exactly what his plan was, I didn't want him to do it." She paused, her hand reflexively going to her temple, where a deep purple bruise had formed. "He... he hit me?"

It was almost comical, how shocked she looked as she felt the bruise, except that it was also sad, because Andrew would never have been pushed to such circumstances were life normal.

"He knocked you out." I said, reaching the bottom branch.

"Yeah, and he tied me on the branch. He left the gun." She handed it to me, looking as though she was frightened it would go off in her hand. I noticed she kept the knife, and I wondered if it was because she forgot she had it, or because she already had a suicide mission planned to retrieve Andrew.

We hit the ground, glancing around to see the rest of the group standing around us. Rhea was frowning at Anne, probably at the bruise that was spreading across her face, and I knew she was horrified by Andrew's actions. They were justified though, and that was the worst part.

"We need to go after him." Anne said, her voice desperate. She was appealing to Sandra, and I knew that it was a bad move.

"No." It was Jason who said this. "We can't. He wouldn't want us to."

"I don't care what he wants." Anne snapped, "I'm going after him, whether you come along is not my problem."

She spun her back to us, about to head off. She was facing entirely the wrong direction, armed with only a knife. She would die.

"Stop." I said. Anne did, probably only because I had rarely ever talked to her. She glared at me, eyes filled with tears.

"Why? Why John? So you can tell me it's a suicide mission? That I'm going to die?" She cried, "I don't want to hear it."

"You're not going to die. You're going to succeed, and you're going to get Andrew back." My words shocked her, her mouth fell open and she had nothing to reply with.

"John, that's a lie and you know it." Sandra whispered, "Don't give her that hope, don't do it. It's cruel."

"It's not a lie." I told her, "It's true. And I'm going to help her do it."

Anne burst into tears, full hysterical sobbing like I had tried to avoid, "Thank you, John."

She stepped forward, as if she was going to embrace me. I sidestepped, and fell behind Rhea's small form. I felt foolish, running from Anne and hiding behind Rhea; but there was no way Anne was going to touch me.

Anne almost laughed, "Still not a hugger, hey John?" She giggled a bit, tears finally subsiding.

I scowled at her, choosing to ignore her comment, "It won't be just me helping her either. It's going to be all of you."

Sandra grimaced, "I had a feeling you were going to say that."

"No. It's a suicide mission! And Andrew does not want this." Zack was angry, and I knew it was because I was about to drag the entire group into danger.

"It's not about Andrew." I declared. "It's about food, weapons, and cold. We're going to die if we don't find more weapons and shelter. We haven't run into any Hungry, and that's a miracle. But we need what those survivors have."

Sandra nodded, "I know. I knew as soon as I saw them. Five of them, fully weaponed and *confident*! I haven't been confident since... god, since before this all started."

"I'm not going. We were doing fine until this happened. And I repeat, this would not be what Andrew wanted." Zack was stubborn.

"Doing fine?" It was Gabby's voice this time, and I was surprised. She rarely took sides in tactical meetings. "You're crazy. We were dying. Starving. There is no way we could have survived another week on roots and tree needles. We have barely enough bullets to load a gun, and we are now missing one of our best fighters. Not to mention that two people *died* on us two days ago! That is not *doing fine!*" Her voice was getting louder at the end of this rant, I wondered if she would be the next one to go into hysterics.

Eva interrupted, "What Gabrielle means is: we are going with John. We need this Zack, and you know it. It doesn't matter that Andrew didn't want Anne in danger, or that he sacrificed himself for our safety. It all amounts to nothing if we die, which we will if we don't get their weapons and food."

Zack looked defeated, and I knew that it was killing him to be wrong. Zack, though, was never one to beat around the bush, and he would come to terms with this battle plan quickly. He loved a good fight.

He nodded, sadly, "Alright. What's the plan?"

"I can track them, and I think that we should ambush them, half of us attack from one side of their camp, the others from the other side." I said.

Rhea frowned, "Not going to work, we don't have enough weapons or fighters for an offensive plan. We should sneak in, and ruin their chances. Steal all their weapons or something, then attack."

I eyed her for a moment, surprised at her tactical knowledge, and proud even though she had corrected me.

"You're right." Jason agreed, "That's our best bet."

"Okay, let's move." Sandra ordered. "We want to catch them before dark."

Chapter Nineteen

It was almost nightfall, and we had reached the camp just behind the group of five that had taken Andrew. There were four more in their camp, which consisted of a huge trailer, a truck that was attached to the trailer, and a large metal table which had a woman strapped to it. The woman was crying, and staring at a tree only about ten feet from her. On the tree was another man, tied down with barb wire around the trunk. He was silenced with a dirty rag, and I could see that there were stains of tears down his dirty cheeks; his eyes never left the woman on the table.

This was a very bad camp. These were very bad people.

"We should have left the women at the trees." Jason whispered. I couldn't have agreed more. It should have just been Jason, Zack, and I, even though the odds were terrible. Even the fighters, like Sandy, Gabby and Eva shouldn't have come.

We knew what had happened to the woman on the table.

Anne was crying silently, "Oh Andrew, what have you done?" She murmured. I wanted to tell her that he had saved her life. I wanted to apologize to Andrew for everything I had ever done to him, for everything that had ever offended him. That man had given up everything for us, for Anne, and he had saved her from a terrible fate.

I turned to Rhea, who was huddled to my right. Her face was drawn and pale, and I knew my expression of fear and horror probably mirrored her own.

There were no words. I turned back to the camp.

Andrew had been dragged in, and the huge burly man threw him against a tree, near the other man. Andrew's skull made a terrible noise as it collided with the trunk, but it wasn't as bad as when the machete man uncoiled some barb wire and started wrapping it around Andrew's body. I was surprised he was lucid, since his head had taken numerous amounts of hits today, but he was stronger than all that.

Rhea was shaking uncontrollably beside me, and I didn't have the nerve to look at Anne's expression. Andrew didn't flinch, but I could see blood beading on his skin and dripping where the spikes dug into him.

"Feel good?" The man asked, his lips drawn back in a sadistic smile.

Andrew spat in his face. I almost cheered him. The man backhanded him so hard Andrew's entire body went limp for a second, and when his face came back it had blood all over it. Andrew focused his eyes on the table where the woman lay, watching the scene unfolding before her eyes.

Andrew reacted the way I expected he would: his eyes widened with realization, and his entire body struggled against the wire, as if to go to the broken woman, as if to save her.

He couldn't, and his eyes that were normally so kind and thoughtful turned back onto the man he had spat on, full of hatred and anger.

"Pig!" Andrew cursed him, "Death is too good for you."

The man laughed and shoved a dirty rag into Andrew's bloody mouth, leaving him on the trunk to rip his skin apart as he struggled to break free.

The woman I had seen with the group of five was frowning at this, as if she didn't approve of such torture, but she did nothing. I almost pitied her, because I would bet on my life she was frightened of taking any action. That didn't excuse it though. How often had she been holding a knife near the machete man while he wasn't expecting it? She could have stopped this monstrosity.

We continued to observe this camp, until the night finally fell fully. Our muscles were cramping, and I doubted I had ever felt such fury as I was feeling now. We may have been outnumbered, but I had so much anger inside me I probably could have taken on the other survivors alone.

"They're siblings." Rhea muttered into my ear suddenly. I turned my eyes to where she was looking, at the man tied to the tree and the woman strapped to the table. I had assumed they were just together, but I could see now that the relation was apparent. They had the same features, same sandy hair. Looked like green eyes.

"Twins?" I asked.

Rhea nodded, "I wonder what he's seen?" Her voice was heartbroken, and I realized what she meant. It would be horrifying, the worst kind of torture to see a sibling hurt while being held powerless.

The man was staring at his twin, helplessness in his features. She was staring back, almost looking like she wanted to comfort him. She was pretty, probably close to my age. Her features were delicate, and her sandy hair hung in waves around her face.

I stared at Rhea. I couldn't even bring myself to imagine what they would do if they ever got a hold of her. I wondered what this woman had been, who she had been, before this table. What she had ever done to deserve this type of humiliation and pain; and her brother? Did he deserve this? Or were they just another pair of siblings, normal jobs and parents, waiting to get their college degrees before the end of the world took it all away from them.

"I'm starved." A man emerged from the trailer. I had seen him wandering around before, but he didn't seem that important. He was skinny, and wore wire rimmed glasses. He looked more like a professor than a torturer.

Machete man stood, his knife glinting in the twilight, "Dinner then, Boss?"

Boss? This skinny, harmless looking man was in charge of this? I wanted nothing more than my hands around his throat, and my knife in his sickening face.

The boss nodded, and walked up to the tree where Andrew was being held.

"Where'd he come from?"

The woman approached him, nervously wringing her hands, "I think he had been travelling with the woman and child before they died. Must have been his van. He was alone. He stole our rabbit."

My stomach dropped. They had been looking for us that long? They had found our van? Sophie, and Dana? They had seen their bodies.

Andrew narrowed his eyes on the woman and started talking through the cloth. It was muffled, and no one paid any attention to him, but I would bet my life he was cussing out the woman and demanding her death, the same as I was.

The boss shrugged, "Okay. He'll pay for the rabbit with his own flesh, I suppose." He turned to the other man, the twin.

His words chilled me to the bone. I suddenly knew exactly what these people were, and how they were surviving so well. I looked at Rhea, she seemed confused still.

"Are they going to torture him for the rabbit? Like, back in the day, take a pound of flesh torture him?" She asked.

I thought I might throw up. It wasn't him that took the rabbit, it was me! "They're going to eat him."

Her skin went white as the snow surrounding us, and I hoped she wouldn't faint. She didn't, but the only sound of comprehension she made was a small gasping 'oh'.

The boss was grinning at the man, and he pulled out the rag to let him talk.

The twin didn't wait for a question, "Please, let her go. Let my sister go, put me on the table. Oh god, please, I'm more than enough, take me instead."

The boss pretended to think for a second, and walked to the table. He ran a finger down her face, and she closed her eyes and let tears drip down her cheeks.

"Stop touching her!" The man growled, "Let her go. Just let her go!"

The boss left the woman and walked back to the man, "Let me think..." He got really close to the man and grinned, "No."

The man yelled, an indescribable noise, filled with hate. "I'm going to rip you apart. You're going to die!"

The boss shoved the rag back into the man's mouth, and he gagged briefly.

The rat-faced man turned back to machete man who had stood watching this entire scene.

"Kill her." He commanded, turning to walk back to the trailer, not even stopping when the man raised his knife.

I wanted to launch myself into the camp, I wanted to drive my knife into his heart, but it would give away my entire group. It would kill us all, and I couldn't do it.

"Don't watch." I said, snatching Rhea close to my chest. She came willingly, her eyes dry but beyond frightened. Blank, she was completely blank and trying to block this entire thing out.

I saw the woman roll her head towards her brother, the rag still in her mouth. She smiled at him, as if to say that it was fine, that this was really the best way to go if she had to die. No more pain. The brother was tearing half his skin off, and so was Andrew, both of them trying with every bit of their power to get free.

Despite this struggle, despite every single one of us wishing for some sort of miracle, some sort of different ending for this poor woman, the knife still came down.

This time, the rag muffled nothing. I could hear the twin screaming through it, pleading with a god that obviously didn't exist any longer. I could feel him crying, and I could feel the hatred that extended past his body into the atmosphere. It was almost more than I could stand. I had never seen anything so brutal.

She was dead, her throat cut, and bleeding out onto the ground. It seemed as though she was content, her eyes had closed and she no longer struggled or cried. Perhaps it was the best for her, to die. She couldn't live through something like that anyway, even in a world as twisted as this one was.

It took another three hours of freezing on the cold ground, reliving the memory of the woman's death, until the camp was sufficiently quiet and dark. It seemed as though most of the group was either in the trailer sleeping, or around the fire at the front of the camp. They had hung the woman up, with rope from her ankles. It had been almost worse to see that, that they were preparing her like you would a deer or a cow for slaughter.

The twin had stopped screaming, instead he was lying limply against his wire, his gaze completely focused on the ground. He looked like he was trying to die. The only thing that livened him at all was whenever the rat faced boss came around, and then he lunged and snapped at him as though he was a Hungry, and the only flesh he craved was the man who had given the order to kill his twin.

Andrew was a literal ghost. He was silent, and he never moved his eyes. I knew that he had clued into the fact that we were here. I don't know why I thought that, but his eyes never strayed to where we were hidden, and he had stopped struggling with his wire, as if he was trying not to draw attention to himself.

"Stop." Andrew's whisper caught all of our attention. It was directed at the twin. "You're going to cut yourself too severely and bleed out."

"I don't care, I just need to get free." The twin replied savagely.

"I can get you free, and you can kill him." Andrew said.

The twin stilled instantly, "You can get me free? Why didn't you do it earlier?"

Andrew shook his head, "I couldn't earlier, wasn't possible." He looked at the twin, his eyes fierce and full of honesty, "I would have done anything to save your sister, if I could have."

This seemed to satisfy the man, and he nodded, "I believe you. I saw how you looked at them after you saw her. You're a good man. I didn't know there were any left."

Andrew smiled sadly, "Thank you. I wasn't alone in this forest. My friends are here, we're raiding this camp." His expression darkened, "And we're going to massacre these people."

The twin grinned, almost insanely, as if the deaths of these people were all he dreamed about, "I'm in."

Andrew finally turned his gaze to the brush where we were hiding, "Do it now."

"Stay." I commanded, slipping out of the bushes and behind Andrew's tree. I tried to stay silent and hidden as I undid his wires. He dropped to the ground, and quickly slipped behind the tree of the twin.

"Make sure he doesn't run into the trailer yet. We need to get their supplies and weapons, so they don't have the advantage when we attack." I murmured to Andrew.

Jason and Zack were meeting me around the back, and I saw that there was blood all over him when he got there.

"Run into trouble?" I asked as we gathered up guns we had seen loaded into an outside compartment on the trailer. We needed to move fast.

"Just the two by the campfire." He responded. I knew that Jason had never killed a human that wasn't infected before, even if these people barely classified as 'human'. His hands were shaking.

"You did a good thing. They needed to die." I told him. We brought the guns and the ammo into the bushes where Rhea was still hidden.

"Where's Anne?!" I asked, frustrated with her. I knew she wouldn't have the patience to sit still.

"I don't know! She ran out to see Andrew, and now she's disappeared." Rhea was obviously upset. I handed her the knife, she looked unsure.

"Keep it, just in case." I said while snatching up a loaded hand gun. It felt good to have it back in my hands. I probably would rip my stitches if I shot it, but no one but my group knew that. It was still a loaded threat.

"Let's go." I told Rhea, and she followed behind me. We walked by the woman and I grabbed the knife I had given Rhea back to cut her down from the tree. We couldn't leave her there. I untied the rope at her feet, and left her lying in the snow. It was the best we could do for the moment.

Gabby and Eva had already unhooked the hitch from the trailer. Sandra was in the truck, searching for keys.

She reappeared, "Nothing, they're probably in the trailer."

"Okay, everyone's got a gun?" I asked. They all nodded, brandishing their weapons. "Take a window, anyone. And shoot. It doesn't matter if you hit anything or not, but it will panic them, especially being shot on all sides."

They nodded, and separated from the hitch. I found Jason and told him to take the door and try and get as many as he could that came out.

"Rhea, go find their food." She looked horrified, "No, the real food." I clarified.

She nodded and disappeared, her knife brandished in one hand. I fought every instinct to let her go, knowing that she would be safer over there, even safer than near me.

Shots started echoing, and I took my position beside the door. Jason and I were trying to cover it, make a small space where everyone had to pass through so we could pick them off.

The first through was a man, another one of the dumb grunts I had assumed were by the fire. Jason shot him down effortlessly. There were only six more people in this trailer if I counted right, and they were as good as dead.

Next was the woman, the one I felt some sympathy for. I knew Jason wouldn't shoot her, and I didn't particularly want to kill a woman, so I grabbed her and knocked her head into the side of the trailer. She dropped to the ground, completely unconscious. Her hands were tied behind her back, and I felt bad that I had hit her so hard. They had probably forced her out here to die first.

I didn't like how these people treated women. I wanted to get creative. The next man that came out I grabbed and spun back towards the door, using him as a human shield.

I prayed my stitches didn't rip, and I started shooting my gun. The girls were doing a good job, it was chaos in the trailer, with shots going off everywhere. I killed the men that were trying to shoot back through the windows. Left alive were only two men, the boss and another. I shot the random in the head, and dropped my human shield.

I walked towards the wiry man, who looked about as harmless as a mouse. I put my gun to his temple, and ripped his arm around his back.

"I have someone you should meet." I whispered cruelly to him, "I believe you're the reason his sister is dead."

I walked him out of the trailer, where Jason, Andrew and the twin stood. The twin had death in his eyes, and I knew the boss stood no chance.

My blood went cold with the sound of a scream. I would know that voice anywhere, and I realized I hadn't accounted for the machete man.

I dropped the Boss at the feet of the three men and took off towards the back of the trailer, towards the table. I don't think I had ever moved that fast for anyone or anything in my life.

I rounded the corner and didn't see anything. I knew they were here, I knew Rhea was here, I could feel it in my bones. I now knew how Andrew knew we had arrived. He could probably sense Anne, sitting barely ten feet from him.

I spun, my gun fully extended. There was nothing back here, and it had gone silent.

There was blood, on the ground. Fresh, and too far from the table to be the woman's.

Five feet from it lay Rhea's knife. She had fought back. She had cut him.

She was probably scared out of her wits. I was going to rip his throat out.

I was jogging, scanning every inch. There was no one around the camp, and it wasn't until I had done a full circle that I took off into the woods where her knife had lain. I found signs of a struggle, ripped branches, more blood.

It took me a full five minutes that felt like eternity until I found them, and I saw nothing but red.

Rhea was against a tree, and he was choking her, her feet dangling off the ground. Her coat was hanging off one arm, and her blouse was ripped down the buttons, exposing her bare skin. He had his machete pressed into her cheek, and I could see a thin line of blood appearing where it was set.

I shot out his left kneecap first, and his scream echoed through the trees in such a way I was almost happy. I didn't have time to deal with him though, not when Rhea was on the ground beside him, dragging herself away and holding her throat, struggling to breathe.

I dropped to my knees beside her, and pulled her against me. She clung to me, like a child. I fumbled until I zipped her coat back up, because her bare skin was both enticing and a reminder of what could have happened.

"Come on." I pulled her to stand and turned to look at the man writhing on the ground behind me. Rhea was sobbing, her tears soaking through my clothes and mingling with the blood from the cut on her cheek.

I had never hated anyone more in my entire life.

His other kneecap was shot out by me and he couldn't do anything but lie on the ground a scream in agony.

"I'd be quiet if I were you." I told him, "They'll find you soon enough. The Hungry. Or the 'Vores, whatever you call them."

His eyes widened and his screams cut off.

"Don't leave me here." He begged, "Have some mercy."

I shook my head slowly, "Let me think..." I repeated the words of the man he called Boss, "No."

He started to cry, weepy sobs that made me want to choke him.

"I hope you die painfully, and understand what you did to other people." I murmured.

Rhea wasn't moving, and I wanted to get out of the area before the Hungry did come. I lifted her, adrenaline still running so high she barely weighed anything. She was still crying, and I wondered if perhaps she had gone into shock.

I got back to the camp, and Sandra had the truck started. The guns were stacked in the back, under a tarp. Andrew, Anne, Zack, and Eva were all in the back as well, covered in blankets and food and rope. They had done a good job of clearing house.

The woman I had knocked unconscious was still lying on the ground, but I could see that she was starting to come around. I took a knife from my belt and set her free.

"I'd start running, the Hungry are coming." I told her. I left my knife in her palm and picked Rhea up and headed toward the truck again.

The back door opened and I set Rhea inside. I climbed in behind her and shut the door. She was almost instantly back in my lap, as if she was stuck to me like glue. The twin was sitting in the back as well, beside Gabby. I didn't like that we were bringing him with us, but I knew we couldn't leave him.

His hands were coated in blood, and I looked back at the camp as Sandra started driving out of a path the other now-dead survivors must have used. I saw the boss, strapped to the table with cuts all over his skin. He was still alive.

"Left him for the Hungry?" I asked.

The twin nodded mechanically, as though he was a robot.

"Same with the one with a machete." I added harshly. The thought of him still made me want to throw up or kill something.

"I left my sister hanging." The man said, his voice soft and desperate.

Rhea finally emerged from my shoulder, her eyes red and puffy and filled with fear. Her cheek was still bleeding, and huge purple bruises were appearing on her throat where the man had choked her. She reached a shaky hand out and set it on the twin's shoulder.

"No." she whispered, "We took her down, me and John. Took the rope off her."

The man started to cry again and it was more than enough thanks to see how grateful he was that we hadn't left his beloved twin sister hanging like livestock.

Rhea undid her coat and threw it at our feet, pulling her blouse together with her hands. She looked down at it and realized it was beyond wrecked and took a deep shuddering breath. I wanted to give her my shirt, but it was the only one I had. It didn't really matter I supposed.

I slipped off my coat and wrapped it around her shoulders. She looked up at me and her lip trembled; for all the world she reminded me of nothing more than some bewildered child who didn't quite understand why she was being hurt.

"I stabbed him." She told me, her voice quiet.

"I know, he deserved it. Do you want my shirt?" I asked. I reached out and wiped the cut on her cheek down, pleased to see it wasn't that deep.

She shook her head and pulled my coat tight around her and leaned towards me, her head against my shoulder.

"Just hold me." She commanded.

My arms pulled around her and I pressed her as close to me as I could possibly get her, and I rubbed her back as I had done under the tree. I didn't want to speak to her, because I would probably say something about the man and it would make me angry. But I didn't want her to think I was mad at her.

"You did a good job, Rhea. I'm proud." I whispered. She breathed heavily again, and was probably crying, but I knew that she was pleased. I knew that it had cleared her conscience.

"I didn't think I would see you again." She murmured into my ear, her voice choked with tears.

I reflexively tightened my grasp, not saying a word.

Her tears finally quieted and I prayed she would find some comfort in sleep as we drove down the uneven path. I was never letting her out of my sight again.

We must have driven for three hours before Sandra finally pulled the truck over. We had found a real road, some sort of secondary highway, but we still had no idea where we were.

"We're lost. I know we are heading north, but we need a map. We need to find a town, an abandoned house."

For the first time since we had started out the twin raised his head. His eyes were dry, and he seemed like he had reasoned out his sister's death. Much more rational. That was all appearances though, and I knew that he would probably never be the same.

"We're in the Northwest Territory. Heading towards Nunavut. Pretty much no man's land." His voice was bland, "There are less Hungry up here, that's why David chose this spot."

"David?" Gabby asked.

The twin scowled, "The one with glasses. The one I killed."

"You were travelling with them?" It surprised me, this man seemed nice and quite rational. I couldn't understand why he would be with a pack of monsters.

He shook his head, "Oh no, I just heard a lot, being camped with them. I've been tied to that tree for over a week. Maybe two. I don't really know, I lost track of time."

"They had your sister that entire time?" Jason's voice was horrified.

"No, thank god." The twin said, "They were torturing me for information on her and my mom, and I wasn't saying anything. They found them though, without my help. Killed my mom on the spot, for food, you understand."

Gabby's breathing was uneven, "That's sick. And they brought your sister back to camp?"

He nodded, "Mostly to rub it in my face I think. To show that they didn't need me. I used to fight back a lot, you know, spit in their faces like your friend back there." He almost smiled, as if the memory pleased him, "But I stopped fighting after they brought her in. They would punish her if I acted out."

He shook his head, as if to rid himself of the memories, and then a small smile flitted back into place. I wondered how he could smile at a time like this.

"I'm sorry." He said, "Thank you for rescuing me. My name is Tanner Clark."

Gabby smiled, "It's nice to meet you Tanner, I'm Gabrielle Fletcher. Driving is Sandra, this is Jason and his brother Zack, and the two over there are Rhea and John."

Tanner greeted everyone again, and turned to Rhea and I. She was still against me, and I knew she wasn't sleeping but pretending to so she didn't have to talk to anyone else. I wasn't going to blow her cover, she could pretend to sleep for the next week if she wanted to.

"I'm sorry about what happened to her. To Rhea." Tanner said softly, "I hope he died painfully."

Rhea stiffened, and I knew why, "Nothing happened. I got there in time. And yes, I assume he's dying painfully as we speak."

Tanner nodded, "Good. He deserved it."

"In the back is Andrew, Anne and Eva." Gabrielle said softly, breaking the tense silence, "Andrew is the one you met, against the tree."

Tanner laughed softly, as if it was inappropriate to ever find humour in a situation and display it loudly again. I thought it was a miracle he could laugh at all.

Sandra and Jason switched spots so Sandy could relax for a while, and I noticed Jason watched the gas gauge carefully as he drove. I wondered how long we would get to sit before we would have to walk again.

Morning came, the sunset appearing to our right over the treetops. It was beautiful: red, orange and pink. I wondered how anything in this dark world could ever be so stunning.

Jason pulled the car over, "We're almost out of gas, only about a quarter tank left. We're best off camping out now, when we have a quick getaway planned."

"The ones in the back are probably freezing too." Gabby added.

I opened the door, carrying Rhea with me as I jumped out of the truck. She was awake, as I had known she would be, and I saw that her eyes weren't red anymore, and the cut on her cheek wasn't bleeding. I wet the bottom of my shirt and ran it over the cut, washing away the dried blood and dirt, leaving only a thin line of pink.

"It shouldn't scar." I told her. She summoned a small smile for me, and I noticed that she was still clutching my coat around her, hiding the ripped blouse. I slipped my shirt off and handed it to her, and then turned around. The freezing air stung my bare skin.

She giggled, "Thank you."

I turned back to her, wondering what she found so amusing, and the sight of her, still grinning and wearing my shirt nearly brought me to my knees. She was holding her ripped blouse out, as if she never wanted to see it again, and I took it from her. I took my coat off her too, putting it back on. It felt weird with nothing underneath it. Rhea was still smiling at me, still wearing the shirt I had worn all day. I pulled her coat out of the back and helped her into it, even though she was fully capable of dressing herself. I just wanted to be near her, touch her.

I almost lost her today.

She clambered into the back of the truck bed, and I followed. Andrew, Anne and Eva had already gotten inside the truck, and I saw that Jason was joining us and Zack in the back. Zack was already wrapped in some blankets and huddled on the other side, facing the truck bed wall. Jason lay down beside him, pulling more blankets around himself.

I put a blanket down for Rhea and I, and pulled some more for over us. She quickly settled herself into my arms again, and I marveled at how soon I had become used to this. My body automatically reacted to her presence, and I opened my arms instantly for her. Her nearness didn't bother me, it pleased me.

"John?" Rhea said, not facing me, her body pressed to mine.

"Yes?"

"Thank you for coming for me. For coming there in time." Her voice broke, "I knew you would."

"Of course I would." I replied, "I'll always come for you."

It seemed silly for her to thank me, it had been an automatic instinct. I would accept nothing but success in finding Rhea and saving her. She was the one thing I cared about, my one responsibility. Of course I came for her.

She turned and came face to face with me, and I recalled the last time she had 'thanked me' properly. I wasn't ready for that again, and I could feel my head start to pound. Instead she brought her hand against my chest, to feel my heart.

"Always?" She whispered, her eyes dancing with something indescribable, but beautiful. I wanted to know what she was thinking.

But I did know, didn't I? She had asked me, the night in the van, before Sophie and Dana died. She told me to stay with her. To never leave her.

I had just promised to always come for her, and in essence, she knew she had won. I would never leave her, not with that promise hanging over my head. She had me.

"That wasn't what I meant." I protested, "I didn't... I didn't mean it like that."

"I know what you meant, John Reid." Rhea said softly, her smile smug, "You meant exactly what you said. You said always, and you're not getting rid of me that easily."

Instead of explaining this comment, Rhea brought herself closer to me, her cheek pressed against my chest, the cut that marred it hidden in my jacket.

I felt her fall asleep, her entire body relaxed and her breathing evened out. She was safe, she was in my arms, and I would never let anything happen to her again. That comfort was enough to make me relax, and even though I didn't want to fall asleep, my body betrayed me, and my eyes closed and I fell into a dreamless sleep.

The rumble of the truck engine woke me, and I shot to a sitting position, my arms empty. Jason was sitting near me, watching the tree line, and I almost attacked him I was so full of panic. He noticed this right away, and answered my unspoken question.

"She's right there, coming back with the women from a bathroom break." He declared, gesturing to the four women emerging from the woods. "You were dead asleep, I don't think I've ever seen you sleep through someone moving, or the sun this bright."

I nodded, "I was tired."

Jason nodded as well, as if he understood by this statement that I meant I was emotionally and physically exhausted, and I needed this sleep, this time to feel safe. The conversation died after that, and I realized why I both liked Jason so much and couldn't be his friend. He was like me, neither one of us liked to talk, and yet, we knew nothing of each other because of this.

I still trusted him, which surprised me.

Rhea jumped back into the truck bed, all smiles. Her cheek was looking healed, it was a shallow cut. Her throat was black and blue, but it didn't seem to bother her. It bothered me.

"John, you sleepy head." She teased. "You almost missed breakfast!" She pulled a granola bar from inside her pocket and winked, "But don't worry, I saved you one!"

I ate it in seconds, I didn't realize how hungry I was for more than just roots. It tasted like heaven, and I was almost full after I finished it.

"I think my stomach shrunk." I told her, completely serious.

She laughed, her blue eyes sparkling with humour, "John, you're ridiculous."

I didn't feel ridiculous, I felt full, and slightly sick from the peanut butter on the bar. It was an amazing feeling. Rhea hugged me, quickly and without preamble. I hadn't expected it, but it was nice feeling her arms around me and her slight giggles in my ear.

The truck started moving and Rhea sat back, watching the trees go by in the morning sunrise.

"We're going to find a house today." She declared, "I just know it."

Chapter Twenty

As it turned out, Rhea was correct about finding a house. It wasn't one we would stay in forever, it was too exposed; but we did search it out carefully, finding a few soup cans and knives, and most importantly, a jerry can full of gasoline. It was barely three quarters full, and it was sealed so tightly we almost couldn't open it, but it was gas.

It only filled the truck up another quarter, and even the sight of the needle rising that much was uplifting. It was a start. During my search of the garage I found string, rolls of it, and I knew exactly what I was going to use it for.

I left the group and ran in behind the house where I had seen some birch trees. Birch was a malleable wood, and even though it was hibernating this time of year, I could definitely shape it into a snowshoe for Rhea.

I stripped two branches off the trunk within minutes, and brought it back to the truck. Sandra gave me an odd look when I dragged the five foot boughs into the back of the truck, but she didn't ask. I was grateful, because I had no idea how I would explain that I was trying to make Rhea a Christmas present.

Rhea went back into the truck, but I stayed in the bed with Zack and Tanner. Zack stayed quiet which was unusual for him, but Tanner was full of questions. It occurred to me that Tanner was my opposite.

"So what's the branches for?" he asked, almost as soon as he had clambered into the truck bed, avoiding the guns and food we had under the tarps.

"Christmas, and keep it to yourself." I added, throwing him a glare.

"Oh, we're having Christmas?" He smiled. "That's my favourite holiday."

I almost wanted to tell him that he was not part of this Christmas our group would be having, but I couldn't, mostly because his smile already wavered enough as it was, and he fit in with our group better than I ever had.

"Yes. But once again, keep quiet about it." I answered, tired again.

Zack perked up, "Is it a surprise for the girls?"

I nodded, whittling away at my boughs, and testing their bendiness. They would be perfect if I decided to beat both the men in the truck bed with me.

Zack smiled, "Great. But I can't make things, like you can. What am I going to get everyone?"

I shrugged, "These are for Rhea."

"What if we made dinner? Christmas dinner?" Tanner asked, "The girls would probably like that, and I'm not a bad cook."

Zack nodded solemnly, as if this was the best he could hope for. I would have helped him out if I knew how. I wasn't really that good with speaking or helping, especially when it came to presents. I had never given anyone a gift before, I didn't even know if I should give these to Rhea, but she had asked for them.

I was bored of whittling soon, and I was too well rested to have a nap while the truck was moving. In truth, I was hungry, and I wanted Rhea beside me so I had someone to talk to. Talking had never been my forte, and I had never wished for a conversation before, but I was bored of sitting in the back with Zack and Tanner.

Tanner was quite funny though, something I wouldn't have expected of him. He had been telling us of his life before this apocalypse hell had started, and from his stories, I was coming to believe he was possibly the luckiest person on the planet. Other than the fact that he had lost his sister and his mother to horrible fates, I would think it was a miracle.

His sister, mother and he had gone camping the weekend this all started, everything they needed packed up and ready. They had all their gear, dried foods and small weapons, like a flare gun, knives and even a regular double barreled shot gun for bears.

They hadn't even known the world had gone to hell until the Monday before they were supposed to go home, and they stopped at a convenience store to find everyone dead.

Tanner had never even killed a Hungry before, they had only run into them once, and by pure luck they had survived. They found food by coincidence, stumbling into underground caches, or fishing.

Tanner was chuckling, "Yeah, I've always been really lucky. I won a lot of money on the lottery on my eighteenth birthday. Paid for my parent's mortgage and a house I have up north here, about three hours or so from where we are. It's my summer cabin, meant for camping, nothing too big, but completely private, on a lake."

Zack and I both whirled to face Tanner, who was still talking as though nothing had happened, as though his sentences hadn't just turned our luck completely around.

"Are you saying you have a deserted cabin up here? With no towns around?" I asked, clearly and concise.

Tanner nodded, "Yeah the closest town is over an hour away. It's still stockpiled from the summer..."

It finally dawned on him why Zack and I were staring, mouths half agape. He had literally handed us our survival.

I opened the small window in between the cab and the truck bed. Rhea was chatting easily with Eva and Gabby in the backseat, and Andrew and Anne were curled up in passenger, leaving Sandy to the driving again.

"Sandra, we found a house." I declared.

Tanner leaned in, "Keep following this highway until you reach Dubawnt Lake then we'll have to go through a few dirt roads to reach it."

"Seriously?" Sandra yelled back, excitement shining on her face.

Zack leaned in and grinned, "Seriously."

The truck went even faster and I could almost feel our anticipation to get to the house, to settle ourselves for once. We hadn't felt like we had a home in so long, and it would be heavenly to sleep on a couch, or a bed.

Or even a floor. I never thought I'd be grateful to have a floor to sleep on.

I continued watching the wilderness go by, seeing nothing on the road for miles, except for the occasional abandoned car. Even those were becoming beyond rare. I knew that we wouldn't have enough gas to get to the cabin and back into civilization, and the thought frightened me. There were already snow drifts piled around the highway and it wasn't even the dead of winter yet. In fact, it was probably unseasonably warm for this time of year.

This winter, this cold, could kill us just as easily as the Hungry could.

It was an hour later, barely, when the truck pulled to a stop on the side of the highway, and Anne and Andrew got out with Eva.

"What's going on?" Tanner asked.

Eva grinned, "Just changing spots so you don't get too cold. We still have a while to go you know."

Tanner nodded, and we all got out of the truck bed and slid into the main cabin. It was much warmer in there, and I didn't realize how numb my ears and nose were until I got in.

Rhea was sitting beside me again, and the relief I felt showed me just how much I enjoyed having her around. I actually truly enjoyed her company, and that was the most miraculous thing of all.

"Have fun in the back?" She joked.

"Not really." I replied.

She giggled, "What's with the trees?"

"Whittling," I lied, "I was bored. Now they're firewood."

"You like to carve?" She questioned. I wondered briefly why I had missed her conversation, she talked too much.

"It's okay."

She grinned, "You should carve something for me!"

I glanced at her and raised an eyebrow; she was seriously telling me to carve her something? First of all, why would I do that? I was already making her snowshoes, not that she knew it, and that was harrowing enough to be giving her one gift! Why would I put myself through this twice?!

Her face fell though, and the grin she had held so easily since I had been in the truck wavered, "Well, only if you want to. Might be nice, you know."

I shrugged, feeling bad for putting her off so quickly. Maybe one day I'd carve something for her, if I was really bored.

"John?" She asked, peppiness returned tenfold, "What's your middle name?"

I gaped at her, confused utterly by her random questioning, "Why?"

"I want to know!"

I scowled, because there was no way I would ever let anyone know what my middle name was. That information had died with my father and public schooling.

"I don't have one." I declared.

"Yes you do!" Rhea sang mockingly.

"Fine, I do. But the day you find it out, you die." I was deadly serious, and I think it shocked Rhea for a moment, because I never threatened her.

"Wow," She giggled, "It must be bad."

I didn't respond to her teasing, because it was true. It was bad, it was beyond terrible; my father had never shown any consideration in anything he did, although I had always wondered why my mother had never had better taste. She had been around to name me.

"When's your birthday?" She asked, a while later after she had given up on the name.

"May 16th."

She gasped, "I just realized I don't even know how old you are!?"

I glanced at her, "Does it matter? I'm twenty-four."

Sandra swiveled and stared at me from the front, "I thought you were nineteen!"

Rhea flushed, "No way. You are not six years older than me."

"Can we say cradle-robber?" Zack laughed.

I glared, "Sometimes it's easy to tell that I'm the oldest person here."

"No, you're not, actually," Tanner interrupted, "I'm twenty-six."

Sandra laughed, "We haven't even graduated, how does that make you feel?"

Tanner shrugged, "Too old for this stupid apocalypse."

Rhea snickered along with them, and for a moment I wanted to smash Tanner's face in. I couldn't figure out where the impulse had come from until I looked at Rhea's smile. I was jealous. Because he had made her laugh, and that was my job.

I was disgusted with myself, but at the same time I had come to terms with the fact that where Rhea was concerned, I had lost my mind. People had called me insane before and I had just gone along with it because I hadn't cared. Because it hadn't been true.

Now it was.

The unbearable jealousy I was now feeling faded when Rhea gently laid her head against my arm and settled into my body. As much as I discouraged it, I was pleased, because she was still mine. I wasn't going to have her, and I would forever push her away even though I did care about her, but for now, for this moment, she was mine.

"I'm so excited to have a home again." Gabrielle said, her voice filled with exhaustion and hope, so much so that I saw Sandra swallow hard in the mirror.

"Me too, Gabby." Sandra agreed, "We'll have to figure out rooms and spaces when we get there, especially if we are staying for a while."

"It's got four rooms actually." Tanner said, "One doesn't have a bed, and the other is a pull out couch, but at least there's some space!"

It was obvious that Anne and Andrew would take one of the rooms, and I wondered if Sandra and Jason would continue to share. I wasn't sure, this trip north had been rough on them, and though I knew Jason still loved her, it might just be too much. Maybe the girls would room up again, and I could take a place close to the front door.

Just the way I liked it.

My satisfaction at this thought was cut short when I recalled the girl so soundly snuggled into my side, and how she had proclaimed she couldn't sleep without me beside her.

Well, she would just have to live without sleep. There was no way I was sharing the floor with her. In the wilderness, where danger was literally around every corner, it was a bit more understandable... but in a house, in a semi-civilized place?

It wasn't going to happen.

Chapter Twenty-One

The house was hidden, and probably the most beautiful sight I had ever seen. It was covered in snow and ice, the lake beside it frozen solid. There wasn't even a driveway, just drifts of snow we skirted or drove through, skidding all over. There was no fear of hitting the ditch, there wasn't even a visible ditch. It was liberating, in a way, and the thick forest of coniferous trees on the other side of the house comforted me. It was shelter, it was firewood.

No Hungry would survive here; although, there wasn't a lot of wildlife I was familiar with hunting. The only thing I could possibly think to bring down would be caribou, or a big horned sheep. I supposed there were polar bears this far north, but I prayed we never ran into one. It was still the Hungry I was most worried about, but they wouldn't come this far north, at least not a lot of them.

We would be safe from them, it was only the cold that was getting bitterer with every minute we drove north that I was worried about.

Sandra killed the truck outside the log house, and the gas gauge barely moved as the engine died. We wouldn't have made it another hour with our gas as it was. I didn't know how we were going to get out of this place.

The cabin of our truck was jam packed, everyone had moved into it not long after I had given up on whittling, it had been too cold outside. I was crushed against the door in an effort not to be touching anyone else. Rhea was basically sitting on me, trying to give room to everyone else.

We clambered out of the vehicle, grabbing anything we had managed to salvage from our raid on the other camp. We had a surprising amount of food and weapons, and for that I was grateful. I knew by the hardened look on Tanner's face that every time he glanced at what we had gained he was reminded of his sister on that table.

There was nothing I could do about that though. We needed it.

The door was practically frozen on its hinges, but after Jason and Zack had lunged at it a few times it flew open. The house was icy cold, but Tanner headed to the furnace room to light the pilot light and increase the heat.

We piled our things in the front room, which held two couches and a wooden stove, logs piled beside it. The firewood was hugely appreciated, as I did not feel like heading out in the barren ice land to chop down some monstrous frozen pine.

The kitchen was small, but held a round table filled with stools. The cupboards were big and chocked full with food, which made all of us happy. There was a lower level, although it wasn't very big, due to the permanently frozen ground, and the bedrooms were all upstairs and tiny, but in the closet there were piles of blankets. Tanner showed us his pride and joy, a small underground room, hidden behind the furnace by a pile of wood. The walls were frozen dirt, and no heat came down there, but immediately I saw the advantage we had with this room.

It needed to be expanded.

Andrew and Anne snatched one bedroom with a bed immediately, and none of us could really refute this, because we knew it would happen.

"Would you mind if I took this one?" Jason asked, pointing to the other bedroom.

Sandra shrugged, "Nope, it's ours."

Gabrielle, Eva and Rhea all stilled, grins breaking out over their entire faces, and it was obvious that they had been worried the two wouldn't make it. I was pleased, because I had been unsure, as had probably the entire group whether or not they would stay together. Sandra was barely human these days, I wasn't sure how Jason could stand her. I couldn't deny that I was happy for Jason though, he had loved Sandra for as long as I had known them, but at the same time I was jealous again.

It baffled me, because I held zero interest in Sandra, but I quickly realized that it was because I wanted a room. I wanted Rhea and I to have a room.

I glanced to the room without a bed and made a split second decision, "Can I take this?"

"No," Eva said, "Take the pull-out couch in the den, then Tanner, Gabrielle, Zack and I can stay in the room without a bed and just pile blankets wherever we wanna sleep."

I nodded, heading towards the room to throw in my weapons, unsure what was going to happen next. It was Rhea's choice, whatever she decided. I had taken the room. Eva hadn't said her name, but wouldn't deny her a spot if she wanted it.

"John?" Rhea's voice had come from my doorway. She was standing holding the only backpack with first aid supplies, and she looked nervous as hell. It was amazingly adorable, and reassuring, seeing her as anxious as I always seemed to feel around her.

"Yes?" I answered, my hands shaking from where they were hidden behind my back.

She shifted, "Um, when you said could you take this room, what did you mean?"

I frowned, "I meant could I have the room."

She giggled, "I know that, I just thought..." She breathed deeply, "I was wondering if you meant for you alone, or if you were talking about us."

"I was talking about me." I said.

Her face fell, and I realized immediately what I had done wrong. She was about to turn out of the doorway, and I had to fix this, I had to explain to her what I meant or else she would be sharing the same room as Tanner! With two other girls, but still!

"Rhea!" I called.

She looked back at me, hurt in her gorgeous blue eyes, "What?" She snapped. I could understand her anger with me.

"I meant that...Well, I was going to say-" I shook my head and cleared my throat, "You never listened to me anyway, do what you want!"

Rhea turned back towards me, and I could tell she was forcing down a smile, but that she wasn't going to let me off the hook that quickly. She wanted me to admit that I had taken the bedroom so that she would be able to stay with me.

I growled, "The room is for us, okay? If you want it."

I tossed down my knives and turned away from her, embarrassment flooding me, and fear that she would reject me despite all the signs to the opposite.

Instead of that fear coming true, I heard the door shut and saw her backpack hit the floor and was turned around by a gentle mittened hand on my coat. Rhea was beaming up at me, her pink cheeks matching her baby pink parka.

"I want it. Thank you, John." She said, her arms coming up to wrap around me. For a minute I stood stock still and let her hang off me like usual, but then I slowly brought my own arms around her.

Tonight was a night for changes.

"You said you can't sleep without me." I explained softly.

Rhea nodded, "I did say that, didn't I?"

I cleared my throat after a moment and unwound my arms from around her. She must have sensed my restlessness, because she stepped back from me.

"Thank you." She repeated. I nodded, unwilling to trust my words. She turned away and placed her backpack beside the couch. She started taking pillows off the couch, about to make the bed.

"John?" She said, not even looking up from her task. I hadn't moved an inch, and was frozen, just watching her make our bed. Our bed!

"Yes?" I responded, purely on instinct.

"Why don't you go help the others unpack, and get the house defenses up?"

I nodded, "Uh, yeah. Yes, uh, good plan."

She giggled slightly as I shuffled out of the room we were going to be living in together and I wondered if it was because she was amused at how wonderstruck I was.

That's what it was: I was struck down with awe. I had thought that it was hate, thought it was fear, resentment, anxiety or even apathy. Yet that wasn't what I was feeling right now, that wasn't what I felt every time Rhea came near me.

I was feeling amazement; absolute, unadulterated gratitude and affection flooded me at the thought that Rhea would share a room with me, let alone the fact that she wanted to.

I ran into Jason downstairs, and his grin showed that he was probably feeling the exact same things I was, only he was showing them better.

"Anything I can do?" I asked, my eyes travelling the house up and down. The weapons had already been stored in various spots, and the food was being put away by Eva, Gabrielle and Anne.

"The branches you broke off are still in the truck, if you want them. But it's freezing out there, prepare yourself."

I nodded, and headed towards the door. The wind shocked me with its bone-numbing temperature as soon as I opened it, and I wondered if perhaps we had made a deadly mistake coming up here. Although the cabin was warming as we spoke, and cold was easier to defend against than Hungry.

"Hey John?" I turned towards Tanner's voice. He was standing by the truck with the branches I wanted in his hands.

"Yeah?"

He gestured towards the side of the house, "There's a small storage shed over there, if you wanted to keep these hidden. No lock on it."

I thanked him and carried my load over to where he had pointed. It was a conveniently hidden shed, nestled into the side of the house and practically covered with snow. It took me a while to dig the door out enough to open it, but the branches fit in it, and it would keep them sheltered enough from the cold that they wouldn't dry too much.

I returned to the house, which had grown warmer still in my absence, although I might have been biased because of the freezing temperature outside, and headed to the kitchen. The girls had finished packing the food away and everyone had gathered at the table. Smiles were pasted on every face, and relief was palpable as we sat there. Eva was making soup, and she had even gotten out a packet of powder potatoes. It was going to be a feast tonight, in celebration of the house, and finally being safe.

I pulled a chair in and sat down beside Rhea. She grinned at me, and set her hand on my arm.

"Cold outside?"

I nodded, pulling my arm out from under hers. She shook her head, probably exasperated that after everything we had been through I still didn't want her touching me for no reason.

The night wore on with jokes and laughter, and I could not help but feel warmed by the company that surrounded me, even if I was not truly apart of the conversation. Our potatoes and soup were the best thing we had tasted in weeks and the house had finally warmed up enough that we had all put our jackets away.

Anne and Andrew were the first to go to bed, and it came as no surprise that they left the table holding hands and grinning. They would finally be getting the rest they needed, and they would have all night to be together, just the two of them.

The thought scared me half to death, because the exact same situation would be happening tonight with Rhea and I.

"Goodnight everyone!" Gabrielle said, standing from the table. Eva stood with her, and I saw Rhea look at me from the corner of her eye. I stared straight ahead.

"I think I'll go too." Rhea followed everyone up the stairs. Jason watched me from across the table, and I held his gaze. We were challenging each other; who would be the first to cave and follow the lead of the others to bed?

Jason smirked, and I knew I had won. He took Sandra's hand and tugged her to a stand.

They said goodnight to everyone while heading up the stairs together.

It was only Tanner, Zack, and I left sitting at the table, and I took the awkward few moments to clear away the plates we had used over dinner.

"So Rhea's yours, huh?" Tanner asked, still seated.

I shrugged, "No, just the only one I can stand."

"Not a people person are you?" Tanner laughed, his green eyes so alike that of his twin, glinting at me with humour.

Zack laughed at Tanner's words, "Basically John hates everyone."

I shrugged again, ignoring Zack's laughter, putting off the eventual moment when I would go upstairs to bed.

"She is yours." Tanner repeated again, a smile playing about his lips.

"No." I snapped, "And why are you so interested?"

Tanner chuckled, "I'm not interested in her at all, she will be a friend, that's all, don't you worry. And I wasn't asking this time, I was telling you. She is yours, that's what she thinks. If she's wrong, you should probably let her know." He started laughing truly, as if the thought of me not liking Rhea was preposterous. Which it was, but there was no need to laugh.

Zack sniffed, "It's true, she's a nice girl, you should snatch her up."

I glared at him, and finally pushed my chair from the table and climbed the stairs. It had been the fear of any more comments from Tanner or Zack that had driven me so far, and of course, the desire to hit him again.

The door to the room was closed, and I wondered if maybe I should sleep on the couch, but I knew that everything I had was in that room, so I had to go in anyway. I opened the door slowly, attempting to slow the creaks it might make and stepped gingerly into the room.

"John?" Rhea's whisper froze me in the dark.

I hesitated, "Yes?"

She sighed, "Oh good, it's you."

"Who else would it be?" I asked, baffled.

She giggled, "I don't know, a Hungry?"

Her laughter pleased me, and I shut the door solidly, deciding right then and there that I would stay in the room. I had claimed it after all, and I refused to be driven out by my roommate.

"I would never let a Hungry get this far." I told her, standing beside the bed.

It was at the bedside that I lost my courage. The blankets were all tucked in, and I just couldn't bring my hand to move them away for me to lay down into them. Rhea sensed my unease however, as she always did, and reached over to pull them down for me.

"Get into bed, it's cold!" She commanded.

I slid under the sheets, the heavy duvet sitting on top and warming me. My clothes were dirty still from our weeks of travel, and I felt bad for not cleaning them before bed, but there was hardly a moment to do so.

I was staring at the ceiling, the only light coming from the moon shining beyond the window. I wondered if I was the only man lying awake tonight, or if everyone was doing the same. I was still afraid to trust the fact that we were safe; my body was still pumping adrenalin full time, waiting for a fight.

Instead of a fight all I got was Rhea's warm body rolling into mine, and her head settling into my shoulder. I put my arm around her, and the feeling that this was exactly where I wanted to be consumed me.

"This happiness won't last." Rhea murmured.

I frowned, she wasn't satisfied with this? This felt like everything I had ever wanted. I moved my arm from where it was on her shoulder.

"No John," She laughed, "I didn't mean with you. I am happy with you, I meant with the house. Our happiness at being here won't last, soon we're going to go back into mourning. We didn't have time to mourn our losses."

She was right, I knew that. I had always had the unshakeable feeling that eventually everything would just break down again, and the losses we had faced and the sights we had seen would come back to haunt us.

I brought my arm back to her shoulder and stroked it gently.

"But we will be safe, and we will have time to be sad." I told her softly, wondering if this was how comforting someone felt. I didn't mind this at all, not when it was with Rhea.

"And you will be here, with me, every night." Rhea said. I didn't nod, but she was correct again. Now that I had done this, now that I had held Rhea in our bed, in our room, I would never go back to sleeping on the couch or on the floor.

I would die before I ever had to be without her again.

Chapter Twenty-Two

December

Waking up was the most incredible sensation of my life. Rhea was wrapped around me, her legs tossed over my own, and her hands curled into my clothes. I hadn't moved in the night, but Rhea had always moved around a lot in her sleep, at least since I had known her.

I crept my way out of her grasp, leaving only her murmurs of discontentment as I left her. She was a heavy sleeper when she felt safe apparently. Her body curled into itself as soon as it lost my warmth, and I pulled the blankets up around her shoulders before I left. The house was still quite cold, and I had a feeling it would never be completely warm.

The kitchen was empty other than Eva, who was cooking up some sort of breakfast.

"The other boys are outside. It's not a bad day out, and I think they're trying to find some sort of firewood." She told me.

I had always respected Eva; she talked to me as though she didn't believe I would hurt her when her back was turned. I knew that she wouldn't put it past me, but she was brave enough to give me the benefit of the doubt and yet still be prepared if I were to try something. Her wicked injury was still healing, yet she never complained, even when our travelling would have been incredibly rough on her. Sandra didn't give her enough credit.

Sandra rarely gave enough credit to the people in this group. I wasn't sure if that was because she loved them too much to put them in harm's way, or because she thought they were all incapable of anything.

I nodded to Eva either way and grabbed my winter gear. I was dressed fully, only eyes exposed to face the bitter cold of the north. The day was deceiving: it was bright and sunny, and no wind blew around us, but it was still bone numbingly cold.

The other men were scattered around the property, and the first one I came across was Andrew, who was going across the now frozen lake. He eyed me with mutual dislike, and I cursed my luck. The day had started out so wonderfully, but I couldn't have run into Jason? Or even Tanner! As much as he may annoy me at times, at least I could stand him. The thought of spending time with Andrew actually made me want to rip his throat out. Although, I supposed it could be worse. It could have been Zack. Since I had helped save Anne in the van incident, Andrew was at least civil to me, but Zack had experienced no such changes.

"Hey." He said.

I nodded at his greeting, "Looking for wood?"

"Yeah, and a spot to ice fish."

After that comment, I knew that I actually had to stay with Andrew for a while, because I was the one in charge of ice fishing. I had been given a drill from the man we had once ran across, and we had only held onto it this long by a stroke of luck. When Sophie had blown the van to hell, it had only been by chance that I had grabbed the backpack with the drill in it.

"Okay. I'll look too." I replied.

Andrew sighed but nodded. I knew he was bitterly resenting me for that, but he would never know how badly I hated myself for sticking around.

We traversed the icy lake in silence for about an hour. The only reason we hadn't frozen where we stood was because we were constantly moving, but even so we were starting to get too cold to continue. It was this that had increased our irritability to the point where we were willing to get into a fight.

"Why do you do it?" Andrew asked, and for the first time since our greeting I sensed he wasn't filling his question with dislike. He was actually curious.

"Do what?" I responded, wondering what in the hell he was asking me about.

He spun on me, giving up our steady march forward for the moment, "Lead her on. Make it seem like you're someone worth loving, and pretend you care about her, when we both know that you're not worth the dirt on her shoes."

I stepped back, shocked at his words. While I had even told myself that on occasion, I had never expected them to come out of another's mouth, and they were especially shocking today, when the thoughts of last night made them so untrue.

"I'm not leading her on." I snarled back, repulsed at the thought that Andrew could actually think me to be that much of a monster, that I would destroy something so beautiful and innocent as Rhea. I may be evil in my own way, but that was something I would never lower myself to.

Andrew closed his eyes painfully, "That's what I was afraid of. You're only going to hurt her."

"Nothing will ever hurt her." I told him coldly.

Andrew shook his head, "Sure, no Hungry will ever get her while you watch out for her, we both know that much, John. But don't you think when she asks if you love her, and you can't respond it will hurt her? Don't you think when she realizes you aren't capable of love she will be crushed?" He scowled, "You're gonna break her heart."

There was nothing I could say. It was true, in a way. I would never be able to love Rhea the way she loved anyone. She cared about everything and everyone more than I had ever cared about a single person. Yet it was also untrue, because I did care about her. I wanted to hit Andrew. "At least I didn't let her mother die." I snapped.

This I had heard from Rhea, that Anne's mother had been killed by Sandra's hand. I didn't blame Andrew for this, but I knew it would hurt him for me to say it. He would always feel guilty for letting Anne go through that.

The hurt and shock registered on his face and I felt sick, "I didn't mean that." I said softly, turning away from him. I didn't want to continue this, I wanted to go back to the cabin where the one face I wanted to see more than any other would be.

There was barely a second's notice before Andrew tackled me, and we both hit the ice hard. My head was spinning from impact, and the gut instinct to snap his neck stormed through me. The only reason I stopped was because it proved every sentence he had ever said about me being a monster right, and there was nothing I wanted more on this earth than to prove him wrong.

His punch was powerful, and it only worsened the instant headache I had developed from the ice; he only got the one hit in before I had him turned around, face down on the ice. His arm was being bent back so badly I knew with a bit more pressure I would snap it.

"John..." He groaned.

"Listen to me," I snarled, "You don't know me. You don't talk to me, and you don't talk to her. I don't care what you say, but you're wrong."

I let go of his arm, and with a black eye forming I started limping back to the house. My knee was sprained, I could feel the pain with every step, and I had a feeling he had bruised a rib with our fall. The house was warm when I entered it though and I felt much better as soon as I saw Rhea peek out from the kitchen, her blond hair braided down her back.

"There you are. Eva and I made pancakes! Come have some." She called me.

I pulled off my winter wear and headed toward the kitchen, but as soon as I reached the kitchen and Rhea's smile turned to shock.

"John! What happened?!" She cried, setting down her plate to rush to my face. Her hand lightly skimmed the left side of my cheek and I flinched away. It was painful, and I knew it must have blackened already. Nothing was broken, but it was definitely bruised.

"I had a disagreement." I answered, "But I'd love a pancake."

She scowled, "No way, you're not changing the subject that easy! What happened?"

I heard the door open and I knew that in about a minute Rhea would have her answer. Sure enough, Andrew made his way to the kitchen, looking significantly better than I felt. I should have pummeled him.

"Andrew, did you see what happened? John's not telling me." At this Rhea threw me a glare, as if it was my job to report back to her.

Andrew frowned, "We had an argument."

Rhea's face turned stony, "You hit him."

"He deserved it."

I hissed at his words, regret storming me that I didn't knock him out when I could have.

Rhea snapped, "Yeah I bet. If he deserved it so much why do you look guilty?"

Andrew sighed, "Because he didn't hit me back. And I deserved to be hit."

"What were you fighting about?" Rhea asked.

I prayed he wouldn't tell her, that he would lie or just keep silent; but the universe had never been on my side, and Andrew would probably rather be tortured than actually do something I wanted.

"You." Andrew said. "How he was leading you on. How he was a bad guy. How he'll never love you."

Rhea stilled, and I could have killed Andrew for the way he had phrased that. He had just done exactly what he had prophesied, now Rhea thought that I was doing those exact things.

"What..." she muttered, "I'm sorry, why... why were you? I mean, what?"

Finally, finally my feet moved. I was glad Eva had vacated early on, and that at least we had some semblance of privacy.

I reached Rhea first, her being my first priority, and I shot a glare to Andrew. "Remember what I said about not talking to us? Start now, or prepare to get what's coming to you."

"John?" Rhea whispered, "Why were you fighting?"

My hands automatically travelled up her arms, until I was holding her shoulders gently, staring straight into her blue eyes.

"We *were* fighting about that. He said that's what I was doing and I disagreed." I said, "Rhea, I'm not a very good guy, you know that. But I am protecting you for a reason. I won't let anything hurt you, and that includes me."

She shook her head, "That answers nothing. Do you care about me? I'm not asking for love, John, I know you wouldn't agree to that. But you need to tell me whether or not you are just doing this because you think it will be better or safer for me. Tell me."

I let go of her and backed up. The counter stopped anymore of my retreat and I threw the biggest glare I could manage at Andrew, who was standing still as a statue and watching this conversation unfold.

It was one thing to admit I cared about Rhea in my head, or even to her. With an audience though? Under pressure?

I would never be able to force the words out.

She was still watching me, fear in her eyes; underneath the fear though, I could see that she believed in me. She thought I would do the right thing.

"I stay *here*, only for you." I murmured, barely loud enough to hear, "Now you tell *him* that you know I care about you."

Rhea nodded, and turned to face Andrew.

He held up his hand, "You didn't let me finish. John, I was wrong. I don't like you, I probably never will. But I was wrong. I know that."

He left the kitchen and I still wanted to kill him for putting me through that.

Rhea smiled at me though, as she faced me again, "John, you *are* wrong about something though."

"What?" I asked gruffly.

"That you're not a good guy. You are." She said this with such determination, and such trust that I wondered how she had come to this conclusion.

"How do you know?"

She grinned. "I know because of the way you hold me, and the way you sometimes glance at me as if sharing a joke, even though you don't smile. I know because every once in a while you do smile. Also, I know because you didn't hit Andrew back."

I shrugged, unsure what to say. She had me down to a tee though, how often had I looked to Rhea to share any amusement I might feel and revel in her laughter?

"Alright, pancakes." Rhea demanded, and sat me down at the table. We ate in silence and I enjoyed the pancakes, which were delicious and fluffy.

"When's Christmas?" I asked.

She frowned, "I'm not sure. I think we're in December now. The beginning?"

Tanner walked in at this moment, grinning, and I knew he had heard our conversation. It bothered me. He bothered me. "We found a trick to finding the right trees for firewood. The ones covered in ice are dry as a bone, easy to light and brittle enough to chop."

"Perfect." I said.

"Also, these pancakes smell amazing, Rhea. And it's December 2nd."

"Really! Thank you." Rhea grinned at me, "Twenty three days until Christmas."

The thought scared me, I still needed to finish her gift and find a tree. I knew that I was going to carve her something as well now, though, I had a perfect image in mind, and the snowshoes she had already asked for. The tree I could get from the forest.

"Tanner, do you have candles here?"

He nodded and spoke through mouthfuls of pancake, "Yeah, millions of 'em."

"Why?" Rhea asked.

I shrugged. "If the power fails."

It was a lie. I wasn't that concerned about the power, Tanner had told me yesterday he had a backup generator hooked up to the cabin, and some solar panels installed. The solar panels would be useless in winter, but in summer when it was long days they'd be perfect. The candles would make beautiful Christmas lights.

Chapter Twenty-Three

The days had been going by, relaxing and healing. Our group had gone back into mourning in a lot of ways, but it seemed like we were getting past it. Tanner was quieter now than before, and I knew he was reliving his sister's death every minute, and mourning his mother. We all were reminiscing about Dana's smile, and Sophie's devil-may-care attitude.

Jason and Sandra had been fighting, and I suspected it was about Dana's death, and Jason wasn't sleeping in their room anymore. I knew he slept on the couch, and probably barely slept at that. It was as if we had traded lives.

I had found my peace in Rhea, as usual, and she had found hers in me. We spent every waking minute together, and it was to the point where the others didn't even look at me strangely if I helped her with something, or did something kind.

The only times I wasn't around her was when I was making her snowshoes and carving. She didn't know that's what I was doing, she thought I was hunting. While I did hunt quite often, I also delegating a lot of time to getting her gifts done, and the perfect Christmas set up.

It had been over a week and I knew that it was December 11th today. I had been keeping track ever since Tanner had given us the date, and I knew that I would continue to do so even after Christmas was over. It was nice to have a timeline, and I couldn't count the passage of time by my memorable nights any longer, since I spent all of them snuggled up to Rhea and too euphoric to do anything but revel in my happiness.

She was curled around me as per usual when we went to bed on this night. I was awake, and I knew she was too, because her breathing wasn't deep and even enough. I wondered briefly what she was thinking about, and debated on asking her, but it wasn't my forte to start conversation. Instead, I tightened my arms around her body, and hoped that she would find a deep and restful sleep, full of dreams of happiness and times before.

It was silent in the house, and I knew that Jason was prowling around somewhere, and Andrew was probably awake listening as well. Jason hadn't slept properly since him and Sandra had been fighting. I heard him sometimes, wandering around at night and muttering to himself. I knew eventually Sandra would come to her senses and tell Jason she was an idiot. Andrew rarely left Anne alone, so he was never found roaming around at night, but I would bet on my life he spent most of the night as I did, wrapped around a sleeping woman and praying for another night of peace.

"John?" Rhea's voice broke into my thoughts and I started.

"Yes?" I answered, my voice only audible because Rhea's ear was underneath my chin.

"Why do you take care of me?" She asked, "I know you said to Sandra I was your responsibility, but why?"

I shrugged, "I don't know. My instincts were to protect you."

"Is it a burden?" Her voice was sad, and I wondered where this had come from. We had long ago determined that I would protect her, it was my job, and I knew that she had accepted it because I would have no other outcome.

"No." I snapped, "We have discussed this before. What brought it up again?"

"I just, I don't know, I saw the way Andrew is always with Anne and concentrating on her and I started to wonder whether I distracted you and you resented me for it." She seemed upset by this fact, and I wasn't sure how I could tell her she did distract me, constantly, and I was always consumed with her safety. It would upset her, and I would never willingly upset Rhea. My goal in life was to keep her safe, and calm, and happy.

"You... you do distract me. But you are not a burden, I don't resent you." I answered. I didn't know how else to tell her this. I had only just had the fight with Andrew about me caring, and she knew I liked her.

"You promised you would never hate me, do you remember that?" She smiled at this, and I couldn't help but think she had a reason to. The first time Rhea and I had truly gotten close was during that moment, when I had promised her I would never hate her, would never even be mad at her. I had never broken that promise, a feat I was supremely proud of.

"Of course I remember."

She turned over and faced me, her sky blue eyes too close for comfort. Her hand rested upon my heart, the steady thudding reassuring her and but making me worry it would give me away. I had long fought my weakness against Rhea's beauty and kindness, there was no one I would allow this close to me, and certainly no one I would want to have touching me like this.

"Do you remember that fight?" She asked, her smile threatening to fall. I knew instantly what she was talking about, it had been the one true fight I had ever had with Rhea. It was my temper that had caused it, and her stubbornness that had continued it. It had ended quickly, with both of us apologizing, but it was still a dark spot in Rhea's memory. It never had affected me as badly as it had her, she was always tortured with the fact that she had been violent towards me, and told me she hated me. I wasn't as hurt by this, because I had never expected anything different, although I had been shocked, because nothing would have prepared me for the fact that Rhea would say she hated me. Rhea was barely capable of hatred.

"Of course I remember." I repeated.

She smiled again, beautifully, a big enough and bright enough smile to light up the world, "I wish you could have seen your face when I said the things I did to you. It's funny now, only because I know I'm allowed to come near you, and you forgave me. But your face was shocked, and almost smug. I felt terribly, I thought you had been trying to make me angry enough to say those things!"

"Why would I do that?" I was baffled.

"To prove that the world is the terrible place you think it is."

I scowled at her, "The world is terrible, look around. But you are not terrible, and you never will be."

"Your expectations of me are too high." She giggled, "But don't ever change them, I like knowing I'm perfect in your eyes."

Her words struck a deep chord in me, and I thought I should probably turn away from the beguiling eyes and smile that had reasoned with my hatred of everything enough to get close to me. It was true, Rhea was perfect in my eyes. She was kind, beautiful, and the strongest woman I had ever met, but without using violence.

Instead of turning away from her words like I knew would be the smarter route, I scowled at her and shut my eyes, pretending to sleep.

The last thing in this world I ever expected was for soft lips to press onto my cheek. My eyes flew open to Rhea's kiss, and I was glad I had restrained my initial reaction to pushing her off the bed, and also grateful that my second instinct, which was to grab her and kiss her back properly had been restrained as well.

She pulled away and smiled at me, and I knew that to her I must have looked wild and frightened, with my wide eyes and clenched jaw. She just brought her hand up and rested it on my cheek; taming me with only a touch.

"I love you, John."

A deep hatred imbedded itself within me, and I knew that it wasn't aimed at Rhea, it could never be for Rhea, it was all for myself. It was instantaneous and powerful; I knew in that moment that I hated myself more than ever before because no matter how I felt about Rhea, or how she felt about me, I was never going to have her. I couldn't love, and I was afraid of being loved. I didn't even believe in it.

Andrew had been right.

I despised myself because I couldn't take what was being offered to me, and at that moment, everything anyone could ever desire was mine.

Then, as soon as the red-hot hate passed, I was furious, but this time at Rhea. Because she had caused this in me, this separation of what I wanted and what I couldn't have, and also the loathing I was now feeling.

"No, you don't." I snapped. I sat up, gently, because as afraid and as angry as I was, I would still never hurt Rhea. As soon as she was situated on the bed safely, I stood and started pacing around our room.

Rhea wasn't shocked at my initial reaction, and I knew it was because she knew me too well. She probably knew better than I did what I was feeling, and that made me mad too.

"Rhea, you are stupid if you think that." She frowned at my words, "I hate everyone. The only reason you think that is because right now, in this world, where it's fight or die, I'm normal. I'm what you want and need, because I belong in this harsh place, I know what death is, and I protect you."

"That's not true!" She stood up, her whisper strong in the creaky house.

"Yes, it is." I was still sneering at her, and I hated myself for doing this too.

She marched towards me, and just like the first time she had done this, I backed away. She followed me until I was cornered against a wall, and I felt like a frightened animal.

"That is not true." She said, calmly and clearly, "I love you because you are amazing, and you're never mean with me, and you look at me as though I am your entire world. I love you because you didn't teach Dana how to fight, and because you stay with me while I sleep even though I know you'd rather be patrolling the house. I love you because I know the only reason you are still with this group is me. You would have left long ago and had a better chance of survival alone, except that you had promised yourself not to let anything hurt me. And you could've taken me with you, I would have come along because I loved you so much, but you never asked me, because you knew that it would hurt me to leave my friends. I love you because you are John, and to me, you are perfect."

I gaped at her. I had nothing to say, nothing smart to reply and nothing cruel to fight back with. Even if I did have something harsh to say, I didn't think it would have come out, not after the speech Rhea had just given me. She was so desperate and amazing, and everything she had said had struck some sort of chord inside of me, something that was forever changed. I would never be the same again, and I had known this since I had seen Rhea, that first time, but now it was written in my DNA, a part of my soul I couldn't scrub out.

She was inside of me, she was my everything.

"John?" She asked, her voice still soft in the quiet of the house.

I wanted out of this corner she had me backed into. I wanted out of this house. I needed to escape her, and her beguiling blue eyes and blonde hair.

"Move out of my way." I commanded, my voice half frightened. Fear was not a normal part of my day, and it felt wrong to be so angry, and sad, and scared, and hateful all at the same time.

Rhea moved, hesitantly, as if she didn't want to. If she wanted to see me again though, she had to move.

It was thoughtless, I just acted, my feet started moving, straight towards the door. I opened and headed towards the downstairs exit, aiming for the forest we had recently found, a dangerous place to be at night, especially in this cold. I didn't care, I didn't even have my knives on me, but I couldn't think about that right now. The only thing that mattered was running away, far away, as far away as it would take to rid myself of her voice and her smell.

I could never run far enough.

My coat and winter wear was pulled on at lightning speed, and I walked out the door without looking back.

"John!" Rhea's voice was frightened, and against my will I turned around to look at her, following me out on the ice with only socked feet and her pajamas; she would freeze within minutes and I couldn't bring myself not to care.

She was holding my knives, and her eyes were full of tears and hurt. The strongest need to pull her into my arms and shelter her from the night sky, and the dangers that surrounded us overcame me, but I fought it; I fought it with everything I had inside me, just like I was fighting my desire for the woman in front of me.

"John, don't go!" She begged, tears rolling off her chin.

The forest was calling me, escape was screaming my name, and I wanted to turn away from her, but I couldn't, not when she was freezing and begging me to stay.

"John, please, don't leave me." She whispered, her hands shaking as she held my weapons out to me.

I snatched them from her hands and attached them to my belt. I fixed her with my best glare, full of every single emotion that was tumbling around inside my head and screaming to get out. Her tears came harder, and I heard her breath catch as she took it all in, everything that I was directing towards her.

"John?" Her voice was barely audible, "Just... make sure you come back, okay? Come home."

Amazement filled me, Rhea was letting me go. She was letting me run away, even after what she had said, and how I had acted. I wanted to tell her I wasn't coming back, that she was completely wrong about me, and truthfully I wasn't staying for her. I didn't need her, I was leaving and never coming back because I would survive that way.

But she was right. That bothered me most of all. So I had to answer, I had to give her something.

After all, she had given me everything, even if I couldn't take what she offered.

"I'll be back." I said, my voice still angry. Rhea nodded solemnly, and I knew she was taking this as an oath, something I would do anything to see through. She knew I would die rather than disappoint her, and I would come back to her, even if I had to come back from death.

She smiled, gingerly and sadly, as if she knew that she couldn't do anything too drastic or it might frighten me again, "I'll wait for you."

This made me mad again —furious— I wanted to hurt her; "I said I'd be back. I didn't say when."

She scowled, "I will wait forever. That's what it means when you love someone."

"Go back inside where it's warm." I commanded.

A wounded animal, I escaped into the forest. I watched her though, for a while, as she stood under the starlight and stared after me. I didn't leave until she went back into the dark house, where she would be warm, safe, and watched over by the rest of the group until I came back for her.

It was the next morning, and I had slept close to the house, inside the shed I had been spending so much time in anyway, whittling away at Rhea's gifts. Sadly, that is what I had been doing while freezing inside the tiny building.

Nothing had disturbed me as I had half-slept, and I knew that we had made a good choice by picking this house, it was too far from civilization for Hungry to be out here. I was half frozen though, and I knew I needed to move.

I headed towards the forest, going straight for the one tree I had mapped out a week ago for Rhea's perfect Christmas tree.

The tree was tall, and I had picked it because I remembered the time we had all slept under one tree such as this, the night after Sophie and Dana had died. The memory was bittersweet, maybe more bitter, because it was full of sadness, hunger and death, but it was also sweet, because Rhea had slept in my arms, and I had known where we had stood together.

I didn't know that now, I was too confused about everything. She claimed she loved me, and I knew that I cared for her more than was healthy for both of us. I didn't even think I was capable of love, though, and I never wanted Rhea to feel like life had stolen something from her. I was not good enough for her. I was a good protector, a good warrior, but I was not boyfriend material. I wasn't even friend material.

Andrew had most definitely been right about that, and I hated him for that. Had he seen this coming?

What was the woman thinking, claiming that she loved me? How could she even know what love meant, and how could she think that I was worthy of it? I was a monster, barely human in the eyes of the group.

Although, she probably knew me better than anyone ever had, and that included my father, who had raised me single handedly. Not that I gave my father much credit, other than for the fact that he had made me capable of survival in almost any environment in the world. I owed him my life, and Rhea's perhaps. I suppose that made up for everything else he had ever done, or not done.

"I'm being stupid." I muttered. The words were truer when I said them out loud, and they just made me more annoyed. It was bright with the morning sun, and I was finally warming up, but I wasn't ready to go back to Rhea. I didn't know if I ever would be, but I would go back anyway. I knew I would, even just to keep the promise to her.

The last thing in this world I would ever do would be disappoint Rhea. She was the only one who believed in me, the only one who had ever even attempted to show love for me, even if I didn't really know if I believed her about it.

There was nothing to be done, I had already caused damage by being angry at her, and leaving her. She would be hurt and angry, and I deserved it completely. Still, I didn't know how to fix it yet, and I probably would have done the same thing if I could go back. I wasn't ready to be loved, and I definitely was not ready to love in return.

I was ready to hunt however, I was ready for a challenge. I brandished my knives and started jogging farther south, towards the civilization we had left. I needed to find some sort of game to take down, or even a Hungry to kill.

My heart was pounding in time to my feet, and all I concentrated on was the blood in my veins and the fury that kept reappearing in my heart. I needed to forget everything. I needed to forget Rhea.

At least for a few days. A few moments.

***

I entered the house silently and looked around; she had to be here, she *had* to. I knew that I had hurt her by leaving her alone, but she also knew I could never have done anything else. I was too frightened by her; even now, my heart was pounding and my skin was clammy. Just the thought of seeing her, of looking into her eyes after over a week of reminiscing about them.

It had been too long, and yet, obviously not long enough because I still couldn't get her out of my head. I never would, and that was the only thing that had convinced me to go back to her. That and I was afraid that without me there to protect her she could get hurt. The bruises she had lining her throat not too long ago mocked me. They were healed now, but I could still see them in my mind.

It was too hard to stay away, I was afraid of losing her, and then we were all better off dead. There was no way I would live without her.

I finally found her outside, on the back porch. It was an unusual spot for her, usually Rhea didn't like to be out in the open unless I was there, and she was frightened of what might harm her without my protection. I knew that she had spent most of her time on the porch now though, since I had left. I had seen her, from time to time as I had come back to check on her, facing towards where the forest would lay. She was waiting; forever, if need be. She had promised.

It wasn't what I wanted, but it did mean a lot to me. She had meant her words.

She was curled up, facing the exact spot she had last seen me, her huge parka swallowing her petite frame in its pillowy softness. I wanted nothing more than to pick her up and take her inside and never let her go. Feelings like that always consumed me around Rhea; she was the only good thing in this life, and the only thing I had ever or would ever care about.

"You came back." Her voice came as a shock to me, and I almost backed away again; I wouldn't back away, not this time. I would never run away from her, not again. I had already done that.

"Christmas is four days away. I promised." I said. It was the other reason I had come home. I had worried about leaving her alone, and I had promised her that we would have Christmas, and it would happen. I had the tree.

"Rhea, you should come inside." My words were soft, and gentle. Sandra would never lose the look of shock she always wore when I spoke to Rhea so tenderly. Even after all this time, she still didn't believe me capable of emotion.

"I don't want to." She muttered, "I want to stay out here, and pout."

I frowned at her, she had never been one to wallow in sadness, "You do want to come inside, I know it, because I know you hate to be cold and its freezing out here."

"John, don't be mean. You know I'm mad and sad, and you know I can't stand being angry with you. Just let me be for now." Her voice was tired, and I was instantly remorseful once more. I hurried towards her and sat down, hesitantly pulling her into my chest. I had never before made the gesture of getting near to her first, and she must have realized this because she came willingly into my arms.

"Rhea, please don't be mad. I had to go, I wasn't ready for... what you said."

Rhea shifted and wrapped her arms around me as well. She felt like a giant marshmallow against my heart. I kissed the top of her head, and inhaled the flowery scent that had so enchanted me from the first. She sniffed, and I wondered if she was crying again, but then she lifted her head, and her eyes were bright blue and soft.

"I love you." She said gently, "I know it scares you. Scares the ever living hell out of you. And I know you don't know how to say it back, but I want to tell you, every day forever, just so you know it. Just so you believe it."

I flushed, as I probably always would when Rhea said those words to me, but I didn't push her away as I had done ten days ago. I wondered if I would ever forgive myself for doing that to Rhea. She had handed me everything I had ever wanted, and everything I would ever need and I had thrown it all back in her face. Only someone like Rhea would be able to see what I truly meant by my anger, and let me go. Waited for me. She knew I was scared, that I would always be scared.

"I don't know if I'll ever be able to say what you deserve to hear." I whispered, fear laced in my voice, "But I know you are the only thing I care about. I figured that much out at least, while I was gone. You're my most precious person."

"That frightens me." She replied, "I know that you care about me, John, even if you can't tell me yourself. I fear what you would do for something you loved."

I didn't reply, but I didn't have to. Rhea stood and took my hand, leading me back into the warmth of the house and the humanity I had found the first moment I had ever looked at her. There was no one else for me but Rhea, and there never would be.

I did love her, I loved her more than I would ever be able to describe to anyone. I feared those words would never come out of my mouth, and she would forever exist wishing that I had been brave enough to tell her, and never truly knowing that she was my sun, my moon, and my stars. Rhea was my everything and always would be.

Her fears were also legitimate, and very possible. If I were to lose Rhea now, especially after I had come to terms with how she felt and how I felt, there would be hell to pay. I would be far worse than Sophie, who had wanted more than anything to die, but her dignity and pride wouldn't allow her to kill herself.

I would truly be a monster. It took this realization to show me how human I was now, how human Rhea had made me. She was my grace, my own personal angel.

She both held my salvation and destruction.

"John?" It was Jason's voice, and I was pleased he was the first person we had run into. I wondered if he and Sandra had resolved whatever fight they had been having. I doubted it, Jason looked tired.

"Jason." I nodded my head. My hand had slipped around Rhea's waist, holding her tight to my side. Jason observed all of this, silently as he always did. I truly liked Jason, he was smart and tough, and he knew how to keep a secret.

"I see you cleared your head." Jason smiled, "Good to have you back, John, we missed you."

With that comment, that both surprised and pleased me, Jason waltzed away.

I glanced at Rhea, to see what she would say, but she was silent, just smiling at me. Hesitantly, I smiled back at her. It was a rare occurrence, me smiling, and Rhea was probably the only person who had ever seen it happen. She lit up though, every time I smiled at her, and I vowed to do it more often.

Chapter Twenty-Four

Christmas

It had been perfect, more perfect than I could have ever asked for. Rhea had gone to bed before me on Christmas Eve, and I had sat up with Tanner waiting for the silence of sleep to surround the house. As soon as it had, we had brought the tree into the front room and stuck it in some sort of holder Tanner had devised for it. I threw a wreath Andrew had made on the door, and we set the candles up all over the room. It was always so dark in the mornings now, we barely got five hours of daylight, and I knew the candles would light this whole place up in the morning.

"I'll be right back, John, I have to get my presents." Tanner muttered and disappeared up the stairs.

I had already put Rhea's snowshoes under the tree, and in my pocket I held the necklace I had made her with a chain and a carving I had done of the sun embellished with designs of flowers around it. Just like her: sunshine and flowers.

The chain I would give her privately, I didn't want anyone to read too much into it. They would see it of course, on Rhea's neck if she would wear it, but I still didn't want to make a show of it. She would get it upon awakening tomorrow morning.

Tanner returned, carrying more small bundles than he could manage. They were all wrapped in newspaper, but I was shocked at the number.

"Jason and I found some stuff for everyone, so at least there's something for everyone to open."

I nodded, "That's good."

Tanner was a better person than I had given him credit for, the idea to give everyone something had never even occurred to me, and I had been travelling with these people for much longer than he had.

He put the packages under the tree and I saw he had written our names upon the newspaper, and sure enough there were two small ones for me as well.

"What's for breakfast?" I asked, remembering that Tanner had offered to cook for everyone as a gift as well.

"We could cook Eva," Tanner told me, face serious. I glared at him long enough that he started to laugh and elbowed me in the side. How was it even possible for him to joke about cannibalism?! The man was more insane than I was.

"Not funny." I informed him, debating on ripping his arm out of its socket for elbowing me. Probably not worth it, Rhea would yell.

He sobered, "In all seriousness, I'm not sure, we don't have a whole lot left."

Something I could help with, "Actually, I put some eggs I found in the back of the fridge, I wanted to save them for tomorrow. There's also some meat in the shed, I hung it up to freeze."

Tanner beamed at me, "John, you are a wonderful man. Bacon and eggs tomorrow, or some version of them! And perhaps a roast for dinner!"

He laughed quietly, joy shining through on his features. I realized that I was probably being foolish to dislike this man; he was a good person, and had a positive view on life despite his misfortunes. Something I obviously lacked.

We headed to bed after retrieving the meat and leaving it in the sink to defrost, and I snuck back into bed with Rhea like a thief in the night. She only rolled over, barely even making a sound. I wondered why I had been so careful and quiet when I knew she slept so soundly nothing would wake her.

I rolled towards her back and wrapped myself around her tiny form. Her shoulder was bare and I kissed it softly, aware that I only allowed myself to make this kind of tender contact when she was asleep.

She stirred slightly in my arms and sighed in what I hoped was a happy way.

"Merry Christmas." I whispered to her in the dark, letting sleep claim me.

For the first time since we had moved into the house Rhea was awake before me, which completely changed all my plans to light the candles. I couldn't regret it too much, because I awoke to her nudging my shoulder with her chin, and grinning hugely at me.

"Hi." I said, sleep still staining my voice.

She rolled farther into me until she was staring at me from my chest, "Hi. Merry Christmas!"

A laugh escaped me, the first since before I could remember, I couldn't help it. She was adorable practically laying on my chest and grinning at me. I would have known, even without her telling me previously, that Christmas was her favourite day of the year.

"I have something for you." I said.

Rhea was smiling widely, "Really?!" She practically leapt off the bed, standing above me waiting for her gift.

I swung my legs out of the bed, and reached into the nightstand drawer. Rhea was staring with so much anticipation I couldn't resist making her wait longer.

"Close your eyes!" I think I was teasing her. I had never done it with another person before, only witnessed it.

She giggled and screwed up her eyes tightly. The chain left the drawer in my hand and I stood before Rhea, her eyes tightly shut and a smile still playing on her lips. I couldn't resist, not on this day. I wondered if I had ever had a chance resisting Rhea; I doubted it.

My hand crept forward, settling against her cheek. Her blue eyes slowly opened, staring straight into mine. The smile fell, but her lips parted, and I could read nothing but acceptance in her eyes.

I pulled her into me, watching as her blue eyes fluttered closed, and finally I kissed her. Fully this time, not like she had done before. Her lips were the softest things I had ever felt, and the heat that stormed through me when she stood on her toes and wrapped her arms around me blew me away. I never wanted to leave her embrace, but I had to. I released her, keeping the chain held tightly in my one hand.

She was breathless and glowing pink, and it was endearing to know I had affected her as badly as she had affected me. "Was that my gift?" She asked.

I smiled at her, "No. This is."

The chain dropped from my fingers, and her eyes went to it with shock. She took it from me reverently, taking in all the infinite detail I had worked so hard on to make perfect for her. I had even decided to carve her name into the back, all in perfect cursive.

"Oh, John..." She whispered, "It's beautiful. You carved this for me?"

"Yes."

Her smile was tremulous, and grateful, "Thank you. Will you put it on me?"

She turned her back to me, and I slipped the chain around her neck, fastening it tightly. When she faced me again I had never seen a more beautiful smile. It was shy, and grateful, and I knew that the emotion I was also seeing was love. I wondered if it shone on my face like it did on hers.

This time, it was her that kissed me, "I love you."

There was still no answer that would come to me, even though I knew the truth of how I felt now. There was something I wanted to tell her however, "There were only two things my mother left for me when she left my father when I was three. The chain was one of them."

Her hand flew to it, stroking it softly, "John, I can't take this..."

I nodded, "Of course you can. I can't wear it, it looks better on you."

She nodded decisively after a moment, and I knew that she would take better care of the chain than I ever had.

Curiosity stained her voice, "What was the other thing? That you have from your mother?"

I shook my head, "Can't tell you, but I have a feeling you'll find out." I had a feeling the other one would end up in Rhea's care as well, eventually.

"Tell me!" She commanded playfully. Her hand was tangled in mine, and the other was still holding the necklace, as if afraid that if she let it go it would have never happened.

I changed the subject, "Rhea, you said you... loved me... because I never asked you to leave the group for me. Was that true?" I asked. I had been truly baffled by her speech about this, shocked at her love and at how easily she had seen through every bit of me.

Rhea blushed, "I love you for other reasons too, but that's one of them. You wanted to leave, even in the house, before we had even talked. I knew you would never kick us out of the house, you knew we needed the shelter more than you did, but I knew you wanted to go, but you would never leave without me."

I nodded, "I wouldn't have. Even back then." I sighed, "Especially now."

"You promise to never leave me?" Rhea asked, shock laced through her voice. It stung, how surprised she was, but I supposed I deserved her doubt after my disappearing act the week before.

"You said I looked at you as though you were my entire world." I stated, monotone, and not answering her question.

She frowned, perplexed, "Yes, I said that."

"How could I leave you, then?" I asked.

Rhea almost jumped on me she hugged me so quickly, laughter escaping her along with her breath.

"Oh John, I love you." She said, "Never leave me."

"I won't," I whispered into her ear, "Not ever."

Her sigh was so full of contentment I knew that I had finally, irrevocably proven Sandra and Andrew and Zack and everyone wrong. So wrong. I would never hurt Rhea; I would never leave her, never break her heart. I may never tell her the words she deserved to hear, but I knew that she didn't want them, not from me, especially when I wasn't ready. Rhea never pushed.

"Come on," I said, "Let's go downstairs."

She followed me down the stairs, and if I had thought that her reaction to the chain was wonderful, I hadn't expected at all what she would do when she saw the house. Tanner was awake and I saw that he had lit the candles I had placed, and the house smelled of caribou bacon and eggs.

The tree was sparkling, and coated with different odds and ends Tanner had collected to be decorations.

"Merry Christmas, Rhea." I said, and she spun with tears unshed shining in her eyes.

"John!" She cried, "You shouldn't have."

I shrugged. "I promised, and Tanner and Jason helped just as much."

I noticed that Jason had slept back in his and Sandra's room last night; I wondered if she had forgiven him out of good Christmas spirit.

Tanner appeared in the doorway, smiling. It was a normal sight, now, to see Tanner happy. I knew that he still sunk into sadness when he remembered his sister and mother, but it wasn't in him to be depressed for long.

"Okay, Rhea, go wake everyone up! Breakfast is ready!" Tanner commanded. Rhea headed up the stairs, joy infusing her every step.

"Thanks." I said, "For the lights. And the breakfast."

Tanner nodded, his eyes still focused on the stairs, "Did you make that necklace?"

"Yeah." I answered, shocked that Tanner had noticed it that quickly.

"It's beautiful workmanship." He said.

I shrugged, "Thanks. My dad was a carpenter." Along with a few other things.

Tanner nodded, and at the sight of some of the sleepy members of our group, we headed to the kitchen where he had prepared a feast the likes of which we hadn't had since before the Hungry had arrived.

Laughter abounded around the table, and I felt more full and happy than I had in forever. After we were finished Gabby and Sandra started cleaning the plates and Rhea's hand snuck into mine under the table. I squeezed it gently, and continued my minimal conversation with Tanner. I had grown to truly like the guy, and he had a quirky sense of humour that I could actually appreciate.

"Presents!?" Eva's cry brought all of our attention to her, "I have just been told that there are even presents waiting under our tree!"

The rush to the tree was hilarious, and everyone sat down around it, eyeing all the bundles that littered the floor.

Eva handed them all out, and everyone had two small gifts, except for Rhea who was also holding her snowshoes. Sandra still hadn't lost her look of shock that I had actually made them for her, and Rhea was still grinning at me, both because she was amused by Sandra's reaction and because she was pleased I had gone to so much trouble for her. I think I had finally been completely forgiven for disappearing for so long.

The bundles were full of different things. It turned out Tanner had a stash of plenty of little chocolates (expired, but still good), and everyone had gotten one bundle full of sweet treats. The others had various other things in them: a small sewing kit for Eva who had been complaining she had lost hers in the van, a pair of earrings Tanner had found for Gabrielle, a collection of dried flowers and pine needles that smelled amazing for Sandra. Anne received three different bars of soap, and I recalled Zack asking me how I made soap a while back. I had thought nothing more of it, but it was obvious he had made it for her.

Rhea received a small medical kit that Tanner had found in the basement. It had a little utensil section, with tweezers and a scalpel. There were some real medicines, since ours had been lost with Sophie, and some medical stitches and tape. She seemed pleased, and I knew that Rhea had enjoyed her role as our 'doctor'.

Jason got a book along with Zack; I briefly let myself wonder if Zack even knew how to read, though I dismissed the thought when I realized I was being petty. Andrew got a sketchbook complete with some sort of artist pencils. I had no idea he liked to draw, but by the smile that spread across his face he enjoyed it immensely. Tanner and I got crossword books, and he didn't seem particularly shocked. I wondered if he had picked it out for himself.

I was surprisingly pleased with the gift, since I had needed some sort of thing to do while I wasted the winter away in this house. I supposed I would try my hand at crosswords.

Everyone thanked each other, and Tanner started playing some Christmas music on a cd player and we all stayed sitting, visiting and sharing one of the most peaceful days we had ever had together.

I wished Dana was here, to see this and to be a part of it.

I had Rhea though, and as I looked to her I saw she was holding her gifts close to her and smiling brightly. I caught her eye and she mouthed a thank you over the din everyone else's voices were creating. It was like we were stuck in our own bubble, aware of nothing but each other's eyes. I put my hand over my heart and nodded at her.

It wasn't over; I didn't know if it would ever be over. But we had this, and for now, for this moment, it was enough to keep us strong.

To be continued…

Follow Shalynn Cavanagh on twitter @shalynncavanagh

Books by Shalynn Cavanagh

The Ravening Trilogy

    The Hungry – October 2015

    The Science – Spring 2016

    The Divide – Winter 2017

Made in the USA
Middletown, DE
06 July 2016